LONDON
HOLIDAY

Also by Richard Peck
in Large Print:

This Family of Women

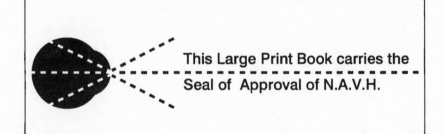

This Large Print Book carries the
Seal of Approval of N.A.V.H.

LONDON HOLIDAY

Richard Peck

Thorndike Press • Thorndike, Maine

LP
Peck

Published in 1998 by arrangement with Viking Penguin, a division of Penguin Putnam Inc.

Thorndike Large Print ® Basic Series.

The tree indicium is a trademark of Thorndike Press.

The text of this Large Print edition is unabridged.
Other aspects of the book may vary from the original edition.

Set in 16 pt. Plantin by Juanita Macdonald.

Printed in the United States on permanent paper.

Library of Congress Cataloging in Publication Data

Peck, Richard, 1934–
    London holiday / Richard Peck.
      p.   cm.
    ISBN 0-7862-1635-2 (lg. print : hc : alk. paper)
    1. Large type books.   I. Title.
  [PS3566.E2526L66   1998]
  813'.54—dc21   98-36372

Again, for
Jack Cook
and
Jean and Richard Hughes

From *Bed-and-Breakfasts in Britain: A Selective Guide*

Somewhere above the top of the list in a class by itself is Mrs. Smith-Porter's in Radnor Walk, Chelsea, with neither TV nor fax to ruffle the tone. Here a narrow row house a stone's throw from the King's Road somehow embodies the fey charm of a Cotswold cottage insinuated into one of London's better neighborhoods. Whether Mrs. Smith-Porter inherited her exquisite clutter or has assembled with an unwavering eye, your bedroom won't feature four unrelated wallpapers from the geometric 1960s. Her mattresses cater to American spines, and the bathrooms, while down the hall, sport heated towel racks.

But the chief feature is Mrs. Smith-Porter herself, the ultimate English landlady. A cup of early-morning Earl Grey appears still steaming in your room, and on departure day the cab is at the door. Continental breakfasts only, though if she likes you and the day is fair, you may be invited for a cuppa and a small sandwich with the crust off in the postage-stamp garden behind. But expect to find yourself telling more about your origins than you learn about hers.

Takes American Express, prefers cash.

Chapter 1

Mrs. Smith-Porter stood at the front window of her best bedroom fingering a strand of artificial pearls. An early rain had greased the street, and it was shaping to be the sort of June morning the Americans mistook for November.

The cab had just taken away her previous visitors: two Plano, Texas, couples and a Virginia woman suffering from ancestor worship. They were always visitors, never paying guests. The *paying* part went without saying, and *guests* seemed to presume in both directions. Visitors then, and she was apt to pack them off early for even a midday flight, panicking them gently about the metal detector at Heathrow and the chaos of Terminal Three if they weren't flying British Airways. Love them and let them leave, as she put it to herself.

It set a measured tone for the rest of the day. Gemma came in to bring down the trays and turn out the rooms and take the bed linens away to do in her own time. She was young, a single mother Mrs. Smith-Porter gathered, and liked to be about her business.

She was up and down and in and out and off along Radnor Walk with a bin liner full of dirty linen before you could say knife.

Mrs. Dowdel, who came three mornings, was the char of earlier times, down to the hat she never took off, the fag stuck to her lower lip, and the unchanging apron. She was evidently the heart and soul of the Coach and Four public house, Tooting Bec, and often seemed to turn up straight from the boozer, pissed as a newt. Mrs. Dowdel's hand shook too dramatically to dust anything breakable, and she was inclined to knock ash into the umbrella stand, but she could be trusted with the floors. She was slow — Dowdel by name and dawdle by nature — and like Mrs. Smith-Porter herself, preferred cash. Nothing kept her from flinging dirty water out the front door, but perhaps that offered an authentic Old World touch.

This wasn't one of her days, so Mrs. Smith-Porter had half an hour alone with her house before another cab drew up to fill it with the jet-lagged, an ailment she couldn't quite fathom but saw a lot. People often fell suddenly like trees an hour after they'd arrived, and it confirmed in her the resolve never to travel farther than the number 19 bus went.

Her house stood in a once modest row

whose fortunes had risen with the neighborhood. Nearly opposite was a restaurant grown wondrously smart back in the 1980s as a favorite of the Princess of Wales, though if royalty had frequented it, Mrs. Smith-Porter would have noticed. There were cries of alarm in those Thatcher days from the hard-left weeklies that spring up in improving neighborhoods. They wrote in reams against the Old Chelsea that had sold its soul for money. Even the most ramshackle house was relentlessly tarted up and asking a million pounds for itself.

Mrs. Smith-Porter saw herself in the window glass, tall as a crane in her landlady uniform. The twin set hung from bony shoulders and fell straight as curtains against her. The Jaeger tweed skirt had found its own shape with the years. She was all flat planes and long knees and jutting elbows, but she compensated with a graceful way of moving when anyone was there to see. Her white hair in a flyaway feather cut balanced the English jaw. It was late days for vanity, but her looks pleased her. They suited the woman she'd become, and make no mistake about it, she'd had to create herself out of exceedingly raw material. She hadn't been born to this station in life, or any other, as it happened. She didn't like to think where she might be if she had allowed life to dictate to her — some wretched council flat, she supposed.

She often reminded her visitors of some *Masterpiece Theatre* character actress, usually now dead. Her commanding height, the throaty voice, the sudden rise of eyebrow, that lingering suggestion that she was playing a part. She might have been Coral Browne come back, or even Martita Hunt. People often said she was too good to be true.

She and her house had come a long way together since that day in the gray 1950s when Mr. Smith-Porter had bought it for her. Two thousand pounds freehold and begging for a buyer. Only a few years ago she'd read in the *Telegraph* of Mr. Smith-Porter's death. She took in a range of newspapers for her visitors and preferred the *Telegraph* for herself. He'd been a husband, though not hers. Older than she was, but not as much older as he'd thought.

It turned out he was something in the City, leaving a wife in Barnes and four children all abroad. More furtive than generous, he'd never given her much before, apart from a box of crystallized violets from Maison Lyons. She remembered that particularly because the box lived on at the top of a shelf in her kitchen, full of nails and all manner of things she never remembered putting there. At the end, he gave her this house. Funnily enough she'd been born not so far away in the very different Chelsea of those times. Then in the war, right at the end of it, she'd lived in a house — squatted, really — along this very row. So she supposed it was meant to be. When it was given her, it was by way of being Mr. Smith-Porter's good-bye gift, or an attempt to keep her quiet. Not that she needed it for that. She knew how to keep herself to herself, and it wasn't much more than a gesture. The house was still on its knees from the war. The whole street was, come to that.

She often thought of the war nowadays. She'd come to that time of life when the past, even hers, returned in sudden flashes more vivid than yesterday, memories detonating like bombs. She'd been young in the war, unimaginably young. Still in her teens, and someone else. It was being cold and hungry she remembered. She supposed she'd been too young to think she could die.

It was in the final summer of the war, the D day, doodlebug summer, that she'd come to live in this row for the first time. She recalled the sound of the flying bombs coming over. The putt-putt of their engines. No

13

point to burrowing in the shelters — people had died like flies in them. By then there was no place to hide, and the bombs came over day and night, anytime.

The neighborhood stood half empty, what with the dead and the fled. You could see right through a good many houses to the gardens that nature was already taking back. She'd lived in a front parlor, the window out and boarded up. Lulled by the sound of seeping water, she'd slept with a bread knife beside her because of the rats. She hardly remembered going out except to queue. There'd been a muddle about her ration book, and the meat ration right down to eightpence. It was all muddle then and usually a way around it. She hadn't been above a fiddle. One way or another, she'd been on the fiddle all her life. Then later by one of those chances, Mr. Smith-Porter had bought her this house.

The row had been thrown up to shelter the workers of some earlier century, jerry-built to begin with and then badly knocked about by Jerry. The ceilings were all down, and the scullery still had its earth floor and a single tap over a stone sink. Above, there were two floors of bedrooms roughly boxed in with a bathroom of sorts added and a leaking loo, though the original lav was still out back.

Once it was hers, she'd had her work cut out for her if this house was to stand between her and starvation. People had put the war behind them by then, and it was every man for himself. Beginning as she meant to go on, she did the work herself. She pulled off wallpaper with her bare hands, scraping floors by day and sleeping on them at night. Under cover of darkness she nicked paint and brushes from building sites, and once a necessary ladder for distempering her ceilings. Like an old rag-and-bone man, she plundered London. Fridays before daylight found her at the Caledonian market doing her deals for furniture and crockery.

Not for her the new rubbish in Heal's window, the randomly glued fake-Danish modern. She bought outdoors straight off the lorries: good old English oak and mahogany, nothing veneered, and towers of white paste plates with their gold bands fading, all at knockdown prices. She carried bedsteads and beveled looking-glasses into the tube and staggered under them all the way from Sloane Square to her door. When the Royal Court Hotel jettisoned a carpet with unworn bits that would do for her parlor, she carried it unfurling down the King's Road. It was a display of enterprise that escaped her neighbors, who were all intently waiting for better times.

Behind her best bedroom was a windowed closet that looked west along the side of the house and caught the afternoon light. From the start she sewed in there, taught herself to sew, and looked to the day she'd never have to let this room. To fit her windows, she hemmed the cut-velvet hangings and old damask panels they were glad to be rid of in the market.

She'd been on the stage in the war, on and off it and always in the back row, and it had taught her something about dressing a set. The cumbersome old furnishings she plucked off carts at the Caledonian market took on a gathering grandeur.

When the house was fit for company, she began with Australians, who stayed six months, stretching their money to cover the time. On the first day she put a card in her window — it was the Suez year, with Anthony Eden's picture in the papers every day and people saying there'd be Russian tanks in the Tottenham Court Road — she filled the rooms that were ready at fifteen shillings a night, full English breakfast. Then the sewing room. Then the box room at the back of the top floor she'd meant to sleep in herself. All her rooms burgeoned with Aussies, and they didn't mind doubling up. She slept on a collapsing cot from the war in the kitchen.

Waking early to light the boiler, she was already at her post.

The Australians were chilled to the bone in all weathers. After closing time at the pub, nothing kept them from the electric fire in the parlor, and lighting one bar didn't thaw them. She'd expected to have the house to herself much of the time, but she liked the company. She'd been short of company most of her life.

Voices seemed to transform her house, and she learned that people come halfway round the world to talk mainly of themselves and home. She heard so many life stories that in time she remembered only odd moments of her own. Branching out, she took in South Africans — Rhodesians, as they were called then — Canadians, and the first of the Yanks — roaming students, mostly, and the retired. Their stays were briefer, and they passed her name along to their friends, who began to book ahead. In time, she could withdraw the card from the front window. Later a card in a window along Radnor Walk wouldn't have done at all, but later she was well beyond needing it.

An American couple were the first to want to buy the bed they'd slept in. It wasn't her best one, an Edwardian stab at Sheraton, she'd have thought. She helped them knock it down. In the end they took the nightstand with it, on the S.S. *United States*. She came away forty quid to the good, and it seemed to set a trend. Most Fridays she was in the market to replace all manner of things bought out of her house. What began as an inconvenience became another income, and replacing improved her taste. When she could give herself a half day, she'd take the number 49 bus up to the foot of Church Street and stroll along to see the prices the antiques shops were asking.

Toward the end of the 1960s, she'd banked eight thousand very lightly taxed pounds under a loose floorboard, and was in possession of a going concern. And she had her health, which was as well because she wouldn't go near the national health scheme. In the war she'd observed what government does when they get a hold on you. Eight thousand pounds looked like more than it was in those days, and she found herself at a crossroads. With the thought, she sold off all but her best things and shut up the house for most of two years. Change of life as she thought of it later.

It wasn't the first time she'd done a bunk, and she knew the value of starting with a clean slate. Though she'd never been west of Windsor Castle, she read of a cottage to let in Devon. Leaving no forwarding address, she went to earth at Dawlish, knowing no one, spending little, biding her time.

Nothing about the country recommended itself. As far as she could tell, it was all goosegrass and stinging nettles. The sea horrified her, an endless, restless emptiness, and anything at all was liable to wash up. There she stopped, along the godforsaken seashore, letting the old days and the old ways fall away from her whilst she planned a future on quite another scale.

She began with herself, inspired by bits drawn from films and ladies' magazines and what she'd observed of the sort of women who had their morning coffee up the top at Peter Jones, their voices and their shoes. When it came to clothes, nothing flashy, mind, and that was a pity because she'd liked a touch of color. She laid a restraining hand upon herself, and practiced old Queen Mary's own posture in her walks beside the terrible sea.

Leaving all her pasts behind, she returned as Mrs. Smith-Porter to a Chelsea no more recognizable than she was.

She'd expected change, but hardly this much. Throughout the sixties, the young had laid waste the King's Road: plastic miniskirts and paper dresses and Mary Quant run amok. All the best bakeries were gone now and in their stead shops selling the most appalling tat, and the pavement thick with toffee wrappers. She hadn't seen so many loud, overpainted young girls since the war, but these were the daughters now. Music meant to inflict pain bawled out of the wine bars where the young flung down the new decimalized currency without thought for its value. The pub at the corner seemed to conduct an endless fancy-dress party, and now the change was creeping into the byways.

None of her old neighbors remained. The houses both sides of hers were divided into bijou maisonettes and let to new people on long leases at figures she could only wonder at. Radnor Walk had achieved its first Daimler, whose anonymous owner parked it with nonchalance on the curb. Mrs. Smith-Porter saw promise wherever she looked.

She spent the rest of her savings to improve her house out of all recognition. The Caledonian market had moved over the Thames to Bermondsey, and she followed, buying now with a practiced eye. Her uniform was a waxy rainproof from the old days, with poacher's pockets, topped with an uncompromising Garboesque hat the dealers came to recognize. She was no favorite of theirs. She arrived early, well ahead of the

20

punters, and drove a wicked bargain. As like as not at the end of the morning when they were packing it in, she appeared again out of the blue to drive a harder bargain still. Then she expected them to deliver to her very door right across London, herself up beside the driver to show the way.

Prices were up, but so were hers. When she reopened her house, her rates were just under Brown's Hotel's, and she'd broiled her last breakfast tomato.

She bought her linen supply at Robinson & Cleaver's last sale, and since David Hicks was making a splash, she ran his carpets up her stairs. She discovered in herself an awakening eye for the right color, neatly avoiding landlady hues. Never cyclamen pink or, on the other hand, any of those boiled-cabbage shades. Taking a flyer, she did up the parlor like a *Country Life* photo of a morning room, heavy on the cretonne with a pair of Barbour-blue Wellies standing guard by the door to the hall. The walls looked papered, but Mrs. Smith-Porter had painted the stripes herself, apple green against ivory, and had stippled in the flyspecks by hand. Just three or four chairs and a banquette slip-covered in bleached damask and bound in old cording. This room looked into the dining room, which was smaller still. Not a lot

21

was asked of this space except as an ante-room to the garden and somewhere for the visitors to have their breakfast.

She'd bought off a barrow a pair of old Pekin yellow curtains. When she added the fringe, they might have been made for the French doors opening onto the garden. As there was no point trying to make this room look larger than it was, she did the walls below the chair rail and above the skirting in a bold marble trompe l'oeil. Above the rail was a deep orange, varnished. She found a wide-waisted Welsh dresser to lay out the breakfast on and a cottagey gateleg table. She would need to seat six at the most as she naturally would not sit down with them. Somebody had wanted to buy the gateleg table, so she replaced it with a black-lacquered one that she rather thought was worth thirty or forty times what she'd paid.

The garden began with lead tubs exploding in chrysanthemum on the crazy paving. She'd had the pocket wilderness out back paved over when the tile setters came to floor the scullery. And she'd set an optimistic little sundial just over the old lav as a memorial. Then she doubled the number of bathrooms to two, both in green marble.

With years of dogged effort behind her, she was an overnight success, the first of the smart B and B's, being reviewed like a play in the newspapers abroad. She hired herself as secretary — she'd worked in an office at one time, she couldn't think when — to cope with the correspondence. She kept her own books too, in a quiet way. She was good at sums and got better, and she was neither the first nor the last to learn that the less you feed them and the more you charge, the longer the queue.

The Germans found her and would have kept her to themselves, but she decided against them. She didn't know the language, and their tread was heavy on the stairs, and she found she rather resented them about the war. Having failed to bomb this island into the sea, they now wanted to be British, if you please, buying up green tweed by the mile and bone china in all the wrong patterns.

The Italians came in an early wave. They'd been on the wrong side in the war too, though you couldn't take them seriously enough to mind. She didn't know their language either, and it went on and on into the night. The French complained even in an introductory letter, and she'd priced herself out of most other entire nations.

She decided to limit herself to Americans, having known her full share of them in the war. They struck a balance between the familiar and the exotic, and she could follow much of what they said. It meant central heating, but she took the plunge. She lacquered her front door in a green to suggest Harrod's, and the Americans beat a path to it.

Over the years since, she'd grown rich on them beyond all expectation. And she found herself looking forward to the life stories they brought with them like luggage. Travel, it would seem, was too desperate an act to undertake for pleasure alone. The Australians had been a clear case. To them, Australia wasn't quite a real place, and they'd make any sacrifice to get to one. The Yanks, a more mixed lot, always seemed to be in flight from something. From her distance she watched these sudden dramas unfolding in this set she'd devised.

Though she was vaguely aware that the better class of the English despised Americans, she found them good value. They were friendlier than she'd ever known people be. Some of them from the southern states invited her to visit them, as if she should return the call. Un-Englishly, she could tell one American from another. The Texans seemed to be southerners with the sound turned up. She didn't mind their instant familiarity, though when they wanted to know her first name, they didn't hear it. She was less keen on the New Yorkers. They weren't considerate about the bathroom, and all their stories were alike. Still, coast to coast they were all a good deal more civil than the English. She'd heard about American children but did not take them.

They didn't stay long nowadays. The exchange rate seemed to work against them. But Mrs. Smith-Porter could still count on the American habit of sudden intimacy. They valued their privacy as little as any people she'd ever known. And they bathed more often than she could believe. She wondered if it hadn't removed a protective layer. An initial touch of British reserve on her part, a hint of Mrs. Danvers, set them off, and they were liable to tell you anything. It was like going to the pictures in the old days when they were about interesting problems, Celia Johnson films and Margaret Lockwood, though the Americans were in full color.

With the palmy days of the 1980s long behind her, she found she could still fill her rooms, though they bought fewer of her furnishings. She couldn't remember when she'd sold as much as an apostle spoon off her dresser. Still, Fridays found her at Bermondsey, picking through, watching the prices rise and the quality fall. Habit took her there, or she liked the company. She wondered if she was altogether too hungry for company as the years moved past her.

She told herself that she went to keep her hand in. Treasures still surfaced. She recalled a pair of gilt candlesticks that looked to be 1920s and proved to be Directoire and the silver ewer that had turned out to be William IV. In truth, she loved the market. It was still the London of her youth, at the mercy of the elements: the gusty rain peppering the stall roofs, the steam rising off the tea wagon, the backchat and the quiet deal. She wasn't sure what she liked best, the anonymity or the villainy.

She passed unremarked from stall to stall, turning over the goods with a gloved hand. Now that she approached the age of invisibility, the dealers were too young to take much notice. She often got the best of the bargain and was away again before they knew where they were.

As today's visitors were due any minute, she turned from this woolgathering to give her best bedroom another look. It was presently in a mood of Gothic revival, dominated by a rather wonderful black oak bed that pointed at the ceiling like the Albert Memorial. She knew the value of overscaled furniture in undersized rooms. The paper behind was a toile print of Strawberry Hill follies. She'd gone over the top with the window: swag upon swag of old red watered silk like a vestment off the back of Cardinal Richelieu. The whole was scented with a bowl of Crabtree & Evelyn's rose potpourri. No fug of cooked sprouts haunted her halls. She didn't cook, not even for herself. The breakfast buns were brought round from a bakery, and she sent Gemma off to Marks & Sparks for the tea sandwiches so often noted in the travel guides.

She'd been hungry every day of her youth, and now she had no appetite. Hearing the shriek of brakes, she looked down to see the cab at the door.

Before the driver could come round, a woman was stepping out. Something young in her face, though almost everyone looked young now to Mrs. Smith-Porter, and fair-haired and quite as tall as she was herself. Then another woman, thin-faced with a cloud of dark hair. On her heels a third, more ample, possibly a little older. It was hard to tell. American women always looked girlish in a group. The tall fair one was belted into the kind of Burberry Americans wore against the British summer. The thin-faced one was in something smarter. The ample one seemed shapeless. Mrs. Smith-Porter looked again to see that her mac was worn over her shoulders and that one of her arms appeared to be in a sling.

Shoppers all, she assumed, and that would keep them out from underfoot. They staggered on the pavement beside a growing pile of luggage. They'd overpacked, but she'd seen worse. They hitched their long-strapped handbags and dithered about the money.

They were from St. Louis in Missouri, at least the woman who'd written was: a Mrs. Hockaday. Three women, and that was all right. She only let three rooms now. The box room above at the back was her bedroom, hers alone. She was too old and rich to doss down in the kitchen. And she liked to keep the sewing room with the west-looking window to herself, carrying on her business correspondence at a little George II game table wedged under the window. She let the sewing room only to oblige in an emergency.

Mrs. Hockaday had written in a large, unformed hand on best-quality letter paper, cream-laid with a narrow blue border. Ordinarily Mrs. Smith-Porter was fully booked for this time of year and had been since the winter, but she'd had a cancellation. The woman paid in full and wrote with a kind of eagerness. Three old friends from childhood, she'd said: a Mrs. Steadman, a Mrs. Mayhew, and herself, getting away together for a much-needed holiday. There were hardly enough lines to read between, but Mrs. Smith-Porter scanned them out of habit. She thought too that they could sort out the bedrooms for themselves and make their own choices. People liked to. It made it less like an hotel and more a house party. Better yet, it rather masked the fact that there weren't quite enough bathrooms to go round.

Then a fourth emerged from the cab below, seeming to hang back. She was quite a young girl, rather large and with a quantity of hair. She stood apart from the women, looking aside.

Mrs. Smith-Porter hadn't counted on four. But that was all right. She'd oblige them, and they'd be grateful. In the last silence she walked down through her house and waited a moment behind her closed door. Then just as they'd be wondering if they'd come to the right place, she opened to them.

April

Chapter 2

The journey had begun in their childhood when they were Lesley Vogel and Julia Englehardt and Margo Skinner. They'd combined forces by fourth grade, and Les always thought it was a miracle. In a bigger place than Cape Vincent they might not have known one another at all. They'd have gone to different grade schools because even as it was, they were from three different backgrounds, different levels of one of those river towns that stairstep up to the bluffs.

Les thought that first friendships take precedence and hoped all through high school that life wouldn't rip them apart and scatter them to the four winds. It was a nightmare when people you counted on and loved and needed walked away and weren't there anymore, like death.

In high school Les had foreseen perfectly logical lives for all of them: success for Julia and Margo, sure things for herself. Marrying Harry Hockaday would solve everything, and she might not even have to leave the Cape. Julia would go. Julia was born to leave and had started announcing her departure in grade school. Margo said less but had the kind of quiet wisdom that might take her anywhere.

It would be up to Les to keep them all together. In study hall she sketched the design for the monogrammed stationery she'd have when she was married, cream-laid paper with a narrow blue border. She'd planned to write a lot of letters, keep in touch. That had all been . . . Les didn't like to think how long it had been, though she kept her high school yearbooks with the years emblazoned on the spines in order on a shelf by her desk for easy reference.

There'd been a moment very early on when all three of them had been married, even Julia, married and nearby. That had given Les hope. It made her think that life really did have a shape, and they could be three married couples together.

But then suddenly they were all over the map. Even Les and Harry had moved up to St. Louis. Nothing had gone according to plan, though she supposed she was herself still playing out the hand that had been dealt her.

You couldn't get a letter out of Julia for love or money, and Margo never had the time. They were all busy — Les too. But she was always the one who had to call, and manufacture a reason. She was always leaving messages on their machines.

She didn't want to cling. She didn't think she was the clinging type, and surely her response to marriage and motherhood had proved that. But she'd catch herself carrying on conversations with Julia and Margo in the mornings when she walked her two miles along the perimeter of Forest Park, chatting away to the two of them, careful not to move her lips.

Then in April Dorothy Englehardt died, and Les had ample reason to call Julia.

Dorothy Englehardt was Julia's grandmother. Les heard she was dead from Harry of all people. He never called from the office, or anywhere, and he hadn't been out of the house an hour. A fraternity brother of Harry's was a broker down home and had called to tell him — big news at the Cape.

Les had almost been out the door for a hospital board meeting. She'd already walked and was showered and changed. She'd just settled sideways to run over the rest of the week on the calendar.

"How?" she said.

"How? Hell, I don't know," Harry said. "She was in her nineties, wasn't she?"

Yes, but somehow that didn't seem reason

enough in Dorothy's case.

"Last night or in the night? At home or where?"

"Honey, I don't know." How typically vague, this news passed from one man to another. "She had somebody around the clock, didn't she? Just thought you'd want to know, babe."

But she was already scanning down the phone list on her blotter, and she cut him off. With Harry, she usually measured her words, but suddenly the day was full of possibilities. She was already punching 1-212 while she was looking up Julia's number.

With the time difference, she was already an hour behind. But then St. Louis got up earlier than New York. She thought about dialing Julia's office, but decided on the home number, though they were two phone lines at different ends of the same apartment. And Julia could be anywhere. She might be out of town on a job or traveling, and nobody could reach her, and she wouldn't even know. Les let it ring.

Julia awoke. She'd slept briefly but with determination, and now she was having to climb up through gray layers to daylight. The dream had been a version of the usual: of herself and Lesley and Margo as they'd been, kids together. Her dreams never had plotlines and seemed refreshingly free of symbolism. She supposed she had too literal a mind for literary dreams.

Now, rigid against the day with a faint ringing in her ears, she was awake in that oversized bed that Mrs. Warburton wouldn't have for Oyster Bay. Julia ran an interior-design business, and part of the deal was to live with clients' rejects. Her bedroom was chockablock with them, going back to the first Reagan administration, back to flame stitch and faux tortoiseshell finishes.

Les let it ring forever, and Julia's machine didn't come on, which could mean anything. Could Julia already be heading this way? Not very likely. Would she come at all? Les distracted herself by drawing up a numbered list of things to do. She tried the office number again in case Mrs. Lederer, who handled Julia's calls, had just come in. Les tried to will Mrs. Lederer out of the unspeakable New York subway and up the elevator and to her desk.

Then she tried Julia's personal number again, and Julia picked up on the first ring. "Hello, Les."

"Julia, how did you know it was me? Then you know why I'm calling." But then she didn't know what to say next. *I'm sorry* didn't cover it. "Harry told me," she said. "Imagine Harry hearing anything first."

You're coming, aren't you? Les wanted to ask. *When are you coming?* All kinds of inappropriate questions were lining up in her mind. *What will you do with the house?* And *You didn't really hate her did you, not in your heart?* "Tell me what I can do for you. I'm just sitting here. Throw me a crumb," which is what Les always used to say.

"You could call Margo." Margo was already on the list Les was making, right under *flowers.* "Tell her for heaven's sake not to come. Just let her know."

Come, Les wrote next to Margo's name. "What else?"

"I'll be flying out this evening."

Les's pen poised for flight number and arrival. "Stay here, and we'll drive down to the Cape in the morning," she said, "unless you need to get there tonight."

"Tomorrow's soon enough," Julia said. "Burial tomorrow. No funeral. And no wake — what do they call it down there?"

"Visitation," Les said.

"She'd outlived everybody anyway," Julia said. Which was far from the truth. Dorothy still knew everybody in town who counted. Julia had had six calls last night, plus the undertaker.

"Did she die at home?" Les asked.

"As a matter of fact, she died in the ladies' lounge at the country club."

Les gripped the phone. "She died in the toilet?" *On* the toilet?

"Well, near enough, I suppose. I don't know," Julia said. "Film at eleven." Which Les didn't get.

"Harry said she had around-the-clock care."

"She did, but that didn't keep her home. She was destined to die either at the country club or the League of Women Voters."

Not such a bad way to go, Les decided, but decided not to say so. Anyway, Julia was cutting her off now, getting busy, but it was all right because she was coming. Les looked over the calendar of upcoming events well into next week: her committees, the Pi Phi alums, those Japanese businessmen of Harry's she was supposed to do something about. They meant nothing now, and she felt like x-ing them all out for the foreseeable.

Margo would be at work. Les kept home and work numbers for everybody. When she got through, a voice with a knife-edge Chicago accent said, "Hillcrest School." But Margo was conducting a story hour or some damn thing and couldn't be interrupted unless it was an emergency.

Les wasn't sure what it was. "Tell her Dorothy's dead and Julia's coming, and I'm just sitting here."

After a moment of profound silence the voice said, "Name please?"

"Mrs. Harry Hockaday," Les said with some dignity. Then she hung up.

Les remembered her version of everything that had ever happened, but she didn't have Margo's orderly mind, so she never remembered in sequence. Sometimes they were all nine years old and at Les's house after school, up in her room or dodging around under the snowball bushes beside the porch, looking for a safe place. Or it would be the night she and Harry had to go tell his parents they were getting married, and she'd been frozen with fear. Then sometimes she'd remember when Little Harry was a baby, and she hadn't known what to do. Then every detail of some country club dance came back in stunning detail, what everybody wore and the songs.

Now while she waited for Margo to call back, she remembered Julia's wedding, when she astounded everybody by marrying Junior Steadman.

All through school Julia had sworn to get out of the Cape and away from her grandparents. Then after she'd graduated from that Communist college in Ohio and Les thought she'd go out and reform the world, she came home and married Junior Steadman.

Les and Margo were both married by then. Margo and Reg were still living over in Columbia, and Les and Harry were back at the Cape after college. Little Harry was three, something like that. Then out of a clear blue sky Julia dashed home and announced that she and Junior were getting married at Christmas. She'd been home three weeks, tops, and they hadn't even particularly known him. He was in the construction business with his dad. All through high school and then when he was at the Rolla School of Mines, he'd gone with Cloris Weatherly. In fact he was still going with her. Julia broke them up.

Margo was thunderstruck, but Les thought, Why not? Then, of all things, Julia wanted a real wedding. She did a complete reversal and pulled out all the stops. Julia, who'd stomped through college in combat boots, wanted to come down the aisle in a winter white velvet dress, calf length, and satin pumps. Les and Margo went down the aisle with her in claret red and bottle green. Happily nobody was pregnant at the time.

41

Virgil Englehardt, Julia's grandfather, gave her away in one of his last public appearances. Julia looked so lovely that Les had to fight back tears the whole time. Julia always had a kind of nervous glamour nobody had a name for. Now when she turned back her veil for Junior, she was beautiful. And Junior, who was gorgeous himself, looked down at her like he couldn't believe his luck.

Dorothy Englehardt sat in the mother-of-the-bride pew, draped in that old fur cape that she alone could get away with. Les's mother was there too, farther back on the bride's side, trying not to die laughing.

The Steadmans, who were new money and plenty of it, gave Julia and Junior a house free and clear, out on the bluffs south of town in that new development. Nobody could quite believe it. Even Harry, who never noticed anything, said it wouldn't last. Hearing Harry on the subject was about more than Les could take.

Then in six months Julia had left Junior and was in New York, taking classes at Parsons. Julia had waltzed down the aisle and collected a new house full of wedding presents. Then she'd just as easily waltzed away. People said you couldn't have it both ways and bad-mouthed Julia because she could. And Junior was up a stump because Cloris had married on the rebound. Les's mother, a tireless, pitiless student of human nature, laughed her head off.

Les couldn't understand any of it, but Margo called it a failure of nerve. And Les didn't understand that either.

The Mayhews, Margo and Reg, moved to Chicago, where Reg had a job teaching in some college. Kimberly was born up there later when they thought they could afford a baby. Harry's grandmother died, so Les and Harry and Little Harry moved into her big old mausoleum of a house up in St. Louis when Harry went into the main office of the family firm. Everybody was in a different place.

The phone rang. That would be Margo. Fortunately tomorrow was a Saturday because she wouldn't miss a day of school if she was having a hysterectomy. Les never called Margo at home because Kimberly always answered. Then when the little brat heard the call wasn't for her, she'd hang up in Les's ear. After Reg and Margo separated, Kimberly's behavior just got worse, as far as Les could tell.

But it wasn't Margo on the phone. It was Madeline Soulard wondering where they were going for lunch after the hospital board meeting, which brought Les back to earth, canceling Madeline and canceling the hospital board too in a quick call in case Margo was trying to get through. After this flurry, Les was lost in thought again, and for some reason back at prom night, senior year.

Julia had said proms were reactionary and bourgeois. Margo, who didn't date anyway, was staying home to rehearse her valedictorian speech. Les was enrolled at the University of Missouri for the fall because Harry was already there. He was coming home for the prom, to please her.

She'd wanted them all to be there together. Without them the prom was like being somewhere else among strangers. Harry sulked until they left. He had a bottle of Jack Daniel's and the top down. She tied something over her head to keep the spray in her hair, and he helped her scoop the pink net of her dress into the car. Since he was coming home for the prom, her mother had let her have this froth of a dress. Then she never wore it again.

Harry drove miles south and parked up over the river. It was hot as noon, and the lights from the river traffic poked holes in the heavy night air. They sat up there while Les's dress went limp. Harry kept passing her the Jack Daniel's, though she never swallowed. They sat there, sticking to the car seat, while she held his free hand, trying to keep it in place. Her finger moved over the smooth stone of his Kappa Alpha ring. He'd taken off his white dinner jacket and was sweating through his shirt. Now he'd wedged the bottle between his thick legs and was reaching up her net skirt. She was wearing nylons and a garter belt — that's how far back this was. He wasn't as drunk as he was acting, so when she said, "No, not yet," he heard.

When he started telling her about all the girls at college he'd done it with, she knew she was all right. Letting him talk, she wondered where he got some of his information, but supposed that's what they fantasized about in bull sessions all night long at the Kappa Alpha house.

After he wound down, he stumbled out of the car, swung the bottle over his head, and threw it as far as he could. He staggered over to the edge of the drop-off. On his feet he was drunker, and for a heart-stopping moment Les thought he might be about to jump. But he stood weaving at the edge, and she decided he was peeing over the cliff.

She reached across to turn on the headlights to show him the way back. They blinded him when he turned around, and he stood there fixed in the glare like a big deer. His blond hair was tangled in every direction, and his face was liquor red. He stood swaying in the light. Then to impress them both he fumbled his wet tux shirt out of his cummerbund and pulled at it until the studs popped away. It took him a while, working behind his back to unfasten the cummerbund. Then he hooked his thumbs in the waistband of the black pants and shimmied out of them and his underpants in some kind of dance. When the shorts were a puddle around his ankles, he turned his hands palms up, presenting his nakedness to her.

Apparently he assumed she'd never seen a naked man — boy before, which was almost touching. Actually she hadn't, and Harry wasn't the best beginning. He was fish-belly white in the car light, with sloping shoulders and a beer belly in early stages. She looked him up and down, this future of hers, and at the thing between his legs. The end of it showed dull pink even at this distance. As she watched, he lunged forward like a diver off the side of a pool and threw up in the weeds. The pants trapped his ankles, and he was down on all fours, then up, then down again. She let him finish, keeping him in her sights.

When she'd talked him back into his clothes, she slid across into the driver's seat before he could get there and told him to get in the back. She slipped off her spike heels, which were mostly straps, because it was easier to drive without them. She got them back to the Cape, using the dimmers when she needed to and keeping on this side of the center line because she hadn't brought her license in her evening bag. She drove them home and thought about silver patterns to keep her mind off prom night.

Chapter 3

The plane lost altitude across Illinois and slanted in over the river and the Arch. Julia felt the weightless, helpless sensation of being reclaimed. Then she was walking through the jetway, unready but there. By leaving everything in the capable hands of Mrs. Lederer and the less capable hands of Mollie, the runner, she'd managed a ten-fifteen hair appointment and then a straight run to La Guardia. Her Donna Karan, not black, and Ferragamos felt vaguely like a disguise. A buttery Loewe bag big enough for a change and a nightgown hung from one shoulder.

Les was there up front in the crowd. She was in uniform too, a springy two-piece and lizard pumps, medium heel. She was always the tallest of the three of them and didn't need more height. Willowy now, not stringy like eighth grade, and still young, something young frozen in her face. And blonder than last time, whenever that was. Her arms were out, and Julia was ready to turn herself in. There was even a minor element of relief in it. And whatever the occasion, they had to begin by giving each other the once-over, as always. Like Christmas of freshman year.

Julia had come home for the holidays, reaping full credit for going east to school, or at least Ohio. Les and Margo were home from the U of Missouri. Then Les had to enlist Margo in a campaign to get Julia to the country club Christmas dance. Julia had spent all fall at sit-ins, barring ROTC units from the armory. No hard-liner like a freshman, and she hadn't even gone to the high school prom last spring.

It was the same Christmas dance the country club always gave, whether the world was going to hell or not. The same white poinsettias on the tables, the same three-man fox-trot combo. Les worked half the evening to corner Julia alone in the ladies' lounge where Dorothy Englehardt was to die all those years later.

"Guess what."

"You've come to your senses and depledged Pi Phi," heartless Julia said.

"Be serious. I am."

But Julia thought not. For Julia that semester serious meant ending the war, now. And serious meant trying to get that rustic Missouri drawl or whatever it was out of her mouth. And serious meant going to country club dances only under duress because there were people in the world being napalmed.

"I'm pregnant," Les said. The formal was ivory taffeta with a shape of its own. Not a good year for formals anyway.

"Not funny," Julia said.

"True."

But Julia pulled back from that, way back. For one thing, she was still a virgin and trying hard to keep that quiet at college. And Les wasn't the type. You got pregnant because you were careless. Or in love, so nobody had the right to blame you. Or as a statement against something: middle-class morality.

"I've told Harry," Les said.

Or you got pregnant, Julia saw, if it was on your agenda.

"You could get rid of it."

Les sighed. "That school back east is making you hard."

"Speaking of school, what do you intend to do about that?" Julia was shaken and trying not to let on.

"I can make it into second semester, until after initiation."

"Haven't you been initiated enough? What initiation?"

"Pi Phi," Les said evenly. "I'm getting that

50

pin." She pointed to her left breast swathed in ivory taffeta. "Believe it."

"And then?"

"Harry and I get married." Les paused long enough for Julia to give some thought to Harry and the Hockadays and Hockaday Hybrid Seed Corn, a four-state network. "You ought to be glad, Julia. I am. Don't tell Margo. She's — you know — an idealist. I'll break it to her after the holidays, back at school."

"How was it?" Julia asked, still only eighteen.

"How was what?"

"I mean, did you get pregnant the first time you —"

"Heavens, no. We started last summer, here."

Julia glanced around the ladies' lounge.

"Not right here. Down in the boathouse. It was fine, really. I didn't mind." Les didn't like what she was seeing in Julia's eyes, the judgment. "I suppose it would be better if it had been some druggie from the poli sci department at a love-in."

Then Margo breezed in to catch them conspiring. Les and Julia whipped around to the makeup mirror, but Julia had nothing to do since she wasn't wearing makeup that semester. She had on a white blouse and the

51

only skirt she owned, a black one, which made her look more like a cellist than a revolutionary. But at least she wasn't some plastic Pi Phi pledge who went to college only to trap some jackass of good family. She wasn't sure what she was, but she wasn't that.

Now, because time is a trickster, Julia's walking off a flight into Les's arms. And the son, Harry IV, Les nearly had in the Pi Phi house is twenty-something, out of college himself after taking six years to get through Colgate.

Julia surrendered. They didn't kiss, though Les wanted to. "You didn't come first-class. You were practically the last one off."

"Les, where do you get the idea that I fly free?"

"But it must be deductible, and you look frazzled."

So much for the two hundred dollars she'd just put into her hair.

"Margo's coming down tomorrow," Les said briskly. "I know, I know, but she wanted to come. I told her to fly down tonight after school, but she said she couldn't leave Kimberly overnight. So we'll have to swing back by here and pick her up from the flight in the morning. Is that all you packed?"

Julia knew Les's plans of old. At their best laid, there was always something ungainly about them. They'd spent the entire summer they got their driver's licenses making elaborate arrangements to pick one another up and drop one another off, with Les at the wheel. They never got out of the Vogels' Plymouth without Les planning the next time.

The Hockadays' house was from 1904: world's fair Corinthian in limestone with a bronze pediment and a marble balustrade. It stood back from Portland Place, black against the evening except for the coach lamps in front and a single square of light from a third-floor window.

Les drove the Infiniti through the porte cochere and parked around back. The garden was muted by evening, a New Yorker's final fantasy: this lavish sweep in the middle of a city, greening with spring and hedged and graveled and trellised, extending to a carriage house that appeared to be the size of the Morgan Library. They entered the house through the arching door of a tiled sunroom with a barrel-vaulted ceiling and beyond that into a pair of drawing rooms big enough to handle two walk-in fireplaces.

"Wow," Julia said.

"I'd just like to put it all in your hands, Julia, from stem to stern. I'd like to rip out and start over with this place right down to bare walls." Les shrugged. "But I've had to work around a lot of Harry's grandmother's furniture."

"And Harry," Julia said.

How often Les had wanted to hand this house to Julia, invite her out for weeks, months, to oversee the job. She'd put her in one of those big square bedrooms upstairs. They could spend days going over paint chips and fabric samples. Les kept a file of Julia's rooms that appeared in *House Beautiful, Architectural Digest,* a spread in the *New York Times Magazine* headlined "Beyond Chintz: Julia Steadman Moves Ahead of the 'Lady Decorator' Pack."

On the other hand, Les could never quite believe that this was the same Julia she'd known. Granted, most people changed more than she had herself. But change didn't begin to explain Julia. If she'd gone to law school, something as serious and political as that, Les wouldn't have turned a hair, but interior decoration? And she was good at it too, famous. The magazines called her work inspired, her taste impeccable, her eye unerring.

Les had always wanted to see Julia's world

with her own eyes. The only time she'd been to New York was some business thing with Harry. They'd stayed at the Park Lane, which probably wasn't even the right hotel, and Julia had been out of town on a job, or said she was. Les had walked up along the park to the apartment building where Julia lived and worked. But it was just another blank-faced building, with a doorman who looked at you if you lingered. Les had never invited herself, though she could go practically on a moment's notice. Harry wouldn't care, and her purse was crammed with credit cards. Les often wondered what money was for if not for this.

They were standing in the gloom, so she switched on a light. It was a ginger jar, wired, with a drawn-silk shade, that had always been there, though it would take ten lamps to light this end of the room.

"Stem to stern," Les said again. "Start over from scratch."

"People pay me good money to *achieve* this look, Les." Julia gestured around the room. "People want — ancestral accretion."

"But they're Harry's ancestors," Les said, "and they don't exactly go back to the *Mayflower*. In fact they really just go back to Harry's grandparents."

"Half my clients can't trace themselves back to their fathers," Julia said.

It crossed Les's mind that Julia's career might go deeper than swatches and paint chips. But now Julia was appraising a wedge of the parquet visible in this light. It was an intricate pattern, beginning to separate. "At least I didn't carpet," Les said.

"No, you didn't," Julia said. "Your mother would have."

"As a matter of fact, Mother's with me now." Les walked Julia out to the hall, toward a sweep of stairs. "Come up and say hello to her, get that over with."

Julia stared. "She's here? How long?"

"Just since the winter. She's settling in. She was rattling around in that house of hers."

As they climbed past the second floor of this public monument, Julia considered Mrs. Vogel's rescue from rattling around her little Dutch Colonial on Lee Boulevard down at the Cape. "Did she mind giving up her own house?"

"Not too much," Les said. "And I've been rattling around in this one especially after Little Harry was away at college."

"Where's Harry tonight . . . Big Harry?"

"I sent him to the club. When else are you and I going to have any time together? Here's Mother."

She tapped on a door and pushed it wide. "Bath of her own on the left. Her own bedroom through there with a big walk-in closet. For her walls I used a Brunschwig & Fils glazed cotton. You used it in one of your rooms. I saw it in *Metropolitan Home*."

The woman herself was in a chair by a high window, just reaching forward to switch off the television. Les's mother sat in the pool of light from a bridge lamp. Julia was suddenly a child again, seeing Mrs. Vogel on her screened porch in the evenings, monitoring the world in the light from this same lamp. "Julia? Come over here and let me have a look at you."

Julia recalled her habit of looking just past you at something more worthwhile. She and Les both hung back and then moved forward, gawky again. As they edged up, Mrs. Vogel smiled past Julia's left ear, apparently at a ceiling fixture. Her long hands were arranged in her lap. Her hair was white, but only a shade off the blond she'd been when she was the Valkyrie of Lee Boulevard. She looked past Julia and said, "You haven't changed a bit."

Julia struggled against the time warp, but she saw the woman in her prime, the rickrack housedresses starchy in the limpest weather, the skeptical hand on the long bony

57

hip, the caw of laughter at their callowness. Though she'd damaged Les beyond repair, all three of them kept reporting back to her in hope of approval forever withheld.

"How are you?" Julia said, steadying her voice.

"As you see — stuck up here like a skeleton in a closet. I don't get out. How could a woman of my age wander around St. Louis even if I had anywhere to go? I'd get my head bashed open and my brains battered out. You ought to see some of the stuff they show on TV." She crowed with laughter and tapered off, working a long finger in under a trifocal lens.

Julia remembered the odd, comprehensive list of what always made Mrs. Vogel laugh: Women who worked, women who didn't. Good housekeepers and slatterns. Prim women and women with pasts. From her safe tree she sniped at them all: maids, wives, and widows. And still she had scorn to spare. Men amused her less if she noticed them at all. Les's late father was on the road a lot, burning up the rural byways in a company car.

"Lesley marches me over to Euclid for lunch, when she thinks about it."

"Every week actually," Les murmured. This too unnerved Julia, who hadn't heard

that sulkiness in any of their voices for de-
cades.

"You know Lesley!" Mrs. Vogel threw up
her hands. "All her busywork. She sits on so
many boards, her bottom's flat." She
clapped a hand over her mouth to stifle a
whoop.

"I hear Margo's coming down. Quite a
party. I was just sitting here trying to picture
Margo divorced. Of the three of you, I always said she was the only one with her head
screwed on right. Now look at her. High and
dry at her age. It doesn't look very good for
Margo, does it?"

Mrs. Vogel tried to muffle a smile and
failed. "You girls. You never change to me. I
bet that dress set you back." She scanned the
air past Julia's sleeve. "I was just thinking today about that time you were married to Junior Steadman for about a minute. When
you left him in the lurch, people said you'd
live to regret it. But I knew better. I said Julia
looks out for number one. Lesley figures
Dorothy cut you off without a penny."

"Mother, I never —"

"I believe everything's to go to Deaconess
Hospital," said Julia, stiff and defensive,
sinking under the immense weight of Mrs.
Vogel.

"That sounds more like it," she said. "If

59

you weren't right there under Dorothy's jurisdiction, dancing to her tune, she'd write you off."

"Mother, I expect Julia wants —"

"Oh don't pay any attention to me. All I can see is you two and Margo with you like you used to be, racing up those stairs to Lesley's room to tell secrets, as if you had any."

"Oh we had plenty of secrets," Julia said in a futile try for lightness.

"Not at the Cape you didn't. Nobody did."

This was a clear reference to Julia's parentage, and she tensed for a frontal assault, but Mrs. Vogel was still playing her version of cat and mouse. "Margo had good sense, but she was kind of old-maidish. Really when you think about it, she didn't have any business marrying at all. You other two were the sly ones. Julia, I wouldn't have trusted you farther than I could chunk a rock. Your grandmother was a hundred years too old to keep you in line, even if she'd cared. And of course Wanda was no use to you, even before she went off the pier."

Julia stood transfixed. Yes, Wanda — Aunt Wanda — had indeed gone off the end of the pier when Julia was in second grade. Wanda had gunned that old Oldsmobile 98 of the Englehardts straight off the Division Avenue pier, leaving a blizzard of angry notes behind. Dorothy Englehardt had to speak sharply to the *Cape Chronicle* to keep them from running a front-page picture of the streaming Oldsmobile being lifted out of the river by a marine crane with Wanda still in it.

"And I naturally didn't know what Lesley had up her sleeve," Mrs. Vogel was saying.

"Mother, I didn't have anything up my sleeve. You had me cocked and primed to marry Harry before I could —"

"Me?" Mrs. Vogel planted a hand on her startled breast. "Harry Hockaday was the last boy in creation I'd have wanted you to marry. I sent you off to the university in great hopes you'd meet a boy going somewhere in life who didn't have to take handouts from his family."

Les moaned, back where she began. Julia stood there yearning for flight and rooted to the spot, fascinated to find that the years had cost Mrs. Vogel nothing.

"Never mind about all that now, Lesley. Marry in haste, repent at leisure. I want to talk to Julia. I hear Dorothy died in the john." Mrs. Vogel slapped at her knee and knuckled her mouth.

The phrase *crapped out* streaked across

Julia's mind like a meteor.

"So it looks like you're the last leaf on the tree. James, your . . . father, is long gone, and of course Wanda. And you're the only grandchild."

She could always isolate you, cut you off and cut you down. "So that simplifies the arrangements," Julia said, reaching for briskness. "Burial tomorrow. Just something at the graveside. Rantsinger's are in charge. No funeral."

"Oh, nothing as old hat as a funeral," Mrs. Vogel said. "Your generation can't be bothered. When I die, Lesley's just going to shovel dirt in my face."

And I'll dance on your grave, Julia thought mutinously.

Mrs. Vogel sat back and made a steeple of her hands. It was her posture of considered opinion, and it had always held them suspended. "That's right, Julia," she said at last. "Keep it short and sweet and then put it behind you. You were always ranting and raving to get out, and you knew the door of your cage was open the whole time." She looked up and smiled in a ghastly parody of sympathetic understanding. "There wasn't a thing holding you back but you."

Les had Julia unnecessarily by the arm and was pulling her away. "I'm going to give Julia some supper. I bet she hasn't eaten all day. Come on, Julia."

They were in disorderly retreat, and the television blared suddenly behind them. When they were at the door, Mrs. Vogel called out, "You girls!" with a caw of laughter over the comfortably nagging voices of Siskel and Ebert.

They fled down the stairs, and the dark house dwarfed them too. They were children all the way to the landing. A servants' stairway wandered from there to the back of the house. Les led along a passage with shellacked tongue-and-groove walls and lightbulbs on chains. St. Louis gothic, Julia thought wildly, complete with the horror in the attic.

The kitchen was vast and updated: a high-tech cube. Two places were set at a corner of the butcher-block island under a looming thicket of hanging pans. The light in here hit them, and they blinked at each other: a dressed-down society woman and a somewhat stylized New York career woman, forties and holding. A couple of slick items, but somehow they weren't convinced.

"I'm sorry," Les said.

"Well, she could always come right to the point."

"Only if it hurt," Les said. "Just try coming to the point with her."

"Why did you bring her here, Les?"

"You tell me."

"Because you thought you could turn it around? Because you thought that in your house you'd be the mother and she'd be the child and you'd finally have some control?"

"Julia, 'you tell me' is just an expression."

Sitting at the butcher-block island, Julia was tired all the way to the ground but somehow diverted. From a long stainless counter across the room Les said over her shoulder, "I loathe cooking," though she was nowhere near the big cold Jenn-Air stove. "Pour the wine. It's breathed enough, whatever that means."

"Do you have somebody to cook?"

"For dinner parties and do's. Harry's out a lot now, so I don't bother day to day. But I have somebody part-time if Mother doesn't run her off."

"She doesn't just stay upstairs?"

"Mother? Are you kidding? She's everywhere I turn. She does aerobics, for Christ's sake. She's only seventy-four. 'Shovel dirt in my face' my ass. She'll outlive us all. She was only upstairs tonight so you could see her posed as fucking Whistler's Mother."

"I never think of you using language like that," Julia said.

64

"Blame the goddamn Pi Phi house," Les said. "We were never what you thought." She brought two plates to the table, curried chicken salad with white grapes and nut bread–cream cheese sandwiches.

"What's this?" Julia said. "The DAR luncheon?"

"Just eat." They didn't toast, but they touched glasses. Then after a little silence Les said, "You always think I'm naive, but I'm not that naive. I don't think I brought Mother here to have power over her. That generation of women didn't give us their power, did they? Your grandmother wasn't much better, was she?"

"Possibly worse," Julia said.

"Why were they like that?" Les asked. "How come they knew everything, and what gave them the right to judge everything without ever putting themselves on the line? And Margo's mother. She was different, but — Jesus."

They both caught a fleeting glimpse of Margo's mother, who'd been married three times before Margo was in high school and never to Margo's father, according to Mrs. Vogel. Methodical Margo had risen out of that boozy world of screen doors hanging by a hinge and trucks parked in the yard, and a hatchet-faced mother sitting in taverns who married first and asked questions later.

"I believe the feminist view is that they were underemployed."

"Bullshit," Les said. "My mother had her wash on the line by seven-thirty Monday morning and spent the rest of the week pulling the rug out from under everybody in sight. They were busy every minute. Your grandmother was never home. Margo's mother may have slept all day, but she was out all night. And they'd never have taken jobs even before they were married because they wouldn't have put up with bosses. They didn't negotiate."

"And college," Julia said.

"But they never went."

"Exactly. They were never in the presence of superior knowledge." Julia looked sharply at her wineglass, wondering where this wisdom came from. Les poured seconds for them both.

"College was another thing that brought down the women of our generation. What did I think I was going to do with that asinine degree in art history?"

"Change the world?" Les offered.

"No, that's what those endless marches on Washington were for."

"But then you went to art school. Why?"

"I don't know why. I suppose I thought if I

66

couldn't burn down the world, I might as well decorate it. I don't know."

"But how did you pay for it?" Les had always wondered. She hoped Dorothy Englehardt had paid. She didn't want Dorothy to be the complete and utter villain. Villainess.

"Junior paid," Julia said. "It was sort of a settlement. So that's where I sold out."

"Sold out?" Les said. "What does that mean?"

"Julia, the committed little revolutionary on alimony at art school," Julia said. "That's selling out. Come to think of it, none of it was Reagan's fault. And Parsons was in New York, and New York was safer than the Cape."

"How was New York safer?"

"Because my grandmother and your mother weren't there, for a start. I went to New York for the reason most people do, whether they know it or not. Nobody cares enough there to delve into your personal history."

Les was well versed in Julia's history, the early part at least. She'd imbibed it from her own mother. Half the Cape had imbibed it from her mother. Officially, Julia was the daughter of James, the Englehardt son. He'd been killed as a soldier in Germany. There wasn't a war on, but he'd died in a jeep accident out on maneuvers.

The body was sent back, and Clifford Rantsinger, who was third-generation undertaker and knew everybody, the quick and the dead, spread it around that the army had botched the embalming job. Virgil Englehardt had to identify his son and was said never to be the same afterward. Another school of thought had it that he'd never been the same after marrying Dorothy.

There was a full military funeral with a bugle sounding retreat and a flag on the coffin, and the minister called James a "cold war warrior." Then within weeks Dorothy Englehardt was putting it around, mostly by phone, that James had fathered a child in Germany. She was canny enough not to say that James had married, so it didn't look like a complete whitewash. He'd just taken up with some German girl who didn't want the baby, so the Englehardts were arranging to take her in.

That didn't take in Les's mother or in fact anybody. Wanda Englehardt at sixteen had been away at school for a semester — Gulfport, Mississippi, or somewhere down south. Now she was back. Then baby Julia turned up. People could put two and two together as Mrs. Vogel never stopped saying. Everybody knew that Julia, a bastard either way you looked at it, was Wanda's child. But no-body was going to cross Dorothy Engle-hardt. The charitable view was that she didn't want Wanda's chances ruined. Doro-thy's bridge club came nearer the real rea-son. It was something she could hold over Wanda's head to keep her in line. And Les's mother was left to say that James's well-timed death was another stroke of good luck for the Englehardts.

Even in high school the whole situation went unspoken among Les and Margo and Julia, taken for granted. Nobody could call it a secret, and Wanda had never been Julia's mother in any way that counted. Wanda was said to spend most of her vertical time at the bar of the golf club picking up guest mem-bers. Les hardly remembered her, apart from getting out of the way when she barreled down the crown of River Road in the Olds-mobile. Then one day she hauled off and drove it over the end of the pier. Mrs. Vogel said that given the circumstances, it was about the best thing that could happen.

"Your mother was right," Julia said. "The door of my cage was always open, and I had to have known it on some level. But I thought I'd get trapped and end up like Wanda. Dorothy could suck all the air out of you whether she wanted you around or not."

69

"But then you came back and married Junior." Les poured the last of the wine into Julia's glass.

"Yes, I came back and married Junior. You should have seen his face when he found out I was a virgin. He loved me, at least at that moment. I just couldn't get out of the Cape without leaving somebody who loved me."

This was more than Julia had ever told, so Les said, "And you loved him?"

"I was twenty-one, twenty-two. You can convince yourself of anything then if you don't have to believe it too long. I don't know if I've ever loved any man," Julia said, omitting one.

I don't know if I have either, Les wanted to say, but it was too perilous. They needed Margo. Les glanced at her watch as if it were time right then to go back to the airport and get her.

Chapter 4

Coming off the plane, Margo spotted them before they spotted her. Somehow she'd put on eight pounds since Reg. And she couldn't remember when she'd seen either of them last. She hadn't seen Julia in years. Certainly Margo's mother's death hadn't brought them all together. When she died in a trailer park outside Jackpot, Nevada, attended by the last in a descending order of male barflies, Margo had her buried out there where she dropped, to Reg's relief.

Margo had spent the hour on the plane going over her third graders' diagnostic reading test scores. She'd decided on a dress she'd wear again for end-of-the-year parent conferences, and a sensible heel. She'd be ready for about anything in this outfit, apart from changing a tire.

Les and Julia were there, Les beginning to wave. Julia's dress, brought for burial day, was more loosely wrapped than she was and a touch too casual for the occasion. Even the sunglasses parked up in her hair said she was going to try to get through the day as a bystander. She'd undoubtedly considered not coming at all. Julia's defenses had always been a mile high and paper-thin.

Margo put out her arms, earth-mothering them, playing teacher though she hadn't meant to do that. It's only with strangers that you don't have to play a role.

According to Les's plan, Julia would sit up front with her, and then Julia and Margo would switch around after they stopped for an early lunch at Ste. Genevieve. The conversation stayed on the tactical level until they'd cleared south St. Louis and were moving down 55. Margo calculated the odds on getting through the whole day without having to review her divorce for them.

In the weeks after Reg she'd written, and they'd both called back, Les often, giving Margo the opportunity to sound strong, organized, getting on with things. Les had offered to fly up to Chicago and be there for her and had to be dissuaded. It was the least convenient moment in human history for a houseguest. Now she didn't want to have to go back over all that. It wasn't why they were here. Margo tried hard to arrange life into lesson plans.

Les stayed just over the limit, both hands on the wheel. The hermetically sealed luxury of the car was beyond Margo's experience. She could cross her legs with room to spare, then felt the heaviness of one leg over the other. Her panty hose rasped. Julia's hand rested along the back of Les's seat, and she was still wearing Junior Steadman's wedding ring. As soon as Reg left last fall, Margo had taken hers off and filed it away the way she filed everything.

"Grayer," Julia said, looking back at her. Margo had started going gray right after college and hadn't done anything about it. Her hair was in a teacher's bob, low-maintenance, and full enough to balance her figure. Julia's hair was dark and convincing. "I wonder how long we can get away with these colors," she said to Les.

"I say till menopause." Les's eyes stayed on the road. "Then I say to hell with it."

"I say a little longer than that," Julia said. By now Margo had exhausted all the possible reasons why Julia might still be wearing the ring from a six-month marriage after all these years.

"Why?" she said, reaching forward to touch it.

"For business," Julia said. "In my field you're not supposed to look like you actually studied. You're supposed to be a very gifted amateur who doesn't need the work and who started out by doing her boarding-school chums a favor. I'm generally thought to be a

Sweetbriar alum married to a venture capitalist. Something like that. Image is all, and you can pull off stuff you couldn't get away with for a minute down at the Cape."

"Smoke and mirrors," Margo murmured, which Les didn't get. "So you did yourself completely over."

"There wasn't enough of me to do over," Julia said. "Bear in mind I turned up in New York wearing two-strap Birkenstocks and thermal underwear."

"And look at you now." Margo smiled.

"Look at me now," Julia said.

When Les pulled off the interstate at Ste. Genevieve, they passed fence-post signs for Hockaday Feeds and Grains. The nameless place where they stopped for lunch was decorated with high-water marks and blown-up photos of the flood of '93. It was one of the last outposts where a waitress still wore a handkerchief with contrasting crocheted trim, pinned across with her name in looping wire: Fern.

Fern saw them get out of the big car and knew them before they got in the door. They took her back. She'd gone to high school down at the Cape a year behind them, so she'd memorized them. She'd climbed down out of the school bus every morning with the rest of the hayseeds in their Goodwill double knits, and she'd watched these three like movie stars. Seeing them now was no surprise. In a way they'd never left her. She had their names mixed up in her mind, and she'd never been near enough to hear their voices. One of them was brainy. One was going with Harry Hockaday. One of them came from a big house up on River Road. They had so much — and each other.

She watched them till the end, but then she solved high school by getting pregnant junior year. Then it turned out to be twins. She married Dwayne Teeter, who was thirty-four and on parole for stealing conduit tile from the Highway Department. They had the twins and three more and then came up here to Ste. Genevieve for work. All they found was this job for her, but now Dwayne had Social Security and Disability.

"Three BLTs and three coffees, please," Les said to her, "and a Sweet'n Low. No fries."

Julia had forgotten about menus that photograph the food in full color.

"Sweet'n Low all around," Margo said. At least they looked at you when they ordered, which was more than most. Of course they didn't remember her because they'd never known her, and anyway she probably looked ten years older than she should. The one who'd gone with Harry Hockaday took out a Kleenex and wiped the Formica table, but stopped when Fern came back with the sandwiches.

After Ste. Genevieve they switched around, and Julia sat in the backseat. "Good," she said, "you two will get there first," because the mileage to the Cape was dwindling sharply. Time was beginning to lose its shape. It seemed to be some perpetual glaring noon. The car's air-conditioning eased on automatically, and Margo recalled how much earlier spring came down here.

The potential pitfalls of this day were beginning to occur to her. Les had everything organized but only so far. Margo remembered Les's plans of old: minute by minute until that moment when they looked at each other and said some version of, "But I thought *you* brought it." Margo wondered if Julia had really thought out why she'd come. It wouldn't be for the sake of appearances, not in Julia's case.

"I found it was easier after my mother was dead," Margo said to her. She shifted around to Julia in the backseat, but the seat belt had her in a vise. "I could finally talk to her — that dialogue that goes on in your mind."

"Does she answer back?" Julia said.

"No. But now she listens."

"I don't think I'm communing with Dorothy," Julia said, overlooking much. "And it would take more than death to make her a good listener."

Julia was still being brittle, but Les felt reassured. This was why they always needed Margo. Margo knew how to break the ice. Les was too busy holding back. Considering the circumstances, she had to repress the sheer inappropriate pleasure of having them all together. But now it was time Julia gave some thought to Dorothy, time they all did.

Square-bottomed, iron-hipped, perpetually seventy-something Dorothy Englehardt in a stretched-shapeless gored skirt with high-calved chicken legs running down to gapping spectator pumps. Her face a hasty gash of lipstick and a flash of bifocals, her hair a tightly sprung thicket of gray that she ran both hands through in a characteristic gesture. The crack of her laughter leading the pack around the card table, the gravel voice barking commands on the phone from first light. Nobody crossed her.

People called her coarse, but well behind her back. Then they qualified it by saying she was a good sport and a grand gal and a pillar of the community. All but Les's mother, who hated her and probably wanted to be

her. Besides, the Vogels' circle didn't inter-
sect with the Englehardts'.

They came past the high school, and still
the town hadn't quite grown out to it. The
sign in the bald lawn out front read:

CAPE VINCENT HIGH SCHOOL
Home of the Rebel Raiders
"HERE WE EDUCATE FOR LIVING"

"If they only had," Julia remarked.

"Remember that afternoon in the audito-
rium when we went over my valedictory
speech?" Margo reached over to touch Les.
"I wanted Julia's opinion. I knew you'd only
have praised it. I could count on criticism
from Julia."

"And where was I?" Les said.

"Probably driving all over town in the
Plymouth," Julia said, "trying to find us."

But Les made herself remember. "No, I
know. I was on the prom committee, decorating the gym. It was a Peter Max theme
with rainbows."

At the light on Third, Les consulted her
watch. "After one already."

"I don't want to get there early," Julia said.
Which was all right because Les had a stop
to make anyway. Their route, Les realized
too late, took them past the house where

Margo had grown up. The street was wider, abbreviating the yards, but the paintless houses were unchanged. People sat motionless in swings on drooping porches.

"It was that one, I think," Margo said, defusing the moment. She remembered the rent, forty-three dollars a month, and her room under the eaves. She lay up there through stifling nights, her eyes puffy from homework, not sleeping until she heard her mother. They never locked the door. Most nights her mother couldn't have found the lock with the key. Margo had waited for the stumble of shoes on the front steps, trying to hear how many. She'd listen for muttered voices in the room below, hear the squeak and then the rhythmic squeak of the sofa. She'd prop her pillow against the sound of muffled moaning and wake in the night at the sound of ice in a glass.

Les turned left on Division and headed downtown, slowing past the old Twain Hotel, now some kind of rehab center according to the sign. But the Paddlewheel Room at street level was still open. It was where people went to eat downtown if they wanted to pay for the linen tablecloth and the rose in the bowl. Margo had worked in the kitchen there the summer after they graduated, trying to save every penny, panicked that something might yet block her getaway.

Les parked and slipped efficiently out of the car.

"What's she up to?" Julia said as they watched her retreating down the street.

"Didn't there used to be a florist on that corner?"

"Jesus Christ," Julia sighed.

"Let her do it. She wants to."

"How often did we used to say that?"

"Did you see Harry last night?"

"Les said she'd sent him to the club."

"And this morning?"

"As a matter of fact, no." Les disappeared around the corner, and Margo looked back significantly at Julia, though Harry had never been able to hold their interest for long.

"But how are you?" they said in unison.

"No, really," Julia said.

"It's harder on Kimberly than on me," Margo said. "I know that in the aftermath of divorce most people say their children are taking it better than they are, but that's just a delusion. It's come at such a hard time for her. If we could just have held out a little longer."

"You would have," Julia said.

Margo nodded. "But Reg wanted out." Which was precisely the sort of thing she hadn't meant to say. She was trying her best to revise this situation as two adults making a reasoned decision. "But I'm fine. If I learned anything from my childhood, it ought to be how to get along without a man."

"But you'd been married a long time, practically as long as Les."

The distant view of Margo had been of the earnest, thick-browed scholarship student in all the wrong clothes who married her history professor, like a quick reading of *Little Women.*

But Reg Mayhew had been only five years older and while bearded, not gray bearded. He was a graduate assistant teaching a section of Western civ. They found each other in class and married just before her senior year. It was the era for quiet weddings, if any, and often outdoors. A JP in Boonville conducted the ceremony on a glassed-in porch, neither family attending. They lived in married housing all the way through Reg's Ph.D., and Margo decided to go into elementary ed because one Ph.D. was really all they could swing financially.

"I hate waste, and that's what those years represent to me now. Reg says not. He says we had some good years, and Kimberly."

"You're in touch with him?"

"Hardly at all, which is just as well, but he isn't keeping in touch with Kimberly. So

81

there we are, mother and daughter. I feel like I'm back where I began."

"Hardly that," Julia said, but Les was at the car door, her purse swinging from an elbow and in both hands an oversized spray of tulips and forsythia that looked like it meant to lie across a coffin. Les knew Julia wouldn't have done anything, so she'd phoned down from St. Louis and said she'd pick up personally. Avoiding Julia's eye, she handed the flowers across to Margo, inundating her. "Pink and yellow," Les said, "and I told them one color." She looked back at Julia. "It'll be from us. The three of us."

The door of the Paddlewheel Room opened, and a bunch of men came out. "Kiwanis," Les said, starting the car, but they were breaking up too early for a lunch program, and they were all in darkish suits.

"They look like pallbearers," Margo said without thinking, a rare slip. The last one out the door was Junior Steadman. He was a little thicker across the front, and his hair was farther back on his head, but it was Junior and still looking good. The whole group had shoeshines.

"Jesus Christ," Julia said from the back.

Les careened down Front Street and on out south. A faint florist smell from the scentless flowers reached Julia in the backseat, tightening her throat.

The Englehardts were all buried on the second knoll in from the gates of Gracewood. Cars were off the gravel almost back to the entrance, and people were walking. When Les parked, the pallbearers pulled in behind. She looked back to prepare Julia. "You remember how this is. People turn out. Just accept it." Then something vulnerable and reasonably receptive in Julia's face made her say, "And take the sunglasses off your head. Either put them on or put them in your purse." Which Margo agreed with but wouldn't have said.

"And people will be coming by the house afterward. It's expected, and it's all arranged."

Julia had envisioned never having to walk in that house again. The afternoon unreeled endlessly ahead of her.

"So just be . . . grown-up about it," Les said. Margo stifled a smile and concentrated on her lap full of flowers.

Then as Julia climbed out of the back door, she found herself virtually in Junior Steadman's arms, again.

"Julia?" Now he had her by both elbows. "Julia."

"And Les and Margo," Julia said as they

83

appeared. Some witless fate had reassembled her entire wedding party. "Let's not say we haven't changed a bit."

"But, honey, you haven't." Julia was confronted again by the blazing blue-eyed sincerity with which Junior could invest any cliché. Her mind skipped out of control, and she remembered Junior naked, looming over her in a motel bed just short of their wedding, that patterned forest of black hair across the football chest, the eyes blue even in the dark. Julia not knowing where her legs went.

"Doggone it, I wish Willa was here." He dropped one of her elbows and reached for wallet pictures. Two kids: Junior junior and, of course, Ashley. You can destroy a man's whole life but only for a couple of months.

It appeared that Junior had continued to think of Dorothy as his grandmother-in-law, no doubt close kin in these parts. Two of the other pallbearers had been ushers at their wedding. They moved ahead in a platoon toward Clifford Rantsinger, who was opening the back door of a hearse. Sunlight struck at the silver casket between their drip-dry suits as they carried it over to a square of fake grass. Les moved on ahead to arrange the flowers across the lid. There was another Rantsinger's car full of flowers, some in shapes: Eastern Star star, Rotarian wheel. Horrified, Julia saw there was a tent with folding chairs for family. Her heel dug spongy earth. "Stick with me," she murmured to Margo. But with the pallbearers, both Pinckneys of Pinckney & Pinckney, Dorothy's lawyers, and Les, they filled the tent.

The minister was young and after their time and kept his remarks scriptural and generic. Dorothy was an offhand Presbyterian and no great contributor. He evidently assumed that she was a ninety-something woman who'd lived out her span and then some and could do you no more harm. Julia kept an eye on the casket under the drooping tulips, waiting for that Vincent Price moment when the lid jiggled and Dorothy's loose-ringed hand emerged, reaching for a phone, always her first waking act.

Then it was over, and Clifford Rantsinger was extending a snow-white hand to Julia. He was showing no cuff, so that meant a short-sleeved dress shirt under the suit coat. It was Julia's moment, and she decided to walk through it and get it over with. Eyes were on her as she stepped up to the casket, so she put her hand on it, feeling nothing. Past it was Virgil's headstone and farther down the rise James's, then Wanda's. The phrase *sole survivor* swept her like the breeze fluttering the florist ribbons. The glare was terrible, and as she turned away she reached around in her bag for her sunglasses.

Devised for tycoons, River Road meandered along the bluffs above the river and the town. The last house went in before the market crash of '29, so it was all old money and doctors. There was a gatehouse but no gate, and people drove through on Sunday afternoons, looking at the houses.

The Hockadays, Harry's parents, had lived in the first one as you turn in. Harry's father told Les that it took twenty-eight tons of coal to heat it through a winter and a team of ten three weeks to paint it. But a urologist had it now, so it was spanking fresh in its original colors with Andersen windows, and the lawn was like a golf green. From there on the houses were Tudor and Italian palazzo and Spanish colonial. Only sixteen or eighteen in all, but they were massive, set in rolling lawns with hedges between, dense as plastered walls.

Julia had grown up at the midpoint of the road in a house built during the First World War, not a good period. An outbuilding around back didn't know whether it was a barn or a garage. The house itself was three stories of patched yellow stucco with deeply overhanging porch roofs that made it evening in every room. The Englehardts had bought it in 1938 for fourteen thousand dollars, cash. Virgil Englehardt had farmland and a share in a barge business and ran the insurance agency. Dorothy ran everything else. James was little when they moved in, and Wanda was born afterward.

Nobody was there yet, and Julia decided to brave the house by herself. An impulse, but she wanted a moment without Les hovering and Margo's eye contact. Julia wanted to give the house one last chance to redeem itself, though she wasn't sure what she meant by that.

Les and Margo watched her walking away over the cracked concrete up to the porch, observing how good she looked even from behind, the acid test.

"Is that the girl who came home from college spouting all that rhetoric with hair hanging down from her armpits?" Margo said.

"I didn't even know who Che Guevara and Betty Friedan were," Les said. Later, in a nod to Julia, she'd read *The Women's Room* and thought it was sad.

They both noticed how Julia had even got a Missouri drawl out of the way she walked. "Who was the father? I never wanted to ask.

Did anybody know?" Margo said.

"Julia's? It was one of the Bassinger brothers," Les said. "You know, they had that discount furniture place. The middle one, I think, who married Doris MacMannis's aunt? They moved on south to Shreveport or someplace. Mother said. I don't think it mattered to Wanda who it was."

And Julia? They both wondered if she'd had lovers, had one still. Or was she as burnished and carefully defended as she seemed? Could she be as alone as she looked? Could anybody? They both wondered but didn't bring it up. They were having that moment of unease they always had when they were left together. Les never knew what she had to offer Margo, who seemed to think on a higher plane. And Margo never knew where to start with Les's preserved innocence. They were left with habitual admiration on Les's part and on Margo's a passing envy of the surface ease of Les's life. The price you paid, of course, was Harry Hockaday.

They descended into motherhood. The picture of Little Harry that Les carried in her wallet was from when he was still at Burroughs. Now he was living outside Boston, having drifted through Colgate. She'd had Little Harry only to kick things off, keep

Harry from being drafted, and provide an heir. She hadn't wanted any more, and Harry didn't care. She hadn't wanted a daughter.

"He's living with some girl out east. We haven't met her. Evidently even he doesn't think she's suitable."

"He'll come back to St. Louis and go into the business."

"Oh yes," Les said. "He'll never get a better offer than that. And he'll marry somebody local. But I'm not mixing in there. I'm not going to be responsible."

Margo had only boilerplate to report about Kimberly, who was seventeen, not quite working up to her academic potential, and as a senior beginning to discover boys. Then she couldn't help saying again how hard the divorce had been on Kimberly, how badly timed, though she was still sure she'd wanted a day off from her divorce. And for that matter, a day off from Kimberly.

Up on the porch Julia was being let in the house by one of the women who'd looked after Dorothy, from a firm called In Our Hands in Your House, which struck Margo as the least reassuring slogan she'd ever heard.

"Shall we give her ten minutes?" Les checked her watch for the hundredth time.

"By then people will be coming anyway.

"Harry's livid, of course," she said, picking up a thread.

"What about?"

"Little Harry living with a girl. Big Harry doesn't seem to remember how we got started. Did you live with Reg before you got married? I forget."

"You don't forget anything, Les. Do you mean sleep?"

Les nodded, looking over the steering wheel down River Road.

"Do you mean sex?"

"You know I mean sex." Les liked hearing about sex but didn't like to be the one to bring it up.

"No, we didn't," Margo said. "Reg was way over on the left politically, and they can be very — prim."

Les never knew what was going on when people talked about the political left and the political right. If left meant you were pro-abortion, then Les was, God knows. But if it meant pouring more federal money down East St. Louis, she didn't know where she was.

The woman who let Julia in wore a size sixteen zip-up pink nylon uniform and, to Julia's surprise, spiked hair. A cross between practical nurse and biker girl and, as it happened, shock therapist. "You're the grand-daughter. I can see her in you."

But no soggy sentiment. "She was an old rip, you know. She kept us hopping. But sharp? As a tack right to the end. You had to watch your step around her."

"Did you ever," Julia said. *And wherever you went for the rest of your life.* The woman went back to the kitchen, and Julia was left to the house, at the edge of the living room. Normal people with normal childhoods return to find that home has shrunk. This room seemed bigger than before.

The living room was webbed in shadows. Rugs of wildly varying values overlapped, and the wallpaper was the familiar repeating ostrich plume, darkened at the cornice. The oldest furniture was from some early generation of Englehardts, pushed back in corners like in-laws. Dorothy was still in full possession.

Above the Roseville pottery on the mantel was her portrait gazing down on the room, taken from a wedding photograph, 1933. She carried a sheaf of waxen lilies, and the veil rode low on her forehead. She appeared more slender than she could have been, but her brows were growing together in a familiar way.

Virgil's only presence was his leather chair,

afghan-draped, still by the fireplace. They were always Dorothy and Virgil to Julia, never grandparents. Grandparents lived down on the farm. Grandfathers whittled, and grandmothers baked. You went over the river and through the woods to get to them.

The In Our Hands in Your House women had set up a coffee urn on the bridge table in the sunroom. The Christmas tree had stood there, looped in strings of fat prewar bulbs and tarnished tinsel, the focal point of the famous Englehardt Christmas Eve parties. Julia remembered the lethal wassail bobbing with clove-studded oranges. Everybody had come: the country club, the bridge club, the garden club, with husbands, and all of River Road.

On Christmas morning Julia had always gotten everything on her list and often opened the presents alone, or with Virgil downstairs in his flannel bathrobe and Romeo bedroom slippers, bleary-eyed and dozing off with a dead cigar clenched in his knuckles. Julia hadn't come home for his funeral, hadn't considered it.

Pulling back, she tried to subdue the room with a professional eye. She gutted it mentally, steamed off the paper, sanded the floor, decided on a stain. She saved the best of the rugs and made a merry bonfire of the upholstered pieces. She hesitated over Virgil's chair, then threw it on the fire and rescued a Centennial secretary and moved it to a better location. But the room was too big and awkward and overbearing — Dorothy again. Decent lighting alone would cost a fortune, as much as the house was worth. Julia wouldn't have touched this room without a budget of a hundred thousand and no back talk.

She turned away, avoiding a mirror for fear it wouldn't reflect her. There'd never been a place for her here. The stairway made three awkward turns to the second floor, and it was still afternoon at the top. A hallway ran north and south the length of the house. In childhood Julia had played hotel in the guest rooms, checking in, checking out forever.

Now she was on the verge of Dorothy's bedroom. The In Our Hands women had kept the rest of the house lightly dusted, but Dorothy had clearly barred them from in here. Julia was swept by a scary, familiar scent, a blend of gynecology and Tabu. The bedspread was familiar, and the bed swaybacked in Dorothy's shape. Two volumes lay on the bedside table under the lamp with cocked shade: Danielle Steel astride Rush Limbaugh.

Julia turned to go and didn't. Dorothy's vanity table with the shepherdess lamps was the same clutter: the glass powder boxes, the hair receiver, a tangled brush left as if she'd just put it down. Photographs were flattened under the glass top.

It was time to go, but she had to have a closer look. Here was the whole reason for her journey, all the way from New York. Julia was swept by the sudden need to find herself there under the glass. She had to discover her face among these overlapping pictures, if only in the background.

She crept across the room, furtive as fourteen. The room was less dim when she took off her sunglasses. The snapshots were etched by drifts of spilled Coty powder, bracketed by hairpins. One shot was of Dorothy and Virgil and the last new car before the war, Dorothy at the wheel. Nothing in any order. One of James in cap and gown flanked by Dorothy and Virgil. One of a long-defunct wirehaired terrier. Then a color print of a bridge foursome and a great many more of Dorothy, on the country club terrace in a New Look skirt, Dorothy in her golfing days with alligator tan and fringed-tongue shoes, Dorothy at a Red Cross tea in her fur cape, pouring. Julia's heart stirred at one with a baby in Dorothy's arms. But the time was wrong: Dorothy's hat gave it away. The baby was Wanda.

Julia thought of Wanda's death. She'd been sent to school instead of going to the funeral, and all she remembered was her second-grade teacher's faint discomfort at having her there that day. Wanda's clothes went to the Salvation Army, and her room was swept clean of clues, becoming another guest room. Julia's status remained unchanged, even though now she was Dorothy and Virgil's only child.

She came to the last picture. She wasn't there either and never had been, and it was no more than she'd always known. Did she really expect to find that hard-as-nails Dorothy had kept a shrine to her bastard annoyance of a granddaughter under this smeary glass? There was nothing particularly intimate about these pictures, nothing very personal about this room. Julia recalled how abruptly Dorothy marched out of it every morning, jerking the brush through her springy hair as she went.

It was Les who kept a record of Julia and a clipping file of her career. For that matter, Margo was the most nearly maternal figure in Julia's life. The room would start blurring soon, and she'd be blubbering for purely childhood reasons: self-pity and solitude.

Another wet, wasted moment here, and it would occur to her why she'd devoted her life to creating rooms for other people's lives. One more moment, and she'd have to know that every house she devised for strangers to live in was this one, every time, the house that had no place for her.

Now beneath her feet the living room began to fill. Julia repaired her face at Dorothy's mirror and started down the stairs.

Chapter 5

Les got them back to St. Louis for their flights, but only just. The Saturday night traffic on the approach to the airport was heavier than she'd bargained for. At the end they were running, and Margo's Chicago flight and Julia's to La Guardia left practically at the same time and three gates apart. Les felt stretched tight and pulled wide. Then hurried good-byes. Julia's getaways were always quick. Les chose her to see off.

"Come back," she said. "Soon. Stay a week for a real visit. Burials don't count."

"Burials count," Julia said. Then Les watched her disappear up the jetway and back into the unknowable void of her life, that world of Carolina Herrera women lunching around fountains and engagement books full of more meaningful appointments than hers.

Julia didn't look back, and Les was alone at the airport, the worst possible place to be if you aren't going anywhere. All the people around her looked like they'd driven in from the Ozarks just to watch the planes take off. Les, who didn't like to leave until the planes were off the ground, stopped in a short-order place for a cup of decaf. She replayed the day, fussing about the funeral flowers that hadn't been right at all. She ought to have ordered another spray for the mantel at Dorothy's house. Her mind always picked at details, and she just had to let it.

The rest of the afternoon had gone off all right. All the pallbearers and Clifford Rantsinger and both Pinckneys came to the house, along with some younger holdouts from Dorothy's bridge club. And some Englehardt cousins of Wanda's generation, the kind that turn up at funerals, some of them in pantsuits. They filled the room, and Les wondered if Dorothy dying in the can at the country club might have sparked additional interest.

She and Margo had gone in to deal with them. Then Julia came down the stairs with her face on and her sunglasses in her bag. It was her house, if only for that moment, but of course Julia didn't make a grand entrance. Nobody there would have understood her dress anyway, with the possible exception of Willa, Junior's wife. He'd gone home to get her, or she'd shown up on her own for a look at the house, and Julia.

Everybody made a point of not staring at Junior between his two wives. Les couldn't help thinking it was a scene Julia would enjoy if it was happening to somebody else. They hadn't known Willa. She was from down around Carruthersville. She oversmiled and looked guarded, possibly wondering if Julia was about to sweep down again and take Junior off her like she'd taken him off Cloris Weatherly.

Then Clifford Rantsinger drew Julia aside, trying to hand her the cards from the flowers. For an awful moment Les thought Julia wouldn't take them, though Les would have written the thank-yous herself. Julia only had to ask. She was just free of Clifford when both Pinckney brothers pounced. They were trying to give her Dorothy's engagement ring, about a carat and a half. Harry'd heard that Dorothy had pretty well lived up all she had, apart from this white-elephant house. Harry thought Deaconess Hospital would tear it down because the lot was worth more vacant.

Les wondered if Julia would take the ring. And then she did, slipping it in her bag with the flower cards. Reassured, Les edged within earshot. The Pinckneys were asking if Julia wanted anything out of the house. But of course she didn't, nothing you could carry away in your hands. She made very short work of the Pinckneys. Then she sailed up to

Les and Margo and said, "Let's beat it." Les thought they ought to stay till everybody else left, but Margo sent her an eye message, and they went.

From the back of the car Julia said, "Step on it," and then on the way out of the Cape, they went down Lee Boulevard past the Vogels' old house. Les hadn't meant to, but the car seemed to find its own way. The For Sale sign in the yard of Les's girlhood Dutch Colonial surprised Margo. So she had to tell her that Mother was with her now in St. Louis. Les felt Margo and Julia making significant eye contact. Julia hardly said two words all the way back to the airport.

Les had been looking at the bottom of the coffee cup for some minutes, and now she couldn't think of anyplace to be but home. Sunday stared her in the face, the one day Harry made a point of being at home, fighting with her mother over the papers. Joining the flow of the concourse crowds, Les occupied her mind by trying to remember where she'd parked.

Margo had planned to drive to O'Hare that morning and leave the car there, but Kimberly needed it to go to Northbrook Court and then wouldn't get up in time to drive her to the airport. This meant a thirty-dollar cab ride each way, the sort of sudden, inevitable expenditure Margo always tried to hedge by packing her own school lunch. The St. Louis airfare was in a different category.

Now she was coming up her front walk, searching in her case through the diagnostic test score sheets for the keys. The house, three bedrooms, bath and a half, no family room, had been well above their budget and then finally a good buy despite the escalating suburban property tax.

Inside, she fumbled for the nearest lamp. The living room looked oddly tentative without the sofa. At first Reg had walked away, wanting nothing but his freedom. But then he'd come back for the guest-room bed and the sofa and finally the cocktail table too since it looked pointless without the sofa. He'd rented an apartment down in Rogers Park, on Pratt off Sheridan, which was in fact handier because he could take the El to work. He'd made much out of sacrificing the car to Margo, who'd need it to get to school.

She assessed the silence and, giving her the benefit of the doubt, decided Kimberly was at home and asleep. She was dead tired herself, hardly remembering where this day had begun. A bath and then bed, but standard procedure took her down the hall to check. She opened the door, and Kimberly's bedside lamp was on. Something — a T-shirt was thrown over the shade. Margo froze.

Someone was there, someone else. Someone had broken in and was attacking Kimberly in her bed. Kimberly's bare legs were trapped, and above her the long naked body of an intruder, pinning her wrists, his greased-back hair buried in her neck. Margo thought of fangs, and a scream echoed up inside her.

But then the boy said, "Oh motherfuck," muffled against Kimberly's neck. He was no intruder, exactly. He was Kevin Bergstrom, the boy whose name Kimberly had lettered all over her notebook cover last year, the senior she phoned so often that Margo assumed he wasn't available. Now he'd be a freshman in college somewhere, so Margo had gathered he was out of the picture.

She could see Kimberly's face — everything in the room seemed to be outlined in little electric squiggles. Kimberly's chin was hooked over the top of Kevin's head, her eyes on the ceiling. They all three had a moment of suspended animation. Kevin's idea of presence of mind was to cover Kimberly's nakedness with his own. In spite of herself Margo had a full view of him. He looked mildly undernourished, and there was a line of curly hair in the crack of his ass. It might have been crossing his mind that if he didn't move, nothing more would happen.

Margo swallowed the silent scream, and her mind lunged for the appropriate words: nonjudgmental, nonstereotypical, above all, measured.

Then Kimberly said, "Goddamn you, Mother. Get the hell out of my room and out of my life."

Julia's cab from La Guardia veered off the Drive at Ninety-sixth Street and stopped short of the perpetual crosstown street repair. Down Second Avenue the cab hit every pothole, and she was braced in the backseat as she'd been braced all day. With the time difference, people were just coming out to dinner, drawn by the spring night. The tables were out all down Second, filling with that mass of twenty-somethings willing and able to dine out every night in the week.

The street scene brought back her first days in New York. Temp jobs and classes during the day, forays into the fading East Village at night in a crowd of Parsons people. It had been her transitional period, somewhere between army issue and the little black dress. She'd knocked a few years off her history then, at exactly the right time, so now she was just cresting forty. Nobody in that arty, aimless group had taken her for a divorcée, though she was the one with the unshared apartment.

Then in the dream movie of those days she was somehow at the Fire Island Pines for a weekend, Fourth of July, and again in a group, watching the muscled boys dancing with each other at the Boatel, that remembered smell of salt air, sweat, and amyl nitrite. One of the last dancing summers, and she couldn't recall the songs, only the beat. But she remembered the boys writhing and slick with their shirts off, tucked into the backs of their white Levi's, rhythmically clapping their hands over their heads in the strobing air. She'd met Dale at the Pines, the first and last person in New York who saw right through her.

During the day he was Dale Pendleton Interior Designs, and he gave her her first real job, as a runner. She had to brave the D & D Building for him, gathering swatches and taking things out on spec. She'd had to come to terms with the hawk-faced Mrs. Lederer, who ran Dale's office and mothered him, and loved him on the sly. Julia was determined to reveal nothing of her origins and then mildly miffed when nobody inquired.

You didn't have to fill out a lot of forms to work for Dale, or write a paragraph about where you saw yourself in ten years' time. But he picked up the leftover Missouri in her vowels. He was from Fond du Lac, Wisconsin. In the midst of one of their busy days he said in passing, "You can stop dressing to shock your mother."

"I haven't got a mother," she said. "Never did."

"You've got somebody of the female persuasion back there in the state of Misery who's larger than life. Walk away."

Dale was the hot young interior designer — never decorator — at the dawn of the eighties, banking on his talent, trading on his looks, working around the clock. *New York* magazine did two pages on him. Thirty-one in real life, he was twenty-six in the story. No narrow double-breasted pinstripe and aesthetic nostril against a Dorothy Draper background. Dale lounged angularly across the centerfold in T-shirt and jeans, shoeless on bare floor against a dragged wall and a king-sized sheet looped over the suggestion of a paned window. "Less is more," he was quoted, "until you do the billing."

He taught her the business with an urgency she was too busy to suspect. She was too busy to think — therapy at last — and now he was walking her past doormen up Park Avenue and down Fifth and into echoing triplexes in need of image. In a T-shirt that broke ground for Calvin Klein, he was introducing a vaguely ancestral country-house look that broke ground for Ralph Lauren.

"Remember," he said, "if they could stand their lives, they wouldn't need us." And from him that sounded more compassionate than cynical.

It was all meant to look effortless, but Parsons hadn't prepared her for the research. He drilled her on period furniture, faux finishes, and profit margins. She learned her sources, turning up for every new shipment at Kentshire down on Twelfth Street, making her first trip to London with Dale to dog the Fulham Road dealers. He showed her how to take his own firm, genial line with suppliers, contractors, especially clients. "Make a little love to all of them," he said. "They're lonely."

He sharpened her eye and showed her how to create a need in the client's mind and then fulfill it. New money was money in the bank but he didn't take music people or show-business types. They were putting their money up their noses and often couldn't pass the boards of the buildings where they wanted to live anyway. There was something of the blond midwestern farm boy on scholarship at Princeton about him, and that opened other doors, Social Register second marriages and Litchfield, Connecticut. When the Hong Kong merchants began bringing out suitcases crammed with cold cash, he seemed almost to meet their planes. Timing was everything, and time was running out.

Julia staggered under the training and the responsibility he heaped on her. "Why me?" she said.

"The boys are dying," he said.

Whole firms in the D & D Building were closed down and wiped out and dead. Sources shuttered. But college had taught Julia that the apocalypse would be political, not medical. Blood in the streets, not death in the blood.

Leaving meticulous instructions, Dale went back to Fond du Lac for a visit. Julia wouldn't let herself think about that time in any detail, or pinpoint the day she knew he wasn't coming back. The months mounted up, and his phone voice faded. She and Mrs. Lederer had to move past veiled rivalry to some kind of partnership of survivors. Mrs. Lederer buried herself in computerized inventory, then shouldered her way home on the subway late every night to a husband in Forest Hills. Julia swamped herself with work.

Then Dale died. Even quicker with his exits than she was, he'd robbed her of these months they might have had. She'd have seen him through, she and Mrs. Lederer. They'd have been there for him for as long as it took. Better them than the faceless family he'd hardly mentioned. He was the one person in the world more elusive than Julia, and she'd loved him within all the limits laid upon them. He left her the business and the Fifth Avenue apartment they worked from, so she couldn't walk away, or run. Now she had to be him.

The firm, Julia Steadman Designs, faltered, then found its feet. She gave up her one-bedroom on University Place and moved into the back of the Fifth Avenue apartment. She lost some of his old clients and got them back when she found new ones of her own. There was a faint air of widowhood about her little black dresses, but that was an image too bogus to promote, though it would have amused Dale. She was shaken by how quickly he was forgotten. Of course the body count was like a war, and half his friends were dead already. Human life was cheap in New York anyway, even at a dinner party. But the clients who'd vied for him for Hamptons weekends developed an odd amnesia. Julia decided to make them pay.

The Reagan years raised her boat, and she weathered the market crash of '87. In the nineties she was working more for less and kiting the occasional check, but so was everybody else. She was an establishment figure now. A few more years in this great impersonal ant heap, and she'd be as tough as Dorothy, though never so strong, never so well attended.

Julia's increasingly hard-bitten history trailed behind her and followed the bouncing cab as it turned off Second Avenue onto Seventy-ninth and over to Fifth. As the cab drew up and her doorman handed her out, she checked her watch to see it was only a little after ten in this never-ending day. Upstairs in her entryway she stumbled over a delivery of Geoffrey Bennison linen at a hundred and a half the yard. Beyond in the living room/front office the message machine glowed on Mrs. Lederer's hunt-table desk amid neat paper piles. Home at last. Returning her door key to her bag, Julia came up with Dorothy's engagement ring, completely out of context here. She decided to take it down to the little man in the Empire State Building and sell it for what it would bring. Then she'd buy herself something you couldn't hold in your hand with the proceeds, so this day shouldn't be a complete loss.

May

Chapter 6

The woman none of them knew woke behind her eyelids. She'd learned to do this, pretending sleep until she could gauge the full danger of the day. It was daylight, not the naked bulb of the shelter where you had to be up at seven, pulling the blanket tight. Sunshine slatted in through the blinds of her girlhood home.

Dreamlike but real, and she was nagged out of bed by knowing this was a special day with something in it to be done: a court date, a clinic appointment, something to give the day purpose and a shape. She stood stoned with sleep and yesterday's medication. In another moment she'd remember what this day meant, what she had to do. She'd learned not to force herself to remember these things. They came.

The room was too orderly now, dusted to death in her mother's way, except for the unmade rollaway bed in the corner where her own daughter slept. Melanie was up and off to school, so that told something about the time. Her own mother would be at work, so the house was relatively safe, as safe as it ever was. The woman stood on the polished floor, her thoughts crowded into the narrow wedge between her mother and her daughter.

She'd slept in a nightgown from adolescence stinking of the lavender sachets that infested the dresser drawers here. For months of her life she'd slept in everything she owned, which seemed less awful now than it had at the time. Those were the stretches when they wouldn't let her have her daughter, long intervals of caseworkers and therapy in a group. The triviality of the problems the other group members shared always astonished her. She'd had to make the kind of compromises nobody could imagine to get her daughter back. Then when they were together again, she wasn't quite the child she'd been. She was a bigger child who used new words and showed signs of independence. Sometimes the woman thought they gave her any child they happened to have on hand. And the compromise this time was that she had to return to her own parents in order to keep her child. It was a deal struck with devils.

Some outside sound pulled her to the window. Through the parted slats she saw the long green sweep of backyard, like a suburban cemetery that forbids gravestones. Her father was crouched at the far end, fussing with miniature tools at a floral border. Careful clumps of purple ageratum, then a low cloud of impatiens, then the irises on stalks. A real father would have felt her eyes boring into his bent back.

She turned away from him and out of habit pulled up the spread on her bed. This shifted the pillow, and there under it she remembered the purpose of the day.

Dressing with care in her mother's clothes, she applied her mother's lipstick, then went all the way with a quick splash of throat-cutting lily of the valley cologne. The skirt strained across her hips, and in the mirror skin showed between the blouse buttons. She'd have to wear her own shoes. She was thinking more clearly now. The day closed around her and showed her the single path. She could hear her heart, and that was always a sign. Needing a purse on a long strap, she dug through her mother's things until she found one.

She walked down the weedless flagstone front walk and along the curving street. All the houses stared empty-eyed across their lawns. The green of the grass pulled at her eyes. Nothing stirred but the sprinkler systems. There was no life here and never had been. She strolled one tree-named street after another, following the old familiar way, invisible and in no particular hurry.

Sensing the school before it came in view, she remembered the chalk smell of the classroom, and her grade-school self hung back. The playground was empty. The lot was full of teachers' cars, and the banks of windows displayed jonquils cut out of construction paper.

They had her child in there.

Margo and her third graders were reaching late morning. Recess was behind them, and the hyperactives had taken their Ritalin. She was looking ahead to a solid half hour of phonics and had arranged some paperbacks, Betsy Byars and Beverly Cleary, in the chalk tray for a read-aloud before lunch. She tried not to limit her class to the textbook primer, though it meant poring over every paperback in her classroom collection for any stray word that might offend a parent power group.

There were always a few tears after recess and some unsettled scores left over from the playground. To wind down, they did deskside aerobics. Margo led from the front of the room, doing a modified version beside her own desk.

The door banged open, and the woman

was standing there, already fumbling in her purse. Margo didn't know her but could match the face with Melanie, something about the eyes and the indefinite color of hair. Margo had to act without the time to think. Every second had a meaning. The children were doing their stretches, and she looked out over the young forest of waving arms for Melanie. On impulse, she pushed another child aside and reached for her. She was the wan child without social skills who'd joined the class in the middle of the semester, the child who drew endless pictures of windowless houses. Melanie saw her mother at the door and fell into Margo's arms.

"Under your desks, boys and girls," Margo said in a carrying voice. Even the best of them needed to be told everything three times, but their arms drooped. Then the first shot rang out.

It shattered the upper pane of a window, and now the room was screaming. Another shot, and Margo felt a bee sting in the back of her shoulder. With strange clarity she wondered if it was meant for her or for Melanie.

Now she needed to be across the room to throw herself at the woman, absorbing however many bullets were left, shielding twenty-eight children. But Melanie clung to her, and Margo looked to find the doorway empty, the woman gone. Then she glanced down at the child buried in her bosom. Melanie's hair was darkening and matting with the blood that soaked through the bodice of Margo's dress. She held the child tight with one arm.

A bulletin interrupted the twelve-thirty news.

"This just in. Frightened parents are converging on a Northshore grade school in the aftermath of an apparent classroom shooting incident. Camera crews and paramedic vans are at the location. An eyewitness observer reports that an adult female has been removed on a stretcher. . . ."

The news flash was picked up by stations around the country and repeated in abbreviated form. But Les was at a Historical Society meeting at the Jefferson Memorial, lunch and a speaker. Julia was trapped in a crosstown cab blasting Haitian creole.

Margo had to be talked out of her classroom. The police from three suburban forces were in the halls, guns drawn. The other teachers were barricaded in classrooms with their children. The principal was on her office phone to the board of ed for the legal posture to take with parents. Conducted by cops, Beryl Kramer came down from the school library to take over Margo's class until the therapists could get there. She got Margo away only by telling her that the blood soaked down to her belt was making the children more hysterical. The cops stood well back until Margo was in range of the TV cameras. People with rubber gloves put her on a stretcher.

She noticed sky when they carried her out to the van past the first of the parents. Then there was pain in hot stabs when the van made all those turns on the way to Lakeside Hospital. In the ER when they were cutting off her dress, she spoke one of her perfectly rounded sentences. "You will need to inform my daughter, Kimberly Mayhew, at Glenburnie South High School." Then they gave her something that made her dopey, and she thought she was registering for first semester at the University of Missouri.

She awoke from that in a double room with the other bed empty. A sling thing was on one arm, propped outside the sheet. Late afternoon light fell in from the window, and she could only assume it was this afternoon. She fussed over a missed faculty meeting. Then it occurred to her that she'd been shot.

119

She was numb all down that side and wondered if good clean bullet wounds were only in Westerns.

She took charge of her mind and composed her thoughts. The woman who'd shot her was clearly Melanie's mother. Margo had worked all spring to get personal and previous school records on the child. She'd ended up making a call in the evening at home, to learn that Melanie and her mother lived with the grandparents. The grandfather seemed to consider the call an invasion of privacy. He'd complained to the school, and the principal told her to back off. Suburban families were increasingly unwilling to disclose background on their children, and their records were riddled with omissions. You knew their medication, but you were lucky to have a home phone number.

Margo drifted and then a conversation outside her door brought her around. With her teacher's ear she monitored two nurses talking, learning that Melanie's mother had been at large for an hour and a half. While three suburban police forces drove up and down every street in the area, the fugitive woman with the gun in her purse had entered a convenience store on Green Bay Road. She fired one shot into a frozen-food refrigeration unit and the other directly into her heart, DOA.

So those were two bullets Margo hadn't had to take.

"Women never shoot themselves in the head," one nurse said from who knows what depth of experience, and the other agreed.

Clinging to just enough of her wits to realize this further development had let her off the hook, Margo felt the dopiness begin to reclaim her. Starting painfully up, she had a sudden anxiety attack about Kimberly. But in the next moment she and Reg were cooking something over an open fire at Illinois Beach State Park.

The incident made the Wednesday deadline for the suburban weekly, but the account was sketchy. Margo lived two suburbs west and so was in fact not local. Suicide in the 7-Eleven took precedence, and there was only brief mention that the dead woman was herself a 1978 graduate of the same school she'd shot up. Stonewalled by the board of ed and stymied by civic pride, the article finished off by wondering if armed guards in local schools would look too much like inner-city Chicago.

The dead woman's father granted a lengthy interview to the *Trib*, stating that his daughter "had always been troubled but was no trouble." He knew she possessed a handgun but wasn't worried as she didn't know how to use it. She had kept it, he assumed, "only to bolster her self-confidence." He blamed the school for not disarming her before she could do violence to herself.

The Living section did a piece on the changing custodial role of parents in the lives of adult children. The *Sun-Times*'s coverage was headlined: "Shooting Challenges Image of Suburbia as the Last Safe Place."

The St. Louis paper picked up the story on the day after that — "Gunslinging Mother Panics Affluent Suburban Chicago School" — and ran it on an inside page. The wounded third-grade teacher was identified as "Mrs. Margo Marlowe," but they got her age on the nose. And once again Harry knew about it first.

He'd glanced over the paper while Les was out walking her two miles. When she got back, he'd left for work, and on the stairs she met her mother going out. She'd begun to develop a St. Louis social life. Les's friends and their mothers invited her to coffee mornings and to go places. They seemed to look on Mrs. Vogel as a colorful character and good fun, which stunned Les.

The sight of her red-faced in a headband and without a dry stitch on after her walk sent her mother into paroxysms. Women who didn't have any more to do than take forced marches along curbs in the blazing heat reduced her to helpless hilarity.

Les had just enough time to shower and change for Symphony Board and then lunch out afterward in a group. She didn't get home till after two. Then something called her into the kitchen, and there was the morning paper under Harry's coffee cup. He'd left a stick-on note: "Could this be Margo?"

Les's heart stopped. She sat suddenly and burned every word of the article into her brain. Remembering that she did her best thinking at her desk, she looked up Margo's school number, but couldn't get through. She got the Lakeside Hospital number, and when she asked if Margo Mayhew was a patient, they wanted to know if she was from the press.

"I'm her sister for God's sake," Les said, and she could have passed a lie-detector test. But they only told her Margo was stable.

She was *always* stable, she wanted to say. Hanging up, she reached under the flap of her Coach bag to make sure her wallet had the full complement of credit cards. She took the stairs two at a time in heels. Then she was pulling down a suitcase and throwing things in.

123

She'd leave the Infiniti at the airport. Harry wouldn't care. He drove a Cherokee to work and wherever else he went. She'd call him from the airport, but then she might be able to walk immediately onto a flight. Standing up at a campaign chest in her bedroom, she wrote Harry a note in her usual style, a sort of marital shorthand.

Of course it's Margo. I'm flying up. I don't know any more than this but her home number is in my book.

She nearly signed off with *In haste, Les,* but didn't have the time. The adrenaline had been pumping through her since the newspaper article. Now she had a fresh blast of inappropriate euphoria. She was about to walk straight out of her life and with somewhere to go.

On the stroke of six p.m. Les approached the desk at Lakeside Hospital. She'd negotiated the incredible tangle from O'Hare in Friday rush hour with the aid of the rental-car map. Normally she couldn't tell one end of a map from the other. Camera crews in the hospital waiting room wouldn't have surprised her, but there was nobody but smokers. She stiffened her spine to do battle with

124

the people at the desk, but they gave her Margo's room number without a quibble, and up she went.

The corridor was almost empty. Down at the end they were bringing out the last of the dinner trays. There was a lull, and the solitary figure at the nurses' station looked reasonably approachable and turned out to be chatty. "She's resting now. I don't know if she's awake. She'll be groggy though. They went in for the bullet today, you know."

Les didn't. She didn't know anything, and the more she heard now, the less she'd have to get out of Margo. She turned her most interested look on for the nurse.

"It was in the papers. She got shot in the back of her left shoulder. It was a miracle she didn't have any nerve damage, but she lost a lot of blood."

"She bled down her back?" Les's forensic knowledge was on the *Murder, She Wrote* level, but there were no limits to her imagination.

"Not that," the nurse said. "The bullet lodged behind the clavicle, and a bone splinter pierced through in front. That's where the blood came from. All gunshot wounds are freak accidents, except they aren't usually accidents. You take the woman who shot her. She —"

But Les didn't want to take the woman who shot her. Since no one was stopping her, she started down the corridor, treading the slick tile on the balls of her feet, reading room numbers.

It was a double room with somebody, Margo, lying absolutely still in the far bed. She was propped at an unnatural angle and outlined by evening light. A man was sitting in a chair past the end of her bed; she thought it must be Reg.

Les couldn't remember when she'd seen him last. Whenever Harry had a meeting in Chicago, she came along. But Reg and Harry didn't have word one to say to each other. Getting the men together was like flogging a couple of dead horses, so she usually tried to see Margo on their own. If it was a Saturday or summer, she'd lure Margo downtown to lunch at the Drake or somewhere else Margo wouldn't go otherwise.

In this light Reg's beard was completely gray, and she noticed a paunch. They carried on a conversation of sorts in the hushed tones people use around the comatose, Les catching glimpses of Margo motionless in the bed. Etiquette rules didn't seem to cover bedside small talk with the ex-husbands of gunshot victims, and Les never had known what she had to offer a Ph.D. in Western civ.

She sensed that Reg didn't find her particularly attractive, though she was sure she wasn't the type who was always wondering that. But it wasn't a real conversation anyway. Reg talked at you.

Apparently the only reason he was here now was to let Margo know that Kimberly was staying with him down in Rogers Park. It seemed to Les that a big lump of a seventeen-year-old girl about to graduate from high school could stay home and man the phone and keep things going at that end, but she didn't say so. Then she realized that after two days Kimberly hadn't even been to the hospital to see Margo.

"The young can be very squeamish about illness and disability," Reg was saying. "It disturbs their universe and challenges their concept of personal immortality."

He shifted one leg over the other, somehow meaningfully. "Margo has always set an impossibly high standard for Kimberly. I sometimes wonder what kind of teacher it makes her. I've often thought Margo was misplaced in elementary education."

Then why didn't *she* get the Ph.D.? Les nearly said. Of course being shot in the back while you were trying to teach your class could make anybody wonder if she'd gone into the wrong line of work.

"Margo has never understood that you have to let children be, and become." Reg turned over a generous hand. "You have to let them go with their flow."

That sounded vaguely 1970s, but now Reg fell silent. Having Kimberly move in on you, in a one-bedroom apartment, could make anybody grow silent. Les had heard how the children of divorce play one parent off against the other.

Margo made what seemed like a long trip and arrived at enough consciousness to find two figures in chairs beyond her own feet. The cool, coiffed finish of the blond woman in the linen suit suggested a Kenilworth society dame. She looked again, and it was Les. And beside her, like people oddly juxtaposed in dreams, Reg. What Margo was doing here herself she would discover any minute now.

Les leaned forward. "Margo, it's me. Tell me what I can do for you. I'm just sitting here. Throw me a crumb."

Chapter 7

Les stayed at Margo's house. It was a cracker box in a whole subdivision of cracker boxes, and Les had a devil of a time finding it. She was prepared to spend the rest of the evening fielding phone calls, but there were no messages on the machine, and the phone never rang. Just to break the sound barrier, she thought about calling Harry. But if he wasn't home, she didn't want to know about it. She puttered around Margo's little house. Things were missing all over it: the bed in what must be the guest room, the living-room sofa. Kimberly's room was a wreck outright with an unmade bed. There was something impermanent about the place, and the ceilings were so low Les kept ducking.

She found a can of tomato soup, heated it up, and ate the whole thing. It was like playing house in somebody else's house, like breaking and entering. Down at the Cape the neighbors would be ringing the bell, pounding on the door to find out who was here. She checked all the windows and doors twice, took a bath with the bathroom door open, and finally climbed into Margo's bed, leaving the radio on. She felt half liberated and half terrified that somebody would plunge in through a window and pounce on her.

On Saturday she was up early, double-locking the house behind her. As soon as Eden's Plaza opened, she was at Carson's to buy Margo a lacy bed jacket and a styling comb. She wanted to be at the hospital before people started coming, to get Margo's hair under control since she couldn't do much herself one-handed. Les meant to get Margo's day started and then leave her to it. She didn't want to hover. Julia and Margo both thought she hovered, and she didn't want to do that.

She found Margo breakfasted and sitting up, clearheaded. "Stitches itch," she said. They had some kind of cast arrangement on her that reached down her arm and left that hand virtually useless. Les worked over her hair, not fussing. Margo looked up once and threw her more than a crumb. "Who but you, Les?" And Les had to look away and keep busy.

Margo wanted to blot off most of the lipstick, but Les thought she was white as her sheets and needed color. What Margo thought of the bed jacket was anybody's guess. Les stood back to admire her handiwork and took the mirror out of her own purse to let Margo see herself. "Like a makeover at Elizabeth Arden," Margo said. "Practically worth getting shot for."

Then it was nearly noon, and there'd been exactly one visitor, a woman from the school library who brought a bunch of painted daisies and three books. She'd said that the school was looking around for a sub to fill out the semester for Margo. A single glance showed Les that Margo had every intention of going back to work even before she was out of the damn cast. The library woman didn't linger, and when she was gone, Les said, "Where is everybody, Margo?" keeping it light, but she really wondered.

"Oh well, Saturday." Margo made a little gesture with her good hand. "Everybody's busy."

Busy, hell. Here was Margo who'd been in all the papers and just had a bullet dug out of her. They might have been burying her today. Reg had done his duty, and Kimberly was making a point of not coming. "But what about the other teachers?"

Margo looked aside. "I expect they're all home, thanking their lucky stars it wasn't them. We're vulnerable now, every day of our lives. We're at the mercy of the next crazed or just plain enraged parent coming in the door. And we're at the mercy of every child's false accusation. We don't have a lot of rights, Les. That's why no other teacher's here today. I'm a reminder. Any one of them could be next."

"Jesus, Margo, is it that bad?"

"Yes."

"Then why —"

"Because I've got twenty-two years in, and now I've got a daughter to educate, if she'll have an education. What are my options, Les?"

This shook Les and threatened to bring down all her illusions in a heap. Of the three of them, Les had always assumed that she alone was the one without options. She sat there. This is what happened when you barged into somebody else's life. You found out these things.

"Neighbors," she said. "What about your neighbors?"

"All the women work. They come home like I do and get ready for the next day and go again. I don't know the neighbors on either side of me. We don't have front porches. We don't even have sidewalks. It's not the Cape, Les."

They brought Margo's lunch, and Les went down to the cafeteria for hers, to keep from hovering. When she came back, she said, "Margo, I still don't get it. You know how you have to spell things out for me. Why did it even happen?" Les felt overwhelmed. "That woman must have been crazy as a loon. According to the papers, she'd been cuckoo for years, probably right from the beginning," Les said, "but she had a child."

"I expect she imagined that having a child would cure her." Then Margo said, unexpectedly, "For that matter, why did we have our children? Why did you, Les?"

Truth-telling time. "I had Little Harry to marry Big Harry," she said, "to jump-start a marriage and get away from my hellhound of a mother." All the ironies of that wafted over her. "Why did you have Kimberly?"

"To save my marriage," Margo said.

Les blinked. "You were trying to save your marriage seventeen — eighteen years ago? That far back?"

"That far back," Margo said. "So who are we to call anybody crazy?"

When Les got back to Margo's house, there was a car in the drive with a Crestwood School faculty parking sticker on the window. But Les automatically unlocked the front door and walked in.

A scarecrow of a boy with hair flopped down on his forehead was in the living room.

He was sitting on the floor, leaning against the wall precisely where the sofa had been. A creature of habit perhaps. His denimed legs and sneakered feet stretched to the center of the room. He was reading *Motor Trend* magazine. "I'm Mrs. Hockaday," Les said, cocking her head at him.

"I'm Kevin." The boy dragged his eyes up from the magazine. "I belong to Kimberly."

Les thought that was an odd way to put it. She looked up to see Kimberly in the door to the back hall, her hands full of freshly laundered clothes. Les smelled the softener. Kimberly had the same already matronly figure Margo'd had in high school. She had Margo's coloring and full face too, but her hair was all her own: a haystack mass of turbulent ringlets. She wore a shift shorter than Kevin's T-shirt. Her legs were real tree trunks, bone white, dropping straight down to sandals.

"I'm an old friend of your mother," Les said. "I don't know if you remember me."

Kimberly's eyes blanked. She didn't remember, and Les wondered if she could tell one adult from another anyway. "Your mother's doing better today."

The girl almost grasped the undercurrent in Les's voice. "Daddy said —"

"Daddy wasn't there today," Les said.

The girl thought about turning away. "I'm just here to do my laundry."

The first load of your life, Les thought.

"I'm staying with Daddy now."

"Your mother's coming home on Monday." They'd have sent Margo home today if there'd been a doctor around. They send you home now as soon as you can stagger.

"Oh, I'm planning to stay with Dad longer than that, till graduation at least." Kimberly tried a little toss of her head under the heavy burden of hair. "I can drive from there."

"In your mother's car?"

"It's the family car." Kimberly inhaled the laundry.

"Assuming your mother can drive one-handed, how is she going to get around? How is she going to get to school?"

Kimberly's eyes blanked again. She hadn't thought that far and certainly not in that direction. Les wondered if Reg knew how long Kimberly planned to stay with him. And she marveled at how clearly she could read the thoughts behind that sullen face, those dull eyes. Surely there must be some spark of humanity in any child of Margo's.

"I'm sure your father would want you to be here with your mother."

Kimberly's eyes widened and met Les's at last. "Why? He didn't want to be here with her." She glanced down at the boy. "We're going," she said, and he climbed up on his stork legs.

Les was still standing those three paces into the room, gripping her purse. They had to walk around her. Just as the boy loomed past, he looked down and grinned, utterly transforming his face. "See ya," he said.

Then they were gone, and there she was. Her feet were killing her, though she'd been sitting all day. She kicked off her heels and felt her toes on Margo's thin carpet.

The door that had just closed behind her opened again, and she whirled around. Kevin's head appeared. "Sorry, Mrs. Holiday, but could you move your car?" He grinned again, lighting the room.

Les had a mad impulse to grab his arm and say, "Kid, you can do better than her." But he was gone again, and she was jamming her feet back into her shoes.

It had been three weeks since they'd buried Dorothy, and not a peep out of Julia. Les called her Monday night. She'd been dying to talk to her for days. Nobody would have told her about Margo, and she wouldn't have heard. Les didn't know if the New York papers even picked up the story. She hadn't called Julia on Friday from St. Louis because she needed to get up to Chicago and see what was what. Then it was always impossible to get through to her on a weekend without Mrs. Lederer at her desk. Julia never returned a weekend call till Wednesday. But something else kept Les from calling her sooner.

Then when she did, the heavens parted, and Julia herself answered. Les meant to be calm and logical, even rehearsed. She'd jotted down a sort of script on her notepad. *"Shot in the back?"* Julia said. Les hadn't known how she'd take it, whether she'd be Julia-as-usual and pull back. Now Les thought she shouldn't have called in the evening when Julia was alone, assuming she was alone. She sounded alone. She sounded near tears. So Les took charge and talked her through the whole thing.

"And where are you?" Julia asked in a small voice when she could get a word in.

"I'm in St. Louis," Les said. "Margo's home from the hospital. I got her settled and some groceries in, just stuff she could microwave. Then I came home. I didn't want to, but, Jesus, Julia, I didn't know what she wanted. She'll be teaching school by Thursday if she can get her car back."

"Surely Reg will send Kimberly home to her."

Les sighed. "Julia, I just don't know. And what good would the little bitch be to her anyway? I swear it's all beyond me. I left Margo swooping around her house with her arm in a sling and still on painkillers, getting back to business the way she does. She said she was going to schedule a Saturday appointment to get her stitches out, so that means she's going straight back to school."

"Surely the school won't let her come back that soon."

"According to her they will. She's got a million sick days accrued, so if she doesn't come back, they have to pay her and a sub too. They won't do that if they can help it, she says. You know Margo, she's got it all figured. Julia, her whole situation is so goddamn depressing, I wanted to sit down and bawl."

This was forty-five minutes into the call, but Les paused for emphasis.

"I wish there was something I could do," Julia said.

And that was why Les had delayed this call till now. Suddenly she saw what she was up to. "Julia, we've got to get her out of all that."

"All what? Her life?"

"Well, yes." The adrenaline was pumping through Les again like last Friday. "Just get

138

her away for a little while. She won't go anywhere till school's out, but let's just take her away somewhere to catch her breath. The divorce is still weighing on her, and Kimberly weighs a ton, in more ways than one. And that awful job and that hopeless little house and all those people who don't give a shit about her. Let's just get her out of it for a week or two. Two."

"The three of us?"

"Yes, the three of us. Who else? Who else does she have?"

The whole plan fell into place in Les's mind. She saw it unfolding before her like a brochure. She fought back a touch of guilt for using the situation, using Margo. But you couldn't just call up either one of them and say, Let's go off on a toot together somewhere, just us. Julia couldn't get away, and Margo couldn't afford it.

"Julia, I'll pay."

"You mean Harry will pay."

"Screw Harry," Les said. "How about it, Julia?"

A long pause followed that Les couldn't read. Then Julia said, "Let me think about it."

"Don't," Les said. "Let's be like we used to be. Do it first and think about it later."

June

Chapter 8

Getting it all arranged was like pulling teeth. Julia took her sweet time about getting back to Les. It was almost a week, and Les hated to leave the phone, wanting it to ring and be Julia.

At her end, Julia was having her slowest season since Desert Storm. Then the Malmquists did a sudden reversal. They'd been dragging their feet on the Santa Fe adobe. Julia was poised for flight to San Miguel Allende for a selection of Spanish doors and Mexican iron, but couldn't get the go-ahead.

Then she read in the *Post* that the Malmquists were divorcing, but all wasn't lost. Irv Malmquist was marrying again on the day his divorce was final. Julia called him on his hot line to learn he was still committed to Santa Fe, but the trophy wife couldn't live with the adobe concept, which had been the original Mrs. Irv's idea. So Irv had bought a territorial style in the Canyon Road neighborhood, handy to the Compound for lunch, and the forthcoming wife was soon on the phone to Julia about it.

She wondered if she could fly in the face of Santa Fe and not go the Spanish colonial/ Native American route. She wasn't very keen on earth tones and faded turquoise anyway, and did Julia think there was a viable alternative?

Julia did. Viable alternatives were Julia's stock-in-trade. She thought there was sound historic precedent for a sort of country English look, pine but no bed warmers, since the original inhabitants of the territorial houses had been Anglos. She delivered a quick, well-reasoned, multicultural minicourse on the diversity of design traditions in the melting-pot American West. Summing up, she thought an English look was justified, modified by Navajo rugs and painted vigas with the grain showing through, a semiformal outpost of civilization in the Great American Desert.

"Perfect," the potential Mrs. Malmquist said. "Go with it, and do it down to details. I broke everything I had over my last husband's head." Julia was the best friend a second wife ever had, often the only one. Irv Malmquist wouldn't stand still for a trip in both directions, so Julia had to work from floor plans and snapshots, but she held out for a trip to London. "As you know, Irv," she told him, "they aren't sending their best-

144

quality pieces here now," and Irv caved.

Then it was time to get back to Les.

"London?" Les said. "Perfect," though she'd have settled for Kuala Lumpur if she could just get a fire lit under Julia. Les had been to London twice, once at the Hilton before a golfing holiday of Harry's at St. Andrew's and Gleneagles. She'd found her way to Fortnum & Mason, and they'd paid through the nose for *Phantom* tickets. The second time was five days on the way to a grain meeting in Brussels. They'd been at the Westbury right in Bond Street, and Les had explored on foot.

"Ideal," she said to Julia on the phone. "You can walk in the parks there, not just around them. This is exactly right for Margo. She minored in English lit, didn't she?"

"She minored in everything," Julia said.

"No, really. It's not like some resort. It's a real place with history, and she's never been. It'll be the perfect getaway. For all of us."

"Let's get one thing straight, Les," Julia said in a no-nonsense monotone. "This is a business trip for me. That's the only way I can justify it. And I'm selling Dorothy's diamond to pay for it. We can't go around joined at the hip for a week."

"Two weeks, Julia, please. Isn't summer

always your slack time?" Les said acutely.

"Ten days, tops."

Les was already jittering to call Margo, now that it was all practically settled.

"Let me give you some advice about Margo," Julia said. "Don't offer to pay her way."

"Julia, it's going to be hard enough to —"

"Don't do it, Les. Don't play Lady Bountiful with her. She's not a pauper, so don't make her feel like one. She makes a good salary, and you know she has money in the bank. Margo would. Don't do that to her."

"Julia, if you could see that little cracker box of a —"

"Les, there are people in this world who think of their houses as places to live, not as some abstract expression of who they wish they were."

"I just don't want her to say no," Les said. "But leave it to me. Leave all the arrangements to me. And, you know, be around when I'm trying to call you back, okay?"

A chastened Les called Julia again two nights later. "First of all, you were right."

"I knew you'd do it," Julia said, "and I warned you."

"I know, I know. All I said was — hinted, really — that I'd help with expenses. Margo

146

got right up on her hind legs about that. Which means she must be feeling better. Naturally she said she couldn't possibly do it. But you know something? I think me offering to pay pushed her over the edge, and she gave in — on her own terms, of course. She's dying to get away, whether she knows it or not, and London is exactly the place."

"So she's going," Julia said.

"Yes. So I'm moving ahead with the plans. I've clipped *British Heritage*'s Hundred Best English Pubs, and I've got a lot of stuff on day trips, that kind of thing."

"Sounds exhausting," Julia said, "but there's something you're not telling, Les. What is it?"

"Julia, how do you do that? But in fact there is one thing I hadn't counted on."

"Les, in your plans there always is. What?"

"Kimberly's moved back with Margo. Apparently staying with Reg didn't work out at all, and she'd completely moved in, taken all her stuff. So . . ."

It took Julia a moment. "Wait a minute. Margo's bringing Kimberly to London? Is this what I'm hearing?"

Les nodded, but Julia picked it up. "Margo won't go without her. She wouldn't dare leave her at home, not even overnight, and Kimberly won't go back to Reg. Margo put it another way, of course. She said the trip would be a graduation present for her. Julia, I tried to talk her out of it, but there are limits. What am I supposed to say, 'Leave your kid home because we don't want her'?"

"Works for me," Julia said.

Les sighed. "Margo went on about how this would be her opportunity to strengthen their relationship. We talked twice. In between, she put it to Kimberly, and she agreed to come."

"Nice of her."

"So that's it. Margo won't go without Kimberly. She said it would be educational for her."

"And for us all," Julia said. "By the way, where are we staying?"

"A bed-and-breakfast, *the* bed-and-breakfast according to all the guidebooks."

Julia's vision of a climate-controlled hotel room with BBC television and bath en suite faded.

"If we can get in," Les was saying. "I'm waiting to hear. Ten days including the Fourth of July weekend. That's for you, Julia. You wouldn't get any work done over Fourth of July in New York, and they don't have Fourth of July there."

Julia professed shock that the British don't

celebrate the American Revolution, but Les got her off that, and they descended into a debate about flight schedules. Les wanted them all to assemble in New York, maybe have a day or so there, and then fly over together. Julia wanted them to fly from their respective airports and meet up at Heathrow. Julia won.

On the night after that, Margo talked to Julia, checking her watch to time the call. As always, they needed to form a united front in the face of Les's plans. And Margo had to say something to Julia about Kimberly.

"Like the old days," Margo said, "back in the Vogels' Plymouth with Les at the wheel grinding the gears."

"I think burying Dorothy gave her ideas," Julia said.

"Julia, we both know this trip is because of me."

"And how are you?"

"Still in the sling, but fine," Margo said. "And rushed off my feet with an end-of-school program. Julia, I hope you don't mind Kimberly being with us."

"Of course not," Julia said faintly.

"The poor kid hasn't known where to turn since Reg left. She's just been up in the air. Her need to go and live with him was perfectly natural. Developmentally, she —"

"Margo," Julia said, "she was trying to punish you."

"Well, 'punish' is too strong a word, Julia. Daughters have a natural affinity for fathers. But then living with him didn't turn out to be a workable arrangement."

"Has Reg got somebody else?" Julia said, cutting to the chase.

Margo paused. "I assume that's what made Kimberly come home. She thought she'd have Reg to herself — at last. I gather she found she had some new competition. I don't know. She isn't saying.

"I thought she might dig in her heels about this England trip and demand to stay home. They all think they're grown up at that age, but something just broke over her face, and she seemed pleased about it. This trip is going to help us turn a corner in our relationship."

"The more I hear about parenting," Julia said, "the better I like color wheels and paint chips." But that was just Julia being Julia.

Les packed and repacked for weeks. She'd squared it with her mother and Harry about being away. Neither one of them had overreacted. Mrs. Vogel was thoroughly entertained at the prospect of three middle-aged women traipsing around a foreign country, trying to be girls again. "Traipsing" was one of her all-time favorite words.

Then on the last night when Les had tickets and passport and British money laid out in the sequence she'd need them, Harry wanted to make love. It threw Les for a loop, but there he was, looming up with his pajama bottoms off. Even with total recall Les couldn't remember the last time. She didn't even know what this meant. But Harry had both hands on her hips under the nightgown, working it up over her head. Then they were in the bed, or on it, and he was saying, "Get me started."

Like an old car, woozy Les thought. She'd already taken two Excedrin P.M.'s, and a bath. Then both her heels were dug into his lower back, and Harry was gasping into her left ear over the whine of the air conditioner. She was half asleep by the time it was over, drifting off.

On the night after that the travelers were in the air. Harry had taken Les to the airport and waited and kissed her good-bye. She wondered where he'd gone from there. She'd bought four folders of brochures and maps, one for each of them, and spent the night on the plane sorting, rereading, and scheduling daily programs. Margo spent the long night aloft from O'Hare reading Jane Austen beside an apparently sleeping

Kimberly. Julia on the shorter flight from New York froze out her computer software traveling salesman seatmate before dinner, and once he was safely back in cyberspace she worked through the night on the Malmquists' territorial, sketching to scale on graph paper. Then they were negotiating their separate ways through immigration and customs in the sudden dawn, and miraculously meeting up in the mobs of Terminal Three.

An hour after that they stood grouped on the damp pavement, weaving slightly above their luggage, as the door in Radnor Walk opened. Mrs. Smith-Porter was there on her threshold, looking down. Margo's eyes rose up the towering figure past the twin set and pearls to the lantern jaw and was suddenly in the pages of *Jane Eyre*, confronting Grace Poole.

Chapter 9

Later, on her midday walk, Mrs. Smith-Porter reflected on her first impressions of this morning's visitors, though first impressions were notoriously unreliable. Barring the young girl, they were a receptive audience for her theatrics as she waved them from room to room.

The tall, fair, handsome woman, the Mrs. Hockaday who had written, seemed to style herself the leader, but Mrs. Smith-Porter noticed independence in the eyes of the other two women and mutiny outright in the young girl's. They were all handsome women in their ways, and even the girl showed some promise, once she was past the pudding-faced stage. They struck her as rather oddly assorted, though she'd seen far unlikelier traveling companions in her time. But they had been girlhood friends, and that explained it.

The glamorous dark-haired woman had an eye for furniture and placement. Mrs. Smith-Porter watched her scan the parlor and dining room in a professional, even calculating way. The woman with the slinged arm said nothing about that, but mentioned she was a teacher. The young girl, her daughter, sat stolidly in a chair while the others trooped behind Mrs. Smith-Porter for a look at the garden as the morning sun was just peeking through and a modest display of wisteria trained up the treillage against the back wall was making a showing.

She led upstairs, and they followed her switching skirts. Even at the top of the flight she said nothing about the obvious need for an additional, unbooked bed for the young girl. But then she condescended to sacrifice her own sewing room, for a consideration, sweeping open its door in a well-timed gesture. It was small, so she showed it from the doorsill: the morning slanting in over the George II table past the candlestick lamp, the weathered old paper of lovers' knots, and the Empire sleigh bed with the fur rug folded at its foot for just a touch of Napoleon on the retreat from Moscow. Fingering her pearls with a ringless hand while her visitors watched, rapt, Mrs. Smith-Porter made clear that as a rule she kept this room for herself, working at that desk. She remarked untruthfully that she often had an afternoon lie-down on the sleigh bed.

She supposed the young girl could go in here and her mother, Mrs. Mayhew, into the best bedroom next door at the front, the Cardinal Richelieu room with the capacious Prince Albert Memorial bed. But in a move so surprisingly swift that it caught them all off guard, the girl stalked in and staked out the larger room. Mrs. Smith-Porter noticed Mrs. Hockaday's mouth open to protest, but close again, and the girl's mother was left to wedge herself into the sewing-room sleigh bed however she might.

The last room on this floor shared the rear of the house with a bathroom, so there was no denying its coffin shape. The advantage was a window looking quietly down on the garden. It might have been a nursery, and so Mrs. Smith-Porter had done it as a gossamer memory of genteel childhood — far from her own. On the white wall above the narrow bed were framed samplers and bits of embroidered lawn that young nineteenth-century girls had worked to show their prowess. An overbearing Victorian dresser with original mirror and candle brackets pointed out the cozy absurdity of the room's dimensions. In the only open corner stood an Edwardian dollhouse that was all pitched roofs and gables and welcoming porches, built at home for some superior child, long grown, long gone. Mrs. Hockaday had stood for a moment on the threshold of the room and then moved in.

Mrs. Smith-Porter led her remaining visitor up another flight to what Americans call the third floor, though it was of course the second. This was the top of the house, with a room right across the front and at the back the box room Mrs. Smith-Porter slept in herself, next to the other bathroom. The ceilings up here were scarcely seven feet from the floor, lower still at the back. But the guest room had three bright windows that gave onto the street with views skimming over the houses opposite and out across London. With a bit of imagination, you could find the tower of Westminster cathedral. She was proud of this room. Stepping aside, she invited Mrs. Steadman in with a sweep of the hand.

It was at first a jumble of oversized oddments and finicking detail even to the educated eye. Mrs. Steadman had stopped dead just inside, and her eye went straight to the geometric washstand with the art-glass drop front smoldering in subdued jewel colors.

She seemed not to breathe. Then: "I thought that was in the Metropolitan." Her hand had come up to her face but hung in the air.

"They have the other one, I believe," Mrs. Smith-Porter said. "I take it you are in the business?"

Fixated on the only Charles Mackintosh washstand she'd ever seen outside captivity, her visitor only nodded. Mrs. Smith-Porter had lowered the ceiling further by darkening the beams to echo the furniture, and she'd used a William Morris wallpaper slightly predating the rest of the room. It was in a mood of Glasgow tea shop, circa 1910, backed up by Liberty stained-oak pieces. The winking hardware throughout was over-wrought copper. Mrs. Smith-Porter herself climbed up here to give it a rub with Sainsbury's metal polish.

"How do you dare?" Mrs. Steadman said in a near whisper.

"Theft? Most of it's too big to shift, and most of my visitors think they've been relegated to the attic with my leftovers."

This visitor turned and looked guardedly up at her. "You wouldn't be interested in selling the washstand?"

"My dear, I'd want two hundred thousand pounds," said Mrs. Smith-Porter, erasing the last hope that this room could have happened by blind chance.

And so the room was a great success with Mrs. Steadman, who took up residence in it as if she were about to bed down in the V & A. It was always interesting to see how the visitors contrived to sort out the rooms for themselves, with only a nudge.

Very sensibly they all took to their beds. Mrs. Smith-Porter only needed to touch lightly on headlong people who drop their luggage and stride out of the house on the first morning, hell-bent for St. Paul's or the Elgin Marbles, and have to come back in a cab by noon, very much the worse for wear. She recalled for them the woman who'd been brought back in a collapsed state by the Metropolitan Police in a panda.

On her way out for a walk, she stopped by the looking glass in her box room. She was more expertly made up than anyone ever noticed. She hadn't been in the back row of the chorus behind Hermione Gingold for nothing. Now she added a trace of lipstick, pillar-box red, because age is so fading. Then, collecting her string bag and a folding umbrella, she was off up the street. It gave new visitors a completely quiet house and herself time to reflect on them.

In her youth she'd walked to get there, lacking the fare. Now she walked to breathe in the life around her, and perhaps to prove she still could. These days she had to get out of bed in stages, and she had her portion of aches and pains, but on her walks age didn't concern her. She considered that life had really begun for her back when she returned from the West Country to make a real go of her house. Taken in that light, she was still quite a young woman.

Her route took her to the top of Radnor Walk with Waitrose, the supermarket, just over the road. It was a general truth that the most convenient supermarket was always the most overpriced. But Waitrose was always her last stop, and in any case you couldn't cross over directly. She went left to negotiate the King's Road at the Chelsea Town Hall corner. Even here you took your life in your hands, for it was neither a zebra nor a traffic light. Mrs. Smith-Porter often so forgot herself that she hiked skirts and galloped across like an old horse in a point-to-point, pausing for breath on the island, then plunging on in a gap between buses, to collect herself and settle her rainproof hat at the Habitat corner. Left from there was the bank and then the newsagent outside the post office. At Heal's, the corner shop, she turned up Sydney Street to the Chelsea Farmers' Market.

Rain spattered across the street, then watery sun, then something in between. The farmers' market, without a farmer in sight, was rather better than a public park: all the pot plants and root-wrapped shrubbery and graduated rows of garden gnomes, all meant for gardens the size of hers. And little sheds like people used to put on their allotments in the war, selling absurdly priced cheeses and exotic coffees.

She could afford their coffee now and settled down for a good sit at an outdoor table, adding a spoon of demerara sugar.

There were days when she wandered farther afield, right across London, to obscure corners where there was a street market or an auction or a house sale. It took very little to draw her. She couldn't walk those distances, but she had her OAP card, which meant she traveled free in all the buses and the tube. The old had these cards, renewed annually, though there'd been a muddle when she had to prove her identity the first time as nobody had troubled to record her birth. This had worked for her in the war when she hadn't been called up with the other girls at twenty. But it rather worked against her later on. In the end she'd had to tell the authorities that all her records had been lost in the bombing of Finsbury Town Hall. This was such a bald-faced lie that it was believed.

Americans were awed that the English old could travel free wherever they chose. Mrs. Smith-Porter couldn't quite imagine what it was to be old in America and didn't think she wanted to know.

160

She made do with the farmers' market today. It was just far enough off the King's Road that one wasn't thrust off the curb by the heedless young plodding along four abreast from shop to dreadful gear-selling shop. A few years ago they were arguably worse, with spikes of parti-colored parrot hair and Union Jacks painted over their faces. They'd charged the foreigners to photograph them, but they were vanished now, bright birds flown, she couldn't imagine where. Perhaps they'd winged their way into adult life, molting as they went.

Now the young, far from putting on a show, slumped between shops, dressed in colorless clothes and buying more. They wore almost unrelieved black, and Mrs. Smith-Porter often wondered what they mourned. Of course England stared moral and financial ruin in the face, but then it always had as far back as she could remember. It was hard for her to imagine being young without a war. Wars and the young are made for one another. During the war the young had kept busier, and someone else chose their uniforms, and with real reason to mourn, they wore very little black. But when her daydreaming turned back in the direction of her youth, she found it all as foreign as this coffee.

She could make a cup last, another legacy of the old days, and didn't know how much time had passed before she gathered up her string bag to go. The sun seemed to be getting over in the sky. She never wore a watch and had long ago learned how to shape a day without one. After all, she never had a train to catch, or a theater curtain. When she stood, she was taller than any tree in view, and people around her looked suddenly up. It was never her intention to draw attention to herself in public, and this always did. She made her stately way out of the market, past the glaring white prefabricated arbors and the piles of terra-cotta.

Then north to Britten Street running along the side of St. Luke's churchyard for a glimpse of the flower beds beyond the tombstones, her alternate route back. Then down Chelsea Manor Street with the King's Road rushing along at the far end past the flower seller. She was lost in thought in this backwater when a young girl stepped out of a telephone box directly in her path. It was the American girl she'd supposed was sound asleep in her first-floor front. Her hand was still on the door of the telephone box. She made a fist and struck it. Mrs. Smith-Porter was arrested by the great tangle of her hair.

"Can I help at all?" she said throatily, and

the girl spun round. She wore a large shirt like a jumper with the word or name NORTHWESTERN across it, white on black. Mrs. Smith-Porter could only envy her the burgeoning bust beneath it. "I am your landlady," she said because there was nothing in the girl's eyes but incomprehension and guilt.

"I was just trying —"

"That telephone only takes phone cards." She was about to tell the girl she was welcome to use the telephone at home. Instead she nodded ahead. "The box down the far end takes coins. Do you have a friend in London?"

The girl looked away. "I don't know. In Richmond. That's where I've written."

"It's not far," Mrs. Smith-Porter said, setting a pace the girl was meant to follow. "You can get there in the tube, the District Line, straight to Richmond." She heard the girl listening, slightly against her will. "You can walk just along the King's Road to Sloane Square to the tube stop."

"How far is it?" the girl asked.

"Just up the way, a quarter of a mile, I suppose." But the girl seemed to think that was well out of walking range. "Or you can take any bus up to the tube from the corner. But mind you take one on this side of the road.

The traffic travels on the opposite side to what you're used to."

"I know," the girl said. "Why?"

Why? Nobody had ever asked that before. "Wiser minds than ours decreed it," Mrs. Smith-Porter said, though she wasn't so sure of that. And then though she was never seen to pry: "How did your mother injure herself?"

"She was shot," the girl said.

Mrs. Mayhew had mentioned that she was from Chicago, and it was well known that people there lived in a constant hail of bullets. "In the street?" Mrs. Smith-Porter asked.

"In the shoulder," the girl said absently. Now they were at the phone box that took coins, and she was fitting herself inside, digging in the pocket of her tight jeans.

Mrs. Smith-Porter strolled on to Waitrose, diverted as always by a chance encounter, though she hoped she wasn't coming to the stage of accosting people in the street. She'd made no systematic study of adolescents, but merely thought that people as large as adults should be spoken to like them. Of course it often didn't work.

But now she was pushing a cart through Waitrose past frosted foods. It was a place she thoroughly approved of: spotless, spacious, well lit, a far cry from the grocers of her childhood and the queues in the war. She took her time at Waitrose, reassured by all those varieties of chocolate biscuits and bottled waters. As she was dithering pleasantly over Dutch butter, she thought again about the young girl, out of the house and braving British Telecom. She wondered if she herself hadn't conspired in some scheme the girl was plotting. But then she remembered orange juice and turned her cart that way. Gemma would have to lay out the breakfast tomorrow because it was Friday, and Mrs. Smith-Porter was always well away early on Fridays.

She was back in Radnor Walk with her shopping heavy in the string bag when she saw the girl ahead of her, on the step fitting a key into the front door. Back home, perhaps before her mother missed her. The three women would be stirring upstairs, ready to set forth for tea somewhere. Mrs. Smith-Porter divined that the girl had no intention of going with them. She could often foretell the immediate futures of her visitors.

In their first change of clothes Julia and Margo and Les went for tea in the orangery of Kensington Palace. Kimberly had pled delayed jet lag and stayed behind, to Julia's relief. They'd gone on a number 49 bus that dropped them when it turned at the gate that led into the gardens, Mrs. Smith-Porter having advised against a cab as there was more to be seen from the top of a bus. They strode in step up the Broad Walk past the Round Pond. "See? I said you could walk in the parks here," Les said.

The orangery, another of Mrs. Smith-Porter's recommendations, wasn't on Les's list and turned out to be ideal. The service was glacial and stately, and the tea leaves were loose in the pot. They sat between marble sculptures in a room that soared above them like frozen seventeenth-century court music. Out the long windows a gravel-trimmed greensward swept down past urns to a concealed rose garden overlooked by a brooding brick palace.

Les set aside her brochures and poured, and Margo appeared near tears. She felt as if she'd wandered at last into the pages of every book she'd ever read. She found herself wonderfully weightless in some parallel universe. "We're sitting here in England," she said, and they all touched teacups. Julia was lulled but determined not to spend every minute joined at their hips.

Sensing the separate agendas of the other two, Les said that at the very least they ought to meet up and have tea some marvelous place every afternoon. She had Margo nailed for a guided bus tour tomorrow morning, and presumably Kimberly. "We're booked into the Ritz for tea on the last afternoon," she said. "They recommend hats."

Julia turned big eyes on her. "You've made tea reservations for the last day already? When?"

"Hats?" Margo said, alarmed.

"I called up from St. Louis," Les said. "Got right through."

"You called from St. Louis for tea reservations," Julia said wonderingly. She was still half in the bag with jet lag hangover. "Les, there's nobody like you, not remotely. You're wonderful in your way."

"You're wonderful, period," Margo said. "We're lucky to have you. We always were."

"Oh well," Les said, turning over a hand to dismiss herself. "You two are the smart ones. I just . . . make lists." She looked down to get busy about the hot buttered scones nestled in napkins. Les spread Margo's portion with brambleberry jam from a little pot because Margo couldn't really manage one-handed. For Les it was like it used to be down at the Cape, the three of them against the world. There are miracles, she thought, but it's like pulling teeth to make them happen.

Chapter 10

Julia awoke at first light, another blow to her body clock. She'd been popping melatonin for days without visible effect. Unbelievably, steam rose from a cup of tea at her bedside. She rolled quietly out and thought about clothes: navy linen slacks and a white pocketed T-shirt. Slightly too Talbots for a down-and-dirty outdoor antique market, but she'd try not to brush up against anything. She didn't know where the rest of the day might take her. She didn't want to come back here to change and end up on Les's bus tour.

By twenty past four she was standing beside the deserted King's Road in the damp dawn air. A cruising cab, glad to see her, drew up and blasted off like a rocket to Sloane Square. They wove through empty Pimlico an hour ahead of the buses. Then they were barreling along the Embankment past the silvering Thames, the iron lacework of the streetlamps, the homeless beginning to stir.

In a sort of fast-forward film they passed a tourist-free Tower of London, and crossed

Tower Bridge, making for the mysteries of south London. Here the traffic was backing up. This hidden quarter had been up for hours, doing business. On the right past warehouses Bermondsey opened to a vast tent city of stalls and trucks selling out of their back doors. A Brueghel scene, Julia thought. Thousands of people milled up and down the narrow aisles ranked with treasures and trash brightening with the day. Out of the cab, she shuddered in the morning chill and stood on the edge. The Bermondsey market wasn't one of her usual sources. Often she wasn't in London on a Friday morning, and rarely in her life was she up at this hour. Overwhelmed and trying to keep the Malmquists in mind, she plunged in.

An hour or two later she came to the end, only to find it was a street and as much market again on the far side. Her feet even in deck shoes were screaming, and she joined a queue at the tea wagon, where the smell of frying onions nearly knocked her sideways. She could manage only tea, milked and presweetened, in a styrofoam cup. Turning, she noticed a black smear clear across the T-shirt pocket, and looking up she saw an unmistakable figure under an indescribable hat.

Mrs. Smith-Porter was moving above the

throng. It was like seeing a familiar face suddenly appearing over a dune in the Gobi Desert. The crowds parted, or she parted them, and Julia got a better look: the waterproof coat with corduroy cuffs and generous pockets and a box-pleated skirt beneath, lisle stockings down to flat shoes. Then they were face-to-face. Mrs. Smith-Porter's eyebrows arched. "Mrs. Steadman?"

"Does the early bird really catch the worm?" Julia said.

Mrs. Smith-Porter pulled a dramatically long face. "You are liable to catch anything here."

Julia thought she was the most arresting-looking human being she'd ever seen. The hat that ought to have made her look like a bag lady at best only added to her magnificence. It was a hat that thumbed its nose at the world and must have gone through the Battle of Britain, the quintessential English hat.

"Finding anything?"

"I don't know where to start. And it's endless."

"That's the joy," Mrs. Smith-Porter said. "Eternal life at last." She'd hooked an arm through Julia's, and they were making their way down a row. "Mind you, it's a thieves' market, always was."

"How much of this stuff is actually stolen?"

"All of it, I should think, at one time or another."

The market scene was unreal enough, but sheltering under Mrs. Smith-Porter's hat brim, Julia seemed to move just above the cobblestones, hallucinating as she went. Half the goods heaped out on the tables were obvious copies. Nothing was as it seemed. You could so easily lose your grip on reality.

"Anything in the silver line?" Mrs. Smith-Porter asked. "The odd Georgian piece still surfaces." Pressing Julia's arm, she dropped her voice a mile. "Some of the younger dealers haven't a clue. It's twenty quid for an electroplated fish fork, and a pound fifty for George III. They simply haven't a notion, some of them, and they're too thick to learn. Thick as two planks." She nodded knowingly. "I look for them particularly."

"I have a whole house to do," Julia said. "I don't think I can get it done a spoon at a time."

"Furniture?" Mrs. Smith-Porter drew them both up short. "Why didn't you say? Nothing but rubbish outdoors unless you're in the mood for old gramophones and questionable rattan. You want over there." She pointed her lethal umbrella past the stall roofs to a line of Dickensian houses. "Furniture worth looking at over there. Hugh Dalrymple's the best of a bad lot."

It must have taken them half an hour to get there. Like all of London, there was no direct way. Mrs. Smith-Porter made occasional stops, looking over the heads of lesser mortals at the heaped tables. Then they were climbing the splintered stairs of a loading dock to warehouse doors. Inside, furniture rose two stories with a kind of loft behind. A man in his shirtsleeves was up there, looking down. "Can I help at all?"

Julia turned to Mrs. Smith-Porter and found herself alone in the wide door. Seven a.m. sun poured in across a wedge of rough wood floor, and Mrs. Smith-Porter was almost supernaturally not there. She'd had that much time and no more. Julia saw how she operated. She got you going, and then she vanished.

The man was coming down open steps, and the cat had Julia's tongue. She was completely off her turf and off guard, and she'd been up for hours, and it was still only seven in the morning. She remembered the woman brought back in a collapsed state in a panda.

"Are you in the trade?"

She nodded.

He was standing at the end of the light, shorter than he'd been in the loft. A little over her age, her real one. Weathered with crows'-feet beside the eyes. Very strong nose. Blond hair with some white mixed in. He wore a really filthy tattersall shirt without a collar, the cuffs turned up his arms, and beltless British trousers, winter weight, cavalry twill, stuffed into gum boots that could never have been new.

"Anything in particular?"

Julia, feeling quite cuckoo now, wondered how slim her figure looked outlined by morning light. Pulling herself together, she said, "Reasonably casual English countryside, top of the line, not too cottagey. A whole house, four bedrooms, living room, dining room, and an indoor-outdoor area, covered. There's talk of a guesthouse."

"New York?"

"No, Santa Fe, so I'll have to cut it with some local pottery and rugs."

"I meant you," he said, "actually."

"Oh. Yes." She reached up for the glasses that weren't in her hair, aware of the smudged T-shirt pocket.

"This isn't my best," he said without apology, "and you're late in the day. Have you had breakfast, because I haven't. Hugh Dalrymple." He came forward, putting out a square hand. They were almost eye to eye.

"Julia Steadman."

"Mrs.?"

"Officially," Julia said.

The next thing she knew, they were farther down Tower Bridge Road at a sticky table in a lorry drivers' cafe. The room was blue with smoke and full of large scarred men all obviously out on parole. First came two chipped mugs of milky tea with the bag tags hanging out. Then two platters with slabs of British bacon bubbling in white fat, two bangers (sausages), both halves of a tomato broiled to mush, a small Alp of French fries (chips), and two very over-easy eggs floating in something and staring blind-eyed up at her. Beyond all reason, Julia was ravenous.

Hugh Dalrymple ate with fork in one hand, knife in the other, and Julia couldn't keep her eyes off his hands. Big, banged-up, work-worn, seamed with dirt, the hands of — Lady Chatterley's lover. Julia fought hysteria. After the first, she hadn't met his eyes — china blue with unforgivably long pale lashes. He wasn't as good-looking as Junior Steadman, but it didn't seem to matter. There were places on his upper cheeks the razor had missed. She vowed to look no higher.

Julia blamed jet lag or maybe one of those viruses the airlines circulate on planes. She hadn't dated, not even down at the Cape, and, God knows, never at college. How she'd bagged Junior she couldn't remember. There hadn't even been a mall at the time. She must have merely called him up and sent for him. Now this indigestible, in fact unspeakable, breakfast seemed to be Julia's First Date with every adolescent overtone, hormones howling their heads off.

She marched her mind back to all the men she'd gone out with in New York down through the unforgiving years, all those men she'd sat with in overpriced restaurants, interchangeable men in Hugo Boss neckties. Give her a minute and she could name names. Dinner, a show, occasionally something more till she put a stop to it or they went home to their wives. Not Dale, of course. Dale was in his own category. In fact she sensed him suddenly here, grinning at her through the smoke. She supposed it was some sort of crush now that she was in the puberty of middle age, but it felt like concussion. She'd be over it in a minute.

"Were you a farm girl to begin with?"

Julia jumped.

"You eat a hearty breakfast."

Pulling her eyes off his hands, Julia looked

down to her empty plate. Not only did she seem to be having somebody else's thoughts, but somebody else had eaten her breakfast. He would think she was half-witted, an overaged bimbo. And bulimic. She gathered herself and looked him in the eye. "You look English and sound it, but there's something else," she said, finding that she'd managed a compound sentence.

"I ask personal questions," he said. "Not British, that. But I didn't spend all my early years here. Navy."

Julia had a quick vision of tight white sailor pants and wondered about tattoos.

"A British bulldog on my backside, I'm afraid," this mind reader said. "National service, and then I misspent the rest of my youth wandering the world, couldn't get enough of it. Cape Town, Perth, Burma when you could get in."

"The States?" Julia asked.

"The Malay States?"

It was like having breakfast with Kipling. "The United States."

"From coast to coast. I bought a Kawasaki in a place called Freehold, New Jersey, and drove it across country till it fell to bits in a place called Ottumwa. Then I thumbed all the way to Haight-Ashbury in the so-called Summer of Love."

"And how did they take to a Royal Navy vet?"

"They seemed to think I was a narc. Couldn't make head or tail of me, and I moved on. Wasn't it one of your lot who said he dared never be a radical when he was young for fear he'd be a conservative when he was old?"

"Robert Frost," Julia said tonelessly. "Why didn't I hear that in time?"

"Surely you're not a reformed hippie." Hugh raised haystack eyebrows at her.

Hay, Julia thought, a roll in the — "Not the Summer of Love part. I took myself much too seriously for that. I was still in camouflage colors by the early Carter administration."

"How beautifully you've recovered," he said in a wonderfully offhand way.

Julia felt she might be undergoing meltdown. "Shouldn't you be getting back to work?"

"Nothing much for it by this time of the morning. Only punters. Tourists wandering in, looking for items they can get into carry-on luggage. Talking of wandering in, what kind fate sent you my way? The elderly party in the hat? I've seen her about. She's something of a recurring character in the market."

"Mrs. Smith-Porter. She's our London landlady. I'm over here with friends. At present they're somewhere between bed and a bus tour."

"And so are you working or hiding?"

"I've been hiding in my work for years," Julia heard herself say.

"Married or not?"

"Not. He's married to Willa now with two kids and regular meals and a nice life once I got out of his way. Are you?"

"Was. She's painting in Prague," he said, reducing a marriage to half a haiku.

Now that they knew absolutely everything about each other, Julia thought she was on the road to recovery. They were on their feet, she glancing down at the empty plates. "Do we pay them, or do they pay us?" So now she saw him grin. They were going now, out into the thundering street, possibly parting.

He offered her his arm even though this wasn't the neighborhood for that. He wasn't a lot taller than she was. "I don't know what I have for you."

Julia reeled.

"Bleached pine any good? I can do you three-drawer, four-drawer, can't promise original hardware."

"Certainly for one of the bedrooms," Julia said, all business. "And a bed, though it can't match. Do you ever get a bleached-pine four-poster? A canopy's going too far."

"Anything's possible," Hugh Dalrymple said while Julia watched her footing. Back in the warehouse he said, "You can have a good look round. I'll be another hour or so. But I keep most of my things and all the better stuff in a barn in the country. Kent, actually, where I live and not so far. Why don't you come down with me and make a day of it? I can arrange for a container. Who knows, you might find everything you wanted." He started up his stairs. "There's lunch in it for you, a suitably picturesque country pub with tables in a garden. A Yankee version of English heaven. Think about it."

Julia thought. She stood among the welter of bleached pine, her mind moving among women who'd climbed into the cars of plausible strangers in foreign countries and ended up virtually unrecognizable on slabs. And Hugh Dalrymple, the best of a bad lot, was bound to be at the least a dealer in stolen goods. Julia thought it was worth a shot.

Kimberly awoke in the weird bed, the headboard looming over her like her mother. Hours earlier, her mother had rapped on the door, something about a bus tour. But it might have been a dream. She couldn't even keep her mother out of her dreams.

Turning to squint at her travel clock, she saw a cup of unsteaming tea on the night-stand, so the old landlady had been in here, watching her sleep, maybe going through her things. With a familiar sense of being invaded, Kimberly edged up in the bed, wondering if she was sick, wondering how much work her hair needed. She barely knew where she was, but at least she recognized the old familiar shirt she slept in, a dress shirt of Dad's with the buttons hanging by threads. Something about the size of the room reminded her of his poky apartment down in Rogers Park. And how Dad had betrayed her.

She grabbed the clock. Ten, and she had to meet Kevin at noon. He'd said he could meet her after morning classes. She still wondered if she was sick, though she never felt much better than this in the mornings. Now she was going to be late. Automatically, she blamed her mother as she dragged herself out of bed and stood swaying.

Reaching around inside the suitcase for something to wear, she came up with a top from the Gap and jeans. The house seemed to listen as she cracked the door and looked out. Her mother's door was open, and so was Mrs. Hockaday's. Kimberly was pushed for time, which she hated. Even before senior year, she'd made a point of being late for school and never did first period, but today was different. It could be the most important day of her life if somebody didn't spoil it. She crossed the top of the stairs to the bathroom.

A quarter of an hour later she burst back into her room, panicking now about the time and Kevin and everything. She jumped back and nearly screamed. Somebody was in her room. Gemma was just smoothing the counterpane on the bed. "Shall I unpack for you then?" she said, looking her over.

And that was a sign to Kimberly, a reminder. Decided now, she reached for her backpack with all her money, the credit cards, her passport — everything. Clean sweep. "I'm out of here," she said, liking the sound of it.

The maid's hands rested on the bed, and she glanced at the front-door key on the table. Kimberly nearly snatched it up, but if she didn't take it with her, there was no way she'd be coming back. With a heart beginning to pound, she zipped the suitcase and grabbed up the backpack. The door was only a step away, and she hung there a moment, giving the maid a chance to stop her, give her an argument or something. Betray her. But Gemma was already going about her business.

Nobody was on the stairs as Kimberly banged her suitcase along the wall. Nearing the bottom, she smelled cigarette smoke and wondered if the landlady was lurking around in the living room. But it was somebody else. Some old crone even more ancient than the landlady was on all fours, slopping a rag over the hall floor. Kimberly kept moving. Then when she pulled the front door behind her and heard the lock catch, it was like that first time she and Kevin had done it. A kind of proof, an answer to everything. Out in the street she realized that all the mornings of her life she'd wanted to walk out and never come back. Turning up to the King's Road, she focused her whole mind on Kevin, rehearsing what she'd say and deciding how he'd react.

She took a bus from the corner the old lady had told her about, the first one that came along. It was weird too, with an open platform at the back. A conductor or whoever showed her a cubbyhole under the stairs where she could stow her bags. The bus was already moving, and she felt hurried. When the conductor came around wanting money and she held out some coins, her hand shook. She said she wanted to go to Richmond, and he told her to "alight" at Sloane Square and take the tube from there, so she did.

Hugh Dalrymple referred to his car as a Mini, or possibly Minnie. Julia hadn't quite heard, being deafened by traffic and terror. They were belting along something called a dual carriageway, and she wondered why the shoulder of the road wasn't littered with wreckage and body parts. Between her feet she saw an irregular patch of pavement racing in reverse beneath a hole in the floorboards. There seemed nothing to cling to, though Hugh's left knee was wedged against her right one. At every swerve, Julia's whole life flashed before her in the bursts of total recall Les seemed to have all the time.

Off the main road, they bucketed along a country lane between hedges that perfectly masked intersections. The car lacked all suspension, but there were unnerving moments of smooth sailing when Julia assumed they were airborne.

Then the two of them were sitting at a table behind a half-timbered country inn. Puffy clouds played across a smogless sky. Willows wept into a burbling river below them. "Extraordinary how slowly Americans drive, I found," Hugh was saying, "given the distances in your country."

The day wasn't getting any more real, Julia observed. It was like sitting in a postcard, faint breeze in the shade, a glareless sun playing over Hugh's blond thatch. A perfectly cast country girl in a long apron came out to take their order and flushed deeply at the sight of him.

But he knitted his haystack eyebrows at Julia. "I hope you weren't thinking along the lines of Pimms and pâté, or Stilton scooped from the round. But they can do you a very passable ploughman's lunch."

The lovesick waitress vanished behind the half-timbering and bobbed back, still smitten, with a lager for Hugh, a lager and lime for Julia. A drink was the last thing she needed, but it had a calming color, and the beaded glass beckoned. "Where are we?" she asked.

"Deepest Kent."

"Then this isn't a theme park?" On cue birdsong trilled high in the sighing trees. A mother duck led a vee of ducklings down the river. Several years of tension began to ebb from Julia. She felt dams breaking gently throughout her regions.

"Not New York," Hugh remarked, mind-reading again.

Another five minutes of this, Julia thought, and I'll be completely defenseless. Putty in his hands. The waitress, also fixated on Hugh, returned, hands full, tripping over her own apron. Julia turned her face to the sun to cover any possible blushes of her own. Then she was plowing through her ploughman's lunch.

They sat on at the table long after, talking shop. Hugh was assembling a container for a dealer on Royal Street in New Orleans. Julia recommended later Victorian as scrolled as possible and all the marble tops he could lay his hands on. She expanded upon the vagaries of American taste: The New Yorkers want anything marked by a maker their friends recognize. You can't go far wrong with ormolu for the Texans. Don't bother with Bostonians who think they ought to have inherited and resent you because they didn't. And the farther west you go, the better the market in other people's ancestors.

She seemed to hold him in thrall, or he was the best listener she'd ever come across. They don't make listeners like this in New York. Suddenly sick of the sound of her own voice, Julia fell silent, and that appeared to be all right too.

They'd been the only two diners on the terrace all along. Now it had a more vacant midafternoon feel. There were dark patches in the reedy river. "Come on," Hugh said, reaching across for her hand. "Let me show you my barn."

More convincingly half-timbered than the inn, it stood overhung by a magnificent copper beech beside a minor country road. Hugh pulled the car into a narrow paved yard. Nothing said it was a place of business apart from some French garden furniture firmly chained and a hill of Tuscan flowerpots. Beside the barn doors a notice read: Hugh Dalrymple. Ring.

Julia thought this trod a fine line between the discreet and the furtive. The padlock fell free, and Hugh rolled back the doors. Inside, it was the mother lode of English country furniture in every state of repair, ranked and stacked to the authentic rafters.

"Where do you find all this?" she said when she could breathe.

"Mostly in this part of the world. Auctions, house sales, that sort of thing. People bring me the odd stick."

"Surely you prey on lonely old ladies in big houses, and you're there the minute they're dead, with a van at the door."

"On the very heels of the undertaker," Hugh said smoothly.

Walkways like wandering mole runs burrowed through the teetering piles. Hugh showed Julia a sort of forest clearing at the back he called his office. It was a badly battered, probably priceless desk. Pearwood, Julia judged. He settled there and let her roam. She spent an hour barking her shins on sharp corners, her mind divided between the merchandise and the proprietor. Once she caught a look at him through the knothole at the back of an armoire. He was at his desk, slightly befuddled and lost in thought, poring over invoices. But she made herself move on. Finally it was all too much, and she was back at his desk.

"What do you think?"

"I can't see any of it, and I think I want it all." Now she was smudged all over with what could easily be mouse droppings. "There's part of a stairway in there that the Petries will want for Millbrook, and it might just be Grinling Gibbons. And that's just one thing."

"It's a fearful muddle, I know. It needs a —"

"You're not going to say it needs a woman's touch."

"It wants sorting through, certainly."

"Do you sell from here?"

"Every day but Friday."

"Well, you're not showing any of it to very

good advantage."

Hugh worked his chin. "I'm forever telling people that I know it's here, but I can't put my hands on it just at the moment."

Julia's mind sprinted ahead toward computerized inventory and the kind of well-lit period groupings Kentshire does in their New York showrooms. Her mouth opened and closed again. This chaotic barn was no more muddled than the rest of England, and it was just possible that Hugh did a brisk business without her horning in. Besides, she wanted to know something else. "You don't live here too?"

"I do. I've boxed off a part of the loft, the bit at the back. I'd show it you, but my etchings are out at the framer."

This dry Britishism was pitched in below her batting range. She blinked. Now he'd come around the desk and was leaning against it, his arms folded. If he kisses me now, she thought, it will just be for today. If he doesn't —

"You're not meant to be anywhere else, are you?"

She stared at him.

"I mean ought you to be getting back? To your friends?"

"I ought. Les wants us to report daily for teatime."

"I'm afraid you won't make that. Les is your leader, I take it?"

"She wishes. Actually she is. Only she could have got us here. And of course Margo being shot."

Hugh looked pensive. "Ah," he said finally. "If you really must —"

"I think missing tea but being back in time for dinner will set about the right tone," Julia said.

"Never mind then. I'll have you back before dark. Lovely long evenings this time of year." And then: "We have plenty of time."

But Julia's mind was already on the aluminum-foil car hurtling back up the dual carriageway in traffic screaming both directions.

"Anyway, there's someone I'd like you to meet." He led her to a low door she hadn't noticed before at the back of the barn. Julia went willingly.

Chapter 11

They stepped through the rickety door into a walled yard littered with lumber. A rusty furniture van stood over an oil slick. "Bit of a tip all this." They were making for a gate in the far wall.

On the other side past a stand of Spanish chestnuts a long half-wild garden rambled. It was subtly some other climate here, dank and dreamy. Overgrown borders narrowed the grassy path. There was faint evidence of a knot garden sketched in weeds. Stone figures in eighteenth-century dress gazed blindly at them as they passed. Julia strolled speechlessly, still lightly attached to Hugh's hand. Then they were walking up a graveled avenue between yew trees, following the contour of a low rise. The sun hung suspended beyond the trees, throwing long purple shadows.

"And at the end of all this," she said, "there's going to be a ruined manor house, some musty masterpiece the National Trust never got its hands on."

"The house itself is something of a cock — mixture of styles," Hugh said. "Not old. Sixteen twenty or thereabouts."

The lane turned and the trees drew back. A house ranged over the crown of the hill, crenellation and chimneys against the sky. "The boxwood and the stone obelisks remain from the early days, but in the 1790s the family fell under the sway of the gothic. They knocked the gables into battlements and let the gardens go in a calculated wilderness way. The original house was mostly brick, that grim brick William and Mary used for redoing Kensington Palace. But plastered over later. Hideous really, but settling in. I suppose the name of the place dates from the late eighteenth century: Ravenscote. It has the ring of Horace Walpole."

Gothic novels blared in Julia's brain. Mr. Rochester swaggered through, brandishing a riding crop. "Who —"

"Sir Ludovic," Hugh said. " 'Ludo' in the village. Baronet, and not an old title. Seems to derive from having entertained the prince regent. Eighteen oh six, something like that."

"Is he your landlord?"

"In a manner of speaking. At one time he was everybody's landlord for as far as you can see, and he wasn't doing anything with that barn."

"When is the house open?"

"Once during the Jubilee Year, I think. Nineteen seventy-seven. Just a few rooms, but Ludo never lived in many. He'll want to meet you."

"Really?" Julia itched to see inside.

"Yes," Hugh said. "He's dying."

As they crossed the last stretch of weedy lawn, the house rose over them, busy with gargoyles. Diamond panes winked in the light. Julia was ready to break into a run on the last stretch despite the dying man inside. Stickered blackberry had invaded the stone porch, and the front door was a triumph of the mock heroic. Surprisingly, Hugh pushed it open. There was a smell of the centuries and rising damp with a hint of the sickroom. "Not much in the way of servants now," he said. "Nurses round the clock, of course."

He led Julia through the rooms, a dusty trove dominated from above by spreading mushrooms of dry rot. "A lot of Regency stuff presumably still in place from the prince's visit. Most of the tapestries are thought to be Louis de Vos, though Charles Lindbergh in an aeroplane figures in one of them, so it's best to keep an open mind."

The morning room moved from mid-Victorian Crystal Palace Exposition to a

Noël Coward cocktail cabinet, mirrored. Tables were overturned on tables, and pictures stood against the walls. From there double doors opened to a ballroom gilded beyond reason. The ceiling, patched with more dry rot, displayed the prince's three feathers, old gold against sky blue. Afternoon beamed through long windows across a dusty floor parqueted in sunbursts. Julia's hand was over her mouth at the sheer unexpectedness of it, and the scope.

"Added for the prince's visit," Hugh said. "Of course it threw the proportions of the house into a cocked hat. Wonderful how well the vulgarity of our ancestors has weathered, isn't it?"

They doubled back to the grand front staircase without retracing their path: An embossed-leather library full of bound copies of *Punch*. A state dining room heaped in gilt chairs. A breakfast room where two kitchen chairs pulled up to a small table with a Marmite pot anchoring a pile of paper napkins.

On the oak stairs, they were looked down on by portraits. "They all want a good clean," Hugh said. "That's the prince regent as George IV, and that's a Copley of the Sir Ludovic of his time, only he was called 'Bertram.' "

At the top they made a turning or two down a corridor painted an institutional green. "No portrait of the present Sir Ludovic?"

"Nothing here that I know of. One as a willowy young man, but that's in the Tate. Rex Whistler. And nothing at all of his wife. She's been dead some years."

"Children?"

"Not that sort of marriage apparently."

Hugh stopped before a door, and this time he knocked. Julia thought she might have heard some murmuring response. Then they were inside, a long room with silvered Chinese wallpaper, dark till the far end. Nearest the windows a bed stood shrouded in very early hangings. Virtually Knole. Then she saw the canister of oxygen beside it and the hospital table. She hung back, and Hugh walked down the room.

"Ah, my dear boy. I thought it was that sadistic woman for my injection, or worse, the vicar." The voice was high-pitched, practically from the grave. Julia considered flight, her usual solution, but she advanced halfway.

"This business of dying isn't the pleasure I'd anticipated," the old man was saying. "It is too like waiting endlessly for the car to be brought round, or rereading *Middlemarch*."

Now Hugh was gesturing behind his back,

so Julia had to gather herself. She could hear the old man's breathing before she saw how small he was, lost in the bed. The covering was crewel, and beyond price. His hand, a loose gathering of bones held together by parchment, clung to the turned-back sheet. Then she saw his face like a doll left out in the rain. But when he noticed her there beside Hugh, his eyes widened. They were a startling blue, lit with curiosity and sudden pleasure. Wildly, Julia color-matched them with the ballroom ceiling.

"This —"

"Introductions entirely unnecessary," he said in his piping voice. "My dear, how lovely to see you at last. You are even handsomer in person. Too kind of you to come." Sir Ludovic put out his fragile hand, and Julia had to take it. "Too kind." The nightshirt cuff was buttoned with a pearl. His grip was firm, though his head never left the pillow. He shot a sidelong glance at Hugh. "You have shown her the evidence of the cannonballs in the upper stories?"

Hugh made some sound.

Sir Ludovic's eyes returned eagerly to Julia. "The house was garrisoned by the king during the Civil Wars, you know. We were always Royalists. You will find a portrait of Barbara Villiers somewhere around." Then he seemed lost in admiration of her. "All the way from America," he marveled, "and still you take the time in your very . . . crowded life to visit an old man on the very verge of eternal damnation. Baltimore, I believe?"

Hugh's hand just brushed Julia's free one.

"Not far," she said.

Sir Ludovic's hand fell reluctantly from hers. "You're not to take any notice of our newspapers. They are quite unleashed now and write whatever comes into their heads, making mischief and calling it news. They are in an ecstasy of rage against their betters. You're not to mind what anybody says." All this in a tone of urgency.

"Ah," Julia murmured. "No."

"He is at heart a good man." Sir Ludovic's eyes searched Julia's. "Weak, of course. Weak as water. You could pour him into a jug. But who would know better than you? An American woman will put him right. You must defer to him in public, but in private . . . ah, but you will know his needs better than anyone."

Julia stared. Hugh's hand brushed hers again. "I will certainly do my best," she said.

"I know you will. The nation leaves him in your hands." Sir Ludovic was gasping now, and his eyes roamed the tarnished hangings of the bed. "My regards to your aunt."

He looked directly at Hugh. "I suppose the borders have got beyond themselves and the lawn at the front looks like a hayfield. See if you can find anyone in the least willing to work, just some light pruning and clearing away. I will pay the going rate." Sir Ludovic spoke with crisp clarity.

A woman with a syringe in her hand appeared through a door disguised by wall-paper. Hugh and Julia were in retreat. Julia wondered if she shouldn't walk out back-ward.

They made it to the grand staircase and halfway down before Hugh crumpled. He sat suddenly, planting his boots, and dropped his head into his hands. He was barking with laughter. Julia went down another step or two and turned back. "That was one of the more surreal experiences of my whole life. Who in the hell did he think I was?"

"Given his preoccupations, I suppose it was natural enough." Hugh tried to pull himself together. "And at this point his mind comes and goes."

"I could see that, but who was I supposed to be?"

"Mrs. Simpson." Hugh's voice was strangled with laughter and his face was wet with tears, two distinct emotions.

"Mrs. Simpson? You don't mean Wallis Warfield Simpson."

"I do. The Duchess of Windsor. He was seeing her in her prime of course. Sir Ludovic has always been preoccupied with the Prince of Wales, not Charles naturally. David — Edward VIII. I suppose he can die happy now that Mrs. Simpson has turned up at his bedside. He was always a little courtier in his heart. Probably in his genes. Anyway, darling, you played up beautifully with only a little prompting."

Darling?

The bus tour ran more than four hours, which Les hadn't counted on. They sat upstairs with the tree limbs batting the windows as the bus lumbered up and down every street in central London. Every time they swayed around another corner, Les wondered if she was going to be seasick, but Margo was all eyes. In something that looked like an attendance book she wrote down every point of interest. Her slinged arm projected out into the aisle, and Les winced for her every time somebody brushed by it. She read over Margo's shoulder, noticing the places she'd put a tick by: the National Gallery, Shepard's Market, St. Paul's, Dickens's house. Les meant to remember so they could go back. When the tour was over, they were famished. They bought tube passes, and Les led them to Harrod's for lunch upstairs in the room with the chandeliers and the piano. They discovered that having lunched there, they could use the Harrod's powder room without paying a pound admission, so they took advantage of that and didn't get out of the place till nearly three.

The bus they boarded outside Harvey Nichols went the wrong way at Sloane Square, and they rode on for who knew how far before they realized they weren't going down the King's Road, and got off.

"Let's walk until we see something familiar," Margo said, and that was all right because it was a gorgeous day, and they weren't carrying anything because Harrod's sale hadn't started. Les thought that maybe the bus tour was about enough organized activity for one day.

The first landmark they came to on their stroll was the Royal Hospital. Margo had ticked that on the tour, and now she wanted to go inside. They saw the chapel and the dining room at the top of the old worn stairs and a few ancient pensioners dreaming in the courtyard. Margo drank it all in while Les waited.

From there they threaded through the

Chelsea streets from window box to window box. Les was wondering where Julia was and finally said so. "Les, Julia's been declaring her independence for as long as we've known her," Margo said. "Let's just cut her some slack." They ambled on until by blind chance they found they were in Radnor Walk, the far end they hadn't seen before. Margo had her key out before they reached the door, obviously with Kimberly on her mind. Les thought Margo'd had Kimberly on her mind the livelong day. Between landmarks that place just above her nose got a pinched look.

Inside, the house was at its sunniest, and the landlady was nowhere in sight. The doors stood open to the garden behind. Margo went straight upstairs, and Les was no sooner in her room than Margo was at the door. "Kimberly," she said. "She's not here."

Les was halfway to the bed for a quick catnap. "She probably —"

"She's taken her things. Her passport. Everything but the key." Margo filled up the door. It was her usual erect posture, but she looked her heaviest. Her brows were a thick line. She seemed pinched all over. Les started to say that Kimberly wouldn't just move out without leaving a note, but thought better of it.

"Les, she's gone."

Mrs. Smith-Porter had returned from Bermondsey at midday. She'd taken her time, three buses by way of Elephant and Castle only because it was a day of such rare weather. Expecting to have the house to herself, she thought she might have a quick look through the post. By the electric kettle in the kitchen she found a note in Gemma's fist:

Dettol
Fairy liquid
Goddard's polish

and then a query:

best front room vacant?

Mrs. Smith-Porter moved at speed up the stairs and through the open door of the Cardinal Richelieu room. The doors of the clothes press gaped, and the key was on the table where people left it on the last day. Vacant indeed. She twitched back the counterpane to see that Gemma had made up the bed with fresh linen.

The day being uncommonly warm, Mrs. Smith-Porter had already shrugged out of her Bermondsey coat. Now she fingered her artificial pearls, wondering what this meant. There was an eerie quality to the moment, and the house seemed remarkably quiet. It was a bit like being first at the scene of a crime, though strictly speaking, Gemma had been here before her. Mrs. Smith-Porter was well versed in the spectrum of disasters major and minor that befell her visitors. People often broke under the strain of traveling for pleasure. And the girl had looked like trouble in the making.

Ructions, Mrs. Smith-Porter foresaw. She meant to be out of the house before her other visitors came back. Where Mrs. Steadman might have gone from Bermondsey she couldn't say. She seemed the sort to go her own way, and the other two women, Mrs. Hockaday and Mrs. Mayhew, appeared to be dedicated sightseers.

Mrs. Smith-Porter had meant to be here to offer them something in the way of refreshment at the end of the afternoon. She promised nothing beyond the advertised buffet breakfast, so anything she provided after that looked like largesse. Then she determined to be down the New Lots Road for the auction by six, and she had no intention of missing it. Now she was persuaded to quit the house as soon as she could manage it and stay away until the evening. It would make a longish day, but she preferred that to the alternative. Let her visitors sort themselves out however they might about the girl, who had clearly bolted. Then if there was anything she could do for them, she'd sweep in later. In half an hour she was aboard the bus, bound for Kensington High Street.

This hectic and charmless provincial high street misplaced in west London always struck her as the least pleasing quarter of the town. But the Marks & Spencers in the King's Road wasn't a patch on the one here, and she was fond of the Boots. She made an afternoon of going round the shops. Then she found herself in front of British Home Stores as she was doubling back from Barker's.

At the top of the escalator on the first floor was a dining room of sorts. Cheap and cheerful, though not all that cheerful. It had the feel of a wartime canteen. There was a stark absence of decor and an institutional steam table: pudding-faced girls behind the puddings and old trouts behind the fish-and-chips. The scones here never held up under the butter knife, and the tea tasted of the metal pot. But somehow Mrs. Smith-Porter kept coming back. The price was right, and you could smoke on one side of the room. She hadn't smoked for years, and so the drifting scent took her back. The clientele was all her own age and then some, eating meager teas to see them through without supper. She blended in here and tended to linger as long as no one came up wanting to share her table. She had long since heard all she cared to hear from people of her own generation.

Soon after seven Julia was on the front steps of Radnor Walk. Behind her, Hugh's car was firing itself away into the evening. He'd wanted to see her to the door and in fact meet Les and Margo, but she hadn't encouraged this. For one thing, she was staggering with fatigue. And she still felt distinctly poleaxed by his offhand charm or whatever it was that made her feel giddy and annoyed with herself, and of course him.

The door leaped open before she could turn the key. Expecting the landlady, Julia saw Les ready to jump over the doorsill at her and looking less than her overgroomed best. Julia was herself a ruin. As far as she could remember, she'd been born in this outfit. Below the chin she was one continual smudge, and her hair was clotted with cobwebs. She felt like Stonehenge and longed for a bath deep enough to close over her head.

"Julia, where in God's name have you been?"

"I was picked up by a strange man in a south London slum who took me to a deserted barn in the country, and then a dying baronet thought I was the Duchess of Windsor."

"I've been worried sick," Les said. She was pulling Julia inside, and they were doing a little dance in the front hall. "Kimberly's gone. Packed her traps and just left."

Good, Julia thought. "Where?"

"If we knew that . . ." Les tapered away to a heavy sigh.

Julia maneuvered them both into the living room. It was still daylight in here, but somebody had turned on the lamps. "Does the landlady —"

"She's not here either. It's like the world stopped. Margo's in the kitchen."

"Cooking?" Julia said, still trying her best to resist this drama.

"There's a phone in there." Les made significant eye contact. "She's calling Reg. In Chicago. She thinks Kimberly may have flown home. This is her second call to him."

"Did she call the airline?"

"Yes, but they couldn't give her any passenger information, or wouldn't. They gave her a runaround. And you know Margo. She couldn't let herself sound too urgent. She's telling Reg to see what he can do at that end. Meet a plane or whatever. Meet all the planes. I don't know."

"What about the police?"

"Well, she doesn't want to call them. Anyway, they'd just give her another runaround, wouldn't they? Don't you have to be gone for days or something before you can be missing? It wouldn't be any different here, would it? Anyway, this isn't exactly . . . foul play."

"Not in the usual sense," Julia murmured. They'd been whispering. Now they just stood there, catching the tone of Margo's telephone voice from the kitchen. Julia's eye wandered, noticing again the perfection of the room. Her eye swept the canny clutter of objects on the mantelpiece — *garniture de cheminée*, to give them their due. A simple gathering of garden flowers in the paste vase would have put Robert Isabell in his place. The effect was all better than professional decorating, she had to admit, though Nancy Lancaster could have achieved some of it. Julia let her eye roam on, and Les saw what she was up to: withdrawing again, doing a mental flit. Not five minutes ago Julia was worried about coming back from the day looking like some lovesick sophomore after the prom. Under normal circumstances Margo would have picked up on that in the first glimpse. Now —

Margo came in from the kitchen. She was relieved to see her, so Julia decided to play it way down and not add to the hysteria. "Margo, I'm sorry."

If it weren't for the sling, Margo would have been working her hands. Julia wondered if she ever cried. When Reg left. When she got shot. "We might as well sit down," Margo said. A moment passed while Julia thought it was too bad they neither smoked nor drank. And what exactly were they waiting for? This could go on indefinitely, but Les came to the rescue.

"Margo," she said, standing up, "you don't want to go out for dinner, do you?" Margo looked slapped at the suggestion. "So I'll make some tea and see if there's anything in the kitchen. I'm sure Mrs. Smith-Porter won't mind." She gave Julia a look that clearly said: Get her to talk, whatever it takes. Then Les sailed hostesslike out of the room.

Margo sat in a chair that was preposterously high backed and low slung, like a throne for a midget monarch. It was going to be hard for her to get out of it. Julia noticed how precisely her ankles were crossed.

"Margo, anything I can think of to say

comes from someone who doesn't have a daughter."

"But Julia, that's all right. That's good. I need another perspective," Margo said in a tone that struck Julia as entirely too measured.

"When I see you now and what you're going through, I blame Kimberly."

"Don't." Margo reached out. "She isn't just what I've made her. She *is* me."

"Margo, how? She's nothing like you. You were never even a kid. You were already — adult." Julia nearly said middle-aged. "You didn't make *enough* trouble."

"What choice did I have? And of course I've wanted something better for Kimberly. I've wanted her to have choices. But I was young for my age just as she is. I was embarrassed by my mother, and Kimberly's embarrassed by me. We're locked in this cycle. She's overwhelmed by having a teacher for a mother. I can hear how I sound to her. That's why she's done so poorly in school. And all this even before the divorce. In her loneliness I see mine. It breaks my heart that I can't do something about that."

"You've done too much," Julia said. "You haven't left her enough to do for herself."

Margo's eyes flitted over the treasures on

the mantelpiece, seeing none of them. "Marrying Reg was the ultimate proof of just how immature I was. I thought marriage would be a safe place."

"Do you think she went home to Reg?"

"I wish she had, but I don't think so."

"Then she'll come back, won't she? She's not going to wander around some strange city in a foreign country for long, by herself."

"No, she won't wander alone for long. I wouldn't have. In my life I didn't. That's what frightens me."

They sat on, hearing the tick of a clock somewhere in the house, which didn't help. But then Les came in bearing a tray with a steaming pot and cups and a plate of finger sandwiches of the DAR sort, which she'd managed to sling together in the English kitchen.

"Let's just eat and not think," she said briskly, and they went doggedly about drinking the tea and chewing the sandwiches. Vaguely, Julia reflected that she'd been stuffing her face all day long. The sandwiches weren't half bad. They were nearly finished when Margo's hand covered her eyes, and her head sagged. She was crying now, almost soundlessly, and Julia thought it was probably for the best. Les was on her feet, bending to hold Margo's good shoulder. Then with life's own bad timing, the phone rang. Julia jumped up and headed for the kitchen.

When she came back, Margo was simulating recovery, her head back against the chair. She and Les had heard enough to know it had been Reg. Julia tried to remember everything. "He was able to get some information out of British Air. Kimberly isn't booked on any of today's flights. There were empty seats on all of them, so she'd have no need to switch airlines."

Margo sat more erect.

"And he says he's ready to fly over if you need him."

The effect on Margo was hard to gauge. She took a deep breath. It might have been relief, or it might have been despair. Then they heard the front door open. Mrs. Smith-Porter stood tall in the living-room door, her eyes climbing her forehead. "Ah," she said, surveying them and the tray.

"I'm afraid we've been eating your food and using your telephone," Les said. "We've —"

"But you are to regard this as your own home," Mrs. Smith-Porter said with grandeur. She set aside an auction catalogue, and Julia watched entranced as she reached up to draw the hatpin out of a weathered summer straw. Only then did she choose to notice

Margo's wet eyes and daubed face. "I hope there has been no trouble."

"Her daughter is . . . gone," Les said.

Mrs. Smith-Porter hung her hat on a rack that seemed to appear there suddenly for the purpose. She was as tall as it was. "She's gone down to Richmond, I shouldn't wonder. She has a friend there. At the college, I expect. Summer term. A young man, wouldn't you have thought?"

Margo struggled out of the chair. "Kevin," she said, scrabbling at Les to help her up. "Kevin's *here*. Why couldn't I figure that out? Why didn't I know that's the only reason she — yes, *Kevin*."

Julia was working hard to keep up, but Les knew Kevin: the scarecrow boy with the lopsided grin, sitting where the sofa had been.

"Thank you," Margo said to Mrs. Smith-Porter. "She told you?"

"She just mentioned it when we met in the street yesterday."

Margo was taking quick breaths. "Richmond College."

"Yes," Mrs. Smith-Porter said, "just at the end of —"

"Margo, do you want to go?" Les looked poised for flight.

"Not tonight," Margo said. "It's not as if I have to go rushing off to preserve her chastity, like Mr. Bennett after Lydia."

Even Mrs. Smith-Porter looked interested at that, and Les blinked. "But what if they're planning to run off somewhere else? Shouldn't you —"

"No, she'll be there with him. He's where she's been heading all along. I'll go out tomorrow and see the bursar of the college, find his dorm and track them down. She'll be ready to be found."

"Margo, do you want to call Reg?" Julia said. "Let him know?"

Something cool and uncharacteristic crossed Margo's face. "No, he can wait." Which caused Les to send Julia a very meaningful look. "I'll be able to sleep now." With half her old composure restored, Margo walked out of the room. Mrs. Smith-Porter had magically vanished.

"Julia," Les said in a plaintive voice, "who's Mr. Bennett? Who's Lydia?"

"*Pride and Prejudice*," Julia said.

"And what does the Duchess of Windsor have to do with anything?" Les looked right at the end of her rope.

Chapter 12

Kimberly woke at a quarter to eleven. Kevin's enormous hand hung motionless from the top bunk. She rolled out and stood, pulling Reg's shirt down. Her luggage took up half the floor. This room made the one at Radnor Walk seem like McCormick Place, and she couldn't remember where the bathroom was: down a long hall, down some stone stairs. The posters on the walls were all of groups she didn't know. Kevin was sleeping as furiously as a child, and she didn't like that because he was going to have to be very grown-up today. From now on, in fact.

She turned to the chest of drawers and met the glazed gaze of the girl in the silver frame: big-eyed, anorexic, boring hair, and a cheerleader smile. Perky. Kevin had sworn she was his roommate's girlfriend, the roommate who was away for the weekend.

Not that there'd been any more sex, not after the talk they'd had. She hadn't brought up anything till evening, to give them an afternoon of just being together, walking hand in hand around the college grounds, sitting in the sun. Cutting afternoon classes was a little gift he could give her.

He'd slipped her into the dining hall on somebody's meal ticket. They'd sat at the end of a long table, and he hadn't introduced her to anybody, which was all right, because they didn't need anybody else. Then afterward when it was just the two of them here in the room, she'd told him. She nearly pulled back at the last minute. She seemed to live a little lifetime then, but she remembered her reasons, and it all came out the way she'd planned, and he just sat there looking too young.

Stubbing a toe on her backpack, she worked her way to the windows. They didn't have screens here, and the plastic curtains had sea horses on them. Kimberly looked out over grass so green it cut her eyes. The campus was deserted on this Saturday morning, but someone was crossing the green on the walk that angled this way.

At first it was just an adult, then somebody with her arm in a sling. It was her mother. Kimberly pulled back behind the curtain, watching through the sea horses. Yes, it was her mother: the planting feet, the poker back, the cheap haircut. Always there and going nowhere. No wonder Daddy . . . It dawned on Kimberly that this is who she'd be if she didn't act now. But when she turned away, something else stirred in her, some impulse to race down the stone steps and into her mother's arms.

Instead, she turned back to Kevin, who hadn't moved. Even a little line of drool from the corner of his mouth to the pillow hung motionless. He wore a pair of Joe Boxers, and his feet stuck out way longer than the bunk, ankles trapped by the metal bar. He was all knobs and narrowness. A line of hair ran down from his belly button into the boxers. She wondered just how attracted she really was to him, but decided that wasn't the point. Putting a hand on his concave chest to wake him, she wondered if she'd always be the first up every morning.

At teatime the three of them sat around a table in the Maids of Honour just outside Kew Gardens gate. Les poured. The day had begun with Les in her nightgown, floating up to Julia to hiss in her ear. "For Pete's sake, Julia, get up. We've got to go with Margo. We can't let her traipse all the way out there on her own."

Julia was still half asleep, but already reflecting that Les created a sorority house wherever she went. "What's wrong with letting her deal with her daughter by herself?"

"Julia, she walked the floor all night, and I

think her shoulder has flared up. She's popping painkillers."

"How many?"

"Well, one that I saw. Julia, we're all she's got right now, and she's already up and dressed."

Never at her best in the morning, Julia struggled up.

"Les, you're afraid if you're not right there monitoring the situation, Margo will grab Kimberly and take the next plane to Chicago and ruin this vacation, or whatever this is turning out to be."

"Julia, I am not. Maybe she is going to take her home. I don't know. I don't think she knows, but she's going to need us."

Julia fell back in the bed, clutching her head. But then she threw off the covers and got up.

So they'd gone to Richmond and walked Margo up the long hill to the college gates. That was as far as Julia was going, so Les restyled the day for all of them. She and Julia would do Richmond, and there was a bus to Ham House, which was National Trust. Then lunch in the garden there, just the two of them. Then Margo could take the train back to Kew Gardens, and they'd meet up here for tea, which was on Les's list anyway.

"First of all," Margo said now, "Kimberly's announced that she's pregnant."

Les never wavered with the teapot, and Julia put out her hand. "So that's what it was about." Julia and Les had speculated on this likelihood all through Ham House.

"So it would seem," Margo said. "What made me think my daughter would want to come to England with me? Or even a quick trip to the mall, for that matter. She had her own agenda. She had something she wanted to tell Kevin."

"How far along —"

"She wouldn't say. She hasn't thought any of this through."

"I'd have thought you had a right to know."

"No, Julia, I have no rights. The only thing she said was that by the time the baby was born, she'd be eighteen. That seemed to justify everything. On the night I came home after we buried Dorothy, I found them in bed, so their — relationship goes back at least that far. But I don't know anything. I wasn't in her confidence."

"She could —," Julia began, but stopped. Kimberly hadn't gotten pregnant to have an abortion. She'd gotten pregnant to have Kevin.

"And I suppose this will be all the reason she needs not to go to college," Margo said.

This struck Julia as a side issue, but of course it wouldn't be to Margo. "I'd filled out her application to community college myself. It was Oakton, and I think they'd have taken her."

Les watched Margo to see if she was going to break down, but Julia thought she was beyond tears. For whatever reason, Margo was dry-eyed. There was some anger too, beginning to surface, which Julia thought was no bad thing.

"And now what?"

"She thought I was going to drag her away with me. As if I could. She wanted a scene, so I left her there."

When a waitress hovered, they fell silent till she moved away.

"I told her to call Reg. She'll have to deal with us as . . . individuals. She didn't want to call him at first, but then she seemed pleased with the idea. She almost smiled. 'It's about time he found out he's going to be a grandpa,' she said. 'That'll give him something to think about.' She wants to marry that boy. Can you believe it?"

"Yes," Les said. "I lived it."

Home at last and up in her room, Julia found a tall Edwardian repoussé silver vase brimming with perfect roses on her nightstand, and an envelope with her name on it. Inside, the card read,

Spend Sunday in the country with me. Don't say unless you have to say no. And please don't say no. Half past nine, if you can manage it.

Hugh

By Sunday morning nothing could have astonished Julia's internal clock. She awoke at the turn of the doorknob to see Mrs. Smith-Porter enter, wearing an incongruously frilly apron patterned in thistles and bearing tea and digestive biscuits. Distantly, Julia remembered the luxury of waking alone in perfect privacy.

"An admirer, by the look of things," Mrs. Smith-Porter said, referring to the roses.

"Yes, and all your fault." Julia was up on her elbows, blinded by another brilliant day already under way. "Your Hugh Dalrymple. Remember? The best of a bad lot? You led me to him like a lamb to slaughter."

"I thought you were merely looking for furniture." Mrs. Smith-Porter's face was all mock innocence.

"I'm having trouble remembering what I was looking for as long ago as Friday morning."

"You haven't done badly, I must say." Mrs. Smith-Porter had lowered the tray. "Nobody down Bermondsey market ever sent *me* roses."

"You've done all right at Bermondsey," Julia said, glancing around the room.

"In my way," Mrs. Smith-Porter remarked.

"Just how much do you know about Hugh Dalrymple?"

"Less than you do." Mrs. Smith-Porter withdrew. Then with a backward look: "Possibly a good deal less."

Sunday in the country suggested slacks, but Julia found her way into a skirt and examined her legs in the long mirror on the back of the bathroom door. The brilliant red silk top looked right with her hair. Catching herself primping, she grabbed up her bag and started for the stairs. Halfway down the last flight she heard conversation.

Bypassing the breakfast buffet, Julia stepped up to the French doors, and there were Les and Margo at a table in the garden. With Hugh Dalrymple.

Already the day had slipped from her grip. A glance showed that Les was dazzled and Margo was at the least distracted. Hugh sat very much at his ease, draped pleasantly against the chair back in a vintage black blazer and white duck pants. Les was pouring what must be his second cup of coffee, and who knew what had already been said? They all three seemed old friends. Never easy with her entrances, Julia made hers. She considered implying that Hugh was strictly a business contact. She'd told them she'd have to keep her nose to the grindstone on this trip, and she'd stick to —

"Good morning," Hugh said, looking up. "I hope you liked the flowers."

Later, only minutes, when they were wedged into the Mini, Hugh said, "What nice women."

"Yes, they are. Much nicer than I am. Les clings and bosses, but always in the name of friendship. And Margo is a very reassuring presence."

"I should have thought Margo was in need of reassurance."

"What did she tell you?"

"Nothing at all, but she seemed preoccupied."

"And with good reason. Shall we not go into it? I'm glad to make an escape today. You're my ticket out."

Every time Hugh shifted down, his knuckles brushed her leg. They were thigh to thigh in the careening car. "I'm afraid I've got you

221

under false pretenses. This isn't merely another day in the country. Sir Ludo is sinking." Hugh reached into the glove box and made a business of finding a pair of sunglasses. "He was noticeably less well yesterday, and he had a bad night."

They were on a bridge now, crossing the Thames. "I'm sorry," Julia said.

"The end of an era, I'm afraid. He could linger, but the doctor thinks not."

"Shouldn't he be —"

"Oh no, he'll die at Ravenscote. He's past caring now, but that's what he'd want."

Silence for a mile or so. "He's being looked after, and there's nothing much to be done. But I thought I ought to be on hand, and I wanted you there, though it'll be a quiet day. Walks in the grounds, that sort of thing?"

"Sounds ideal," Julia said. Why me? she wondered. "Surely other people —"

"Yes, and they'll gather once he's gone. Not much in the way of family, but people materialize at such times. This is the calm before that storm, and I wanted to spend it with you."

Julia couldn't rid her mind of the notion that she was performing in the second act of a play, reaching for every line, and she couldn't remember a single scene from act 1.

After sailing past any number of Sunday drivers, they were in deepest Kent again. Julia had learned how to plant a foot on either side of the hole in the floor. Hugh pulled up at the inn, carried in a wicker basket, and brought a picnic back in it, along with quite a large bottle of wine.

This time they drove the turning lane to the house, to Ravenscote, drawing up at the circle in front. It was less mysterious at midday, but just as imposing. "We won't go in," Hugh said.

"A picnic in the park?"

"Something nicer."

It was a cottage in a clearing down a fall of ground beyond the last of the other outbuildings. Hidden.

"Older than the main house. Elizabethan at its core, and not a lot more than plumbing added after, say, 1850."

To get there they'd walked through fields where daisies and monkshood had seeded themselves. The house looked long abandoned, deeply sunk in a garden. Hugh set down the hamper and pulled out an antiquated key as long as his hand.

"Not a state-of-the-art security system," Julia said.

"No, and watch your head."

The first beam would have brained her,

and the staircase winding up to the rooms under the eaves was built for trolls. To the right was a pocket-sized dining room with a Jacobean dresser at the far end that sent Julia's mind whirling.

To the left past a longcase clock frozen in time, a dusty drawing room extended low-ceilinged to doors onto a terrace. The paneling was silvered linenfold oak, and the furniture was draped in sheets with here and there a claw foot exposed.

"Not the gamekeeper's cottage," Julia said when they were outside again, unpacking the hamper.

"No, my parents lived here. My father was in the army, but they always had this to come back to."

The picnic was portable pub grub: sausage rolls, Scotch eggs, Smith's crisps, a selection of hand-cut sandwiches. Julia sat back from the rustic table, getting some sun on her legs. Hugh had taken off his blazer and sat in shirtsleeves. "Darby and Joan," he said, and she half caught the reference.

"Tell me more about your family," she said.

"I didn't know my father. He died in Korea before I was born. My mother died when I was at school."

"School."

"Harrow."

"And so Sir Ludo took charge of you."

"Nothing so paternal. He was a bit elusive all round. Quite a distinguished war record, mentioned in dispatches and that kind of thing. But he made nothing of it, and it isn't known in the village. Then when he finally married and settled here permanently, he didn't hunt. The rest of the local gentry thought he'd let down the side, and everybody else felt cheated by the lack of lawn fetes. But in time people came to respect his privacy and respect him for demanding it."

"Like Queen Victoria," Julia said.

"Actually quite a lot like Queen Victoria."

There followed one of their silences, smoothed by the wine. It was almost too hot to sit full in the sun on this weedy paving. The ruined garden beyond was enclosed by a brick wall that blocked any breeze. Hugh broke the silence.

"What could you be thinking of?"

"If you must know," Julia said, "I was mentally redoing this cottage."

"How far did you get?"

"The lighting has me stymied. I have to keep boring into beams infested with deathwatch beetle."

"And you haven't even seen the kitchen," Hugh said.

"Didn't you ever want to live here?"

"It's Sir Ludo's, and he never offered."

"And yet it's just as it was when your parents had it."

"Yes."

"He was fond of them?"

"I think he was, in his remote way."

"What do you remember about being a child here?"

"Not a lot, apart from coming home in the holidays. It was just the two of us, my mother and me. She felt rather buried here in the country. I believe she and my father had been very happy together."

A scent of mown grass came from somewhere far off. The heat of the garden rippled the brick walls. It occurred to Julia that Hugh had delved about as deeply into childhood as an Englishman could be expected to go. But she said, "You were a private child?"

"Yes. Quite private. Weren't you?"

"I suppose I was. Always in a rage and always off with my friends. But yes, lonely."

"Then how lucky we found one another."

He stretched out a hand across the rough planks of the table, and Julia took it. She was perfectly willing, she noticed, to sit forever at this sun-soaked table, clasping this man's hand in the hope that nothing more would ever happen in the history of the world. She calculated the wine level in the bottle, wondering if she'd had more than her share.

The moment shattered when a fairly tough-looking customer barged through the gate in the garden wall, an unnerving invasion. Julia's hand jumped in Hugh's. Her wineglass fell over. Hugh stood up. "Luke. What?"

"You're wanted. The doctor's here, and he doesn't like the look of Sir Ludovic."

He was gone as Hugh reached for his jacket. "Will you be all right here while —"

"I'll come with you. I won't be in the way."

"Yes, come." He shrugged into the blazer. Now he shot his cuffs and held out a hand. "You can sit in the library. It'll be cooler there."

They walked hand in hand away from the cottage, up the rise to the house. The back way was a path between stone walls cutting through a village of sharp-roofed sheds. Then around a kitchen garden and across the rose garden, where Hugh let them in by way of a long window to the breakfast room. He showed her through to the library, and then he was gone, swallowed by the house.

The room was dim as evening until her eyes adjusted. Gilt bookbindings winked, and damp had loosened long panels of the stamped-leather walls. Julia slipped a careful fingernail under the leather for a quick look at the original color of the plaster behind, a once-glowing red that had weathered to Pompeian. A library table dominated the room, along with an upended Ping-Pong table, tangled in its net. The only sittable chair was drawn up to the window. Julia was dazed by the sun and the wine and just possibly Hugh. She settled, and the chair sighed as she sank deeper. She was halfway to sleep before she knew it.

When she awoke to utter silence, the room was darker. She was desperate for the loo — the wine again — and considered slipping back outside to find a convenient bush. There might be somebody in the kitchen, if she could find her way that far, who could point her to the nearest bathroom.

A door in the breakfast room opened onto butler's pantries and a back stairs beside a row of old bells. Growing more desperate, she crept up treads like butcher's blocks. Now she was on the floor where Sir Ludovic's bedroom was. Up another flight she pushed through a door and found a wide corridor flooded with dusty light. She thought of Dorothy's house, and Dorothy herself, the house where she'd been a child and played hotel among the rooms.

Plunging on, she went past doors standing

open to bedrooms in various states of decay. Then she was in a sort of boudoir: oriental screens covered in cranes and bamboo tables and settees overflung with paisley throws. At last, there through another door, was the hint of white tile. In two strides she was standing in what might have been Edward VII's own bathroom, with a real throne of a john up on an Off Broadway–sized stage. And not a moment too soon. It was a Georgian chair with a buttoned leather back and carved arms fitted over a toilet, a *chaise percé*, in fact.

Feeling faintly ridiculous, she sat at her leisure longer than necessary, absorbing the room. The proportions said it had begun as a bedroom. The tin-footed tub could have accommodated a toboggan team. A menacing length of leather hung by the sink, for stropping some long-absent straight razor. The wall tile was crazed, with a border of acanthus leaves at the top. Fortunately she'd brought Kleenex. She pulled the chain, and Niagara roared beneath her, flinging spray. The maker's mark in the toilet bowl proclaimed in a flourish: Thomas Crapper. Then she washed her hands with a dry soap fossil. Something might have whispered a warning to her then.

She turned to the boudoir door and nearly

fell over backward in surprise. In this awesomely empty part of the house someone was there. A fireplace angled across a far corner, and a woman was standing before it. She'd been examining herself in the mirror over the mantel. Now she was watching Julia. Their eyes met in the mirror.

Chapter 13

"I couldn't think who you might be."

When she turned, she wasn't much more than half Julia's age and almost unreal in her prettiness. It was a long-stemmed, long-faced English beauty that was too good to last. But she was stunning now: porcelain skin and the reddish hair that goes with it.

Her dress must have come off the best stall at Camden Locks, or somewhere better than that. It was either vintage or a canny copy: throwaway retro-chic in one of those swirly underwater summer prints that only the English would dream up. Every shade of beige and taupe with green tendrils. She was bare legged, and the heeled sandals were vintage too.

"Who did you say you were?"

"Julia Steadman." This much insolent poise in one so young tended to bring out the beast in Julia, but she was too awed.

"I'm called Sylvia." Her bag was propped on the mantelpiece. She reached in it and drew out a silver, perhaps platinum, cigarette case. Julia stood unmoving, almost not breathing. The girl's — Sylvia's — every ges-

231

ture was beautifully choreographed.

She dropped the Dunhill lighter back in the bag and took a deep pull on the cigarette, her head back against the mirror. The length of the room stretched between them, and something still held Julia in thrall.

"I rather dread this house, don't you?" Through the wreath of smoke Julia saw the wide wedding band on Sylvia's hand and with it another ring with an enormous square-cut stone, an aquamarine possibly, bordered in diamonds. The cigarette hung somehow gracefully from her lips as she turned the aquamarine, her hands moving in a mesmerizing pattern. "It wants a king's ransom to do up properly, and even then central heating is beyond thinking about. And, my dear, servants. Of course it could be grand again, but I'm quite happy with something smaller. Are you awfully in love with him?"

Julia stared. Sylvia's cut-glass intonations were daunting enough without that last zinger of a question.

"We're just — we hardly —"

"Ah, as serious as that." She examined Julia with a hint of controlled curiosity. "I knew in the first moment too. It's simply that way sometimes, and very little to be done about it. Besides, you've waited quite long enough, haven't you?"

Julia wondered why this observation didn't raise every one of her hackles. Instead she heard herself say, "I'm only here because Sir Ludovic —"

"Oh! Of course. And here we are nattering on." In her first abrupt gesture the girl threw the cigarette behind her into the grate. For some reason she looked at the watch on her wrist. She seemed ready to go, even pressed for time. A sense of urgency swept Julia too, and she turned back to the bathroom for her purse, the long-strapped Loewe bag. She thought it was missing and then found she'd wedged it beside the sink. When she returned, the girl was gone, though smoke still hung in the room.

Julia found her way along a threadbare maze without a soul in sight. She located the top of the main staircase and at the foot of the last flight Hugh stood. She tried to read his face, but couldn't get past the sea blue eyes. "I thought I'd lost you," he said.

"I went looking for a loo. And looking and looking. How —"

"He's comatose now. I thought for a moment he was gone. The doctor isn't committing himself. A matter of hours, a matter of days."

Julia had stopped on the last step. She

reached out to Hugh, and they stood there witnessed by all the framed ancestors cheek by jowl up the staircase wall. "I'm sorry about all this, but very glad you're here. What a dull day you've had."

"Not in the least. I just met —"

"But where were we? Weren't we in a picturesquely untidy garden lingering over the remains of lunch? And wasn't I on the point of kissing you?"

He drew her off the step, and she was in his arms. The stubble on his chin grazed her cheek, and Julia handed herself over. They kissed in the shadowy hall, and the former Julia cried out only faint, halfhearted warnings to the new one. "Are we too old for this?" she said against his ear.

"We'll never be younger."

Someone was coming down the stairs. Julia thought of Sylvia, but it was the doctor carrying his black bag. "I'm just going home for my tea," he said, coming past them. "I'll call in later." When he was gone, Hugh said he'd run her back to Chelsea.

"If there's a train —"

"Of course not. We have far too much to say."

On the drive back, Julia seemed to say most of it, over the whine of the car. She spilled out her life story, the edited edition

— she hadn't taken complete leave of her senses — and she found herself weaving in more of Margo and Les than she'd have thought. The evening held until they'd turned into Radnor Walk. There was a place to park only a house or two along from Mrs. Smith-Porter's. Hugh swung in and parked with a wheel on the curb.

He took her in his arms. "Have I heard it all?" he said a little later.

"Every minute," Julia said. "Every other minute."

"But there's something you've missed out."

Julia's head was on his chest, safe from eye contact. "I'd like to hear about my rival," he said. "I don't mind competition, but I'd sooner know what I'm up against."

She looked up surprised. "There's no one else."

"Then there has been."

"There have been several, but they didn't —"

"I mean the one who mattered. I take it he isn't your former husband. He sounded a very early phase."

"Hardly a phase," Julia murmured. "Hardly a nanosecond."

"Then?"

Dale. Of course Dale. He might well be

wedged angularly in the backseat, taking all this in, grinning. He was often with her, looking over her shoulder, standing at the edge of her life, offering occasional oblique advice. Without him there, how could she cope with the ironbound loneliness of New York? But she couldn't say any of that. Dale was one of her walls against the world, and bare mention of his name could bring down all that rickety fortress she'd built up around herself.

"Dale," she said. "But it wasn't a love affair. It couldn't have been. He trained me in the business, and he died and left it to me. He gave me my career and took everything else with him. He died of the plague."

Even now she couldn't say the word or wear the glib red ribbon or in fact acknowledge that Dale was actually dead. He'd gone too soon, and she couldn't give him up, unless that was what she was doing now.

"You loved him."

"I loved him," Julia said, shaky on this new ground. "On that evidence I can only love what I can't have."

"Oh, I hope not," Hugh said.

"And what about you?" Sylvia streaked across her mind, Sylvia so nonchalantly at home at Ravenscote, already there in advance of Sir Ludovic's death. A shirttail rela-

236

tive of Ludo's perhaps and nothing at all to do with Hugh. Too young for him certainly — please, God, let her be too young. And married if the wedding band meant anything. Julia was damned if she'd ask.

"Nobody at all," he said, "not for a long time, too long."

She'd spilled her guts, and now he was coolly stonewalling her. For two cents she'd confront him with Sylvia, but the well-defended part of her didn't want to know. "There's something grossly premature about this whole conversation," she said, reaching around for the door handle.

On Mrs. Smith-Porter's front step, she half expected Les to fling open the door to report some fresh crisis. "Heaven knows what's happened today," Julia said over her shoulder. She'd offered Hugh coffee for the return trip.

"If it's all too much for me, I'll bolt my coffee and disappear into the night."

They were inside, and sure enough Les was looming. There was a scent of coffee already made. Les had a cup and saucer in her hand and a look on her face. The three of them jostled in the hall, Hugh beginning to grin.

"Thank goodness you two — first of all, Julia, Reg is here." They were nose to nose in the little space at the foot of the stairs. "Well, not *here*. He and Margo are out in Richmond with —"

"The happy couple."

"Julia, keep your voice down." Les's had dropped to a stage whisper, and she was nodding to the living room.

Who? Julia mouthed because somebody was in there. Les was in her hostess mode and more than usually rattled. She mouthed something, a name, but Julia didn't catch it.

In the living room somebody was unfolding himself out of Margo's low chair. Another perfect stranger in this expanding cast of characters, as far as Julia could tell. A tall, pale young man, very tall, very pale. Black body shirt, black jeans, square-toed boots. Rather academic-looking. Could this be Kimberly's Kevin? Surely not. He wasn't that young: mid- to later twenties, something like that. Getting out of the chair was a feat of skill, and he was doing a balancing act with a cup and saucer.

"Chris Barnabas," he said, extending a hand. He needed a shave, unless this was a look. There were dark smudges under his eyes, which may or may not have been permanent.

"Julia Steadman."

"Oh yes. Julia. I've heard about you."

"Hugh Dalrymple," Hugh said, glad-handing like an American Rotarian, playing along. Les hovered, and her eyebrows were practically sending out semaphore signals.

In the bustle to get a cup of coffee into everybody's hand, Les nearly ran Julia down. Then it seemed to be small-talk time, but Julia cut to the chase. "Where are you from, Chris?"

"Chicago. Naperville originally. Reg flew over when he heard from Kimberly, and I came along. His travel agent really went digital and got us last-minute reservations. An overnight flight, so we were both pretty wiped. I had a nap this afternoon. We're staying at the Wilbraham."

Julia was taking this a step at a time, and it would have helped her concentration if Les hadn't been staring holes in her. "You're a friend of Reg's?"

"I started out as his graduate assistant. A poli sci/Western civ split. Now I've got the course work done for a Ph.D., so I'm looking at orals and the dissertation."

After Sylvia, this was another member of the twenty-something generation Julia had encountered today. She ruminated on their cool confidence. Hugh, she sensed, was vastly diverted. Her brain gunning in neutral, Julia nearly fell back on the weather. Discussing the Kimberly problem didn't seem entirely appropriate with a stranger, if stranger he was.

"I told Reg that Kimberly was putting the screws to him," Chris said, "but you know old Reg. He can't handle anything like that. He can't get past the idea that some horny kid has, you know, deflowered his little girl. It took me all night on the plane to talk him down from his outraged-father-with-a-bull-whip position."

"You've met Kimberly?" Julia said. Pensive, probing.

"Sure. I was at Reg's the day she rolled in with all her gear and her sound system. I guess I'm part of the problem as far as she's concerned. Probably a big part, but I don't know how long she and Reg could have done the father-daughter thing anyway. Frankly, I don't think Reg ever got into the paternal role."

Silence fell. Julia let it linger with the oddest sensation that Mrs. Smith-Porter was standing on the stairs, just outside the room. She was somehow so ostentatiously not in evidence.

"Chris, tell me. Who are you?"

In a fluid gesture he set the cup and saucer on the floor. Shrugging slightly, he turned up

240

his hands. "I guess you could call me the Other Man."

"Julia, take it from the top and really spell it all out for me."

At the end of the day they'd come back to Radnor Walk, rested up, changed, and now they'd gone for dinner at Le Dome down the King's Road, bistro ambiance and deafening. Julia had inherited Les since Margo and Reg were back at Richmond, presumably still negotiating.

This was a business day, and Julia had made that clear to Les, but it looked a lot like shopping, and Les was more than willing. A light rain had fallen on them wherever they went, making London look like London. They took umbrellas and began early at the Monday-morning antique market in Jubilee Hall at Covent Garden. Julia was looking for accent pieces and something in the Victorian jewelry line to take back for Mrs. Lederer. She found a superb amber, set as a brooch in gold wire, very old and possibly Russian. Les looked on in admiring horror as she talked the price down to seventy pounds. They lunched at Crank's and cabbed to the Furniture Cave, which convinced Les to do two of her guest rooms over from stem to stern with as much advice as she could pry out of Julia.

Then back to Sloane Street and Jane Churchill's and after that across the street to the General Trading Company. They'd started on the antique-furniture floor, which made Les weak in the knees. "Julia, can these prices be even higher at home?"

"Les, did you or did you not marry money?"

By then it was teatime, and Les took back enough of the leadership role to choose Justin LeBlanc's, though they had to sit inside and watch the rain fall on the garden behind.

"Let's go whole hog and order a pastry apiece," she said.

"Whole hog indeed," Julia remarked, taking out her Malmquist file. She talked Les through the Santa Fe floor plan, sticking to business.

They hadn't talked about anything important all day, and Les was holding back. She was going to try not to say anything till Julia did. Besides, it was too good a day to spoil, a day out of her favorite fantasy, skating around some fabulous city with Julia, living a little in Julia's life. She held out till they'd ordered dinner at Le Dome.

"I mean it, Julia. Just start talking. I don't get it."

"Are we talking about Chris Barnabas?"

"Well, yes."

"You met him first. You take it from the top."

"Right after you and Hugh left yesterday morning, Reg turned up. He'd flown overnight and looked like death warmed over."

"How did Margo react?"

"Just as you'd expect. Very calm. Very kind. You know —"

"Solicitous?"

"Probably. I left them alone, and then they went off to see Kimberly. I had to pinch myself to remember they were divorced. It was just Margo and Reg like always."

"Not quite."

"Anyway, I had a quiet day and sort of unwound. Wrote some cards and did some hand washing. In fact I found some of yours and did it. Mrs. Smith-Porter was in and out. Julia, where do you suppose she is when you don't see her? Do you think she just stays up in that little room at the back on your floor?"

"Is she what this conversation is about?"

"Well, no. But anyway I had a quiet day. You know, I'm just going to give up trying to keep on a schedule for this trip."

"Very wise."

"So I gave myself a walking tour of Chelsea. I went down to Cheyne Walk and worked my way —"

"Les, you came home. Then Chris Barnabas turned up at the door."

"He was looking for Reg, and Mrs. Smith-Porter showed him into the living room and called me down, and there he was."

"And you didn't get a thing out of him."

"Well, I found out he was a grad student or something, but I was waiting for you. Then you two came dragging in finally. So what's this all about?"

"Les, what don't you know?"

"I don't know what I don't know. Just tell —"

"Chris said it himself. He's the Other Man. He's Reg's lover."

"You mean some kind of male-bonding thing?"

"Les, I mean gay."

This was the moment the waiter chose to bring the ratatouille. It gave Julia a moment of leisure to notice Les was looking her absolute best. Too dressed up for Le Dome, but dressed down in that way that worked so well, her hair in the careful, perpetually blond coif, the Hermès scarf caught at her shoulder with the circle pin. And in profile she was a cool cameo with that sort of coloring. Les could have passed herself off as a grown-up almost anywhere. *Julia*, she

244

mouthed. *Not Reg.*

"Why not Reg?"

"Because, how could he be?"

"Les, what are you picturing? Boys marching in parades with their shirts off and rings in their nipples?"

"Rings in their *nipples?*" Les looked away from her plate, offering that cameo profile that would fool anybody. "Julia, could he be — what's the word — ambidextrous?"

Julia goggled. "Les, do you mean bi-coastal?"

"I don't know what I mean."

"Les, you can't be as naive as you're sounding. It's physically impossible. You're fighting this."

"Maybe, but, Julia, did you know?"

"Not till last night. Never crossed my mind. I'll tell you the truth. I've never given Reg a lot of thought."

"But when?" Les's tone grew whiny.

"What?"

"When did he turn? . . ."

"Les, you can say gay. Trust me, the waiter can handle it."

"Julia, keep your voice down. I mean, did he just wake up one morning and —"

"Les, I wasn't there."

"But Margo and Reg have been married for more than twenty years. Does a man just suddenly go off the deep end and —"

"Probably not. Margo thought marriage was going to be a safe haven. Maybe that's what she and Reg had in common."

"Julia, do you think she knew? About Reg? Before now?"

"I don't know. She wouldn't have told anybody, and maybe she wouldn't have told herself. You know we've always seen Margo as wiser than she could possibly be."

"I bet she didn't know. She couldn't have. It would be like being in love by yourself, wouldn't it?"

"That's not a bad way to put it," Julia said with a look in her eyes so distant that Les couldn't begin to interpret it.

"What if she still doesn't know? We know, but does —"

"I think we can safely assume she knows now. I expect they're having their moment of truth out in Richmond."

"Julia, how much can one woman take, even Margo? As if she hasn't been through enough rejection. Kimberly alone —"

"This *is* the Kimberly problem, as Chris said. After the divorce she thought she'd have Reg, and Margo wouldn't. Then she found out Reg didn't need a woman at all."

"No, Julia. That's going too far." Les was suddenly sure. "No man can do without a woman. I don't mean sex. I mean no man can do without a woman. They just can't manage."

This stunned Julia into silence. They hadn't eaten three bites of dinner between them, and now Les was doing origami with her napkin. She was working up to something. "Julia, we're really going to have to be there for Margo."

"If you ask me, we're all over her as it is, and what good are we to her? She'd undoubtedly rather be working through all this in more privacy than she has. She's got her pride, Les, as I have to keep reminding you."

"I don't mean just right now, Julia. I mean the future. I've seen her life, and you haven't."

"Les, tell me you aren't hatching some plan to link us all up for eternity. Margo's perfectly capable —"

"Well, Julia, think about it. Reg has a plan. Kimberly has a plan. What's Margo's?"

They walked back in the dark, over the rain-slick pavement, past the music thumping out of the pubs, lingering at the shop windows. They were looking in at Heal's when far off in Kent, Sir Ludovic's mind surfaced.

He'd seemed to be deeply asleep. Now he

woke to nighttime, relieved to find the room empty of nurses. The shaded lamp cast an angle of light across his bed. He was a child momentarily, being tucked up in his nursery cot by Nanny. Then he was being sick over the side of the landing craft, but safely out of sight of his men. The rose garden at Ravenscote burst brilliantly into bloom under a summer sun. Then he had just time to compose his hands atop the turned-back sheet, and he was gone forever.

Chapter 14

Reg Mayhew stood in Sloane Square, alone for the first time in days. London was a darker city at night than Chicago, and the big red double-decker buses pulling around the square glowed like lanterns. One of them was carrying Margo off down the King's Road. They'd come in from Richmond on the tube at the end of this harrowing day, and now they'd parted.

This was Reg's first time in England. Luckily he had an up-to-date passport. He'd kept one current since the early Sandinista years in Nicaragua, just in case he could get down there and be of any use. But he was off his turf here. Oddly, Margo seemed already at home. With a practiced air she'd slung the strap of her purse over her head and pulled herself by one hand up on the back of a bus, almost light on her feet. Now she was gone, and he could just about find his way back to the Wilbraham if he made the right two turnings.

It had rained all day, but now only a clinging dampness hung in the air. He began to stroll the glazed pavement around past the

Royal Court Theatre. The day hammered his head, and considering the lack of reasoned discourse, there was another day coming just like it, maybe more.

The first encounter yesterday had been a complete washout. Today they'd all four crowded into Kevin's minuscule dorm room, dragging in extra chairs. Reg could hardly stomach rat-faced Kevin at quarters this close. He couldn't endure the thought of the scrawny son of a bitch in bed with Kimberly. On her, in her. Yet there were long moments when Reg couldn't think about anything else.

The concept that Kimberly could be sexually active at all triggered some abject grieving process in him that seemed to have a life of its own. True, all of his own students apart from a few outright losers were going at each other like rabbits, practically in class. But that was a totally different construct.

She was punishing Margo of course, as Margo admitted. And Kimberly had her reasons. Margo had ridden the poor child every day of her life, trying to make her something she wasn't. For one thing, she'd rammed beginning reading down Kimberly's throat long before she was developmentally ready. How the kid had avoided dyslexia, he didn't know. So even without the divorce, this was the logical outcome. Here Reg had to shoulder a degree of blame, within limits. He should have found some way of making Margo ease up on Kimberly long ago. But he'd been on that damn tenure-track treadmill, giving it all his time, burying himself in his work.

Still, all this career commitment had kept him focused and basically faithful to Margo, apart from some lapses. He'd stuck out a good deal more of that marriage than most men with his orientation, including a few he could name. He had to give himself some credit for not terminating an unworkable life choice earlier than he did, say, when Kimberly was pubescent and with far fewer coping skills.

Even if Chris had appeared in his life at that point, Reg was confident he could have exercised the necessary restraint. People talked about the midlife crisis, even the male menopause, and Reg had seen ample evidence of it right in his own department. But there was always that element of the self-delusional in those other cases that didn't apply to his. He was walking *away* from the delusion in the pursuit of utter honesty: word, deed, and partner choice. He'd even shaved off his beard as a token of this, as a refusal to hide any longer behind any obfuscation. And since his beard was gray, he looked younger without it. Reg walked on up Sloane Street, sure of his direction now.

He'd tried to shape the day just past, using the scheduled priorities of a faculty meeting, though Kimberly screaming through most of it had been counterproductive.

Pregnancy termination needed to be on the table, so to speak, as an option, and Reg had kept a close eye on Margo, who sat there entirely too composed. Presumably anybody capable of forcing beginning reading on an unready child was capable of imposing an invasive medical procedure on an adolescent.

The nightmare thought of Kimberly in stirrups brought Reg to a dead stop. Now he began to harbor some suspicion about why Margo had remained silent during the abortion discussion. Was it her posture of resignation, or was it a pose? Without her marriage, without him, was she reaching for a grandchild to fill the emotional void? Margo deluded herself if she thought she could be a better grandparent than she'd been a parent.

She'd harped on the college issue, how important it was to let nothing stand in the way of Kimberly's education, and for that matter, Kevin's. Reg, who prided himself on being able to see all sides of most issues, was inclined to agree that college needed to be factored in. Kimberly's test scores were low, and her grades weren't commensurate with her abilities. But considering what turned up in his own college classes, he thought she'd have a fighting chance.

Margo was going to have to put together a package of loans and scholarship money, unless she tried to stick Kimberly into some community college. But as a teacher and a single parent, she ought to be in line for some assistance. He would himself help out, though a new lifestyle understandably was more expensive than he'd foreseen. This trip, for example, and having to cover his airfare and Chris's.

But Kimberly saw Margo's push for education as another attempt to set her up for failure and block her from independent decision making. In any case, Kimberly wasn't really coherent on any option but marriage.

Here again Margo would lapse into one of her enigmatic silences, though to be fair it was hard to get a word in. Reg had altered the tone briefly by blurting out, "Marriage? Kimberly, we just brought you home from the hospital."

It meant nothing to Kimberly, but Margo looked up, and they had a moment between them that came from earlier times.

If Reg had ever thought about it at all, he'd have seen Kimberly marrying much later. No sooner than thirty and needless to say to a grown man, possibly someone significantly older than herself, established and with well-thought-out political impulses. Possibly someone from the academic community to provide balance for Kimberly's more intuitive intellect.

But this didn't address the present situation. Toward the end of the day Margo seemed to lean in the direction of allowing the marriage. At least that could be what turning up her hands meant, or at least one of her hands. There was even talk about contacting Kevin's parents, though Reg didn't think that was immediately indicated. The Bergstroms were Glencoe people and thus evidently fairly well-off. Almost certainly Republicans, and that would bring out Reg's combative spirit if it ever came time to play hardball.

But he was willing to hold out a while longer simply in the name of responsible parenting. He wished he could give Kimberly what she wanted, his blessing in the secular sense, if marriage could offer her the personal empowerment that Margo had systematically withheld from her.

Of course the day went on too long for all

of them. He suspected that Kevin had dozed off a couple of times, and the whole thing finally pushed Kimberly over the edge. You can't expect an adult attention span from an adolescent.

"What do I care what you think anyway, Daddy?" she'd screamed. "You're nothing but a goddamn fag."

This introduced a new element, but it was just as well to have the situation in the open at last. Evidently Kimberly had never told Margo about Chris. Margo simply didn't have enough of Kimberly's trust to keep their lines of communication open. Now Margo reacted with no more than considerable surprise, and Reg told her about Chris. Sensing Kimberly's hostility, he didn't expand, apart from invoking bisexuality, which was true at least in the mechanical sense. Margo asked him nothing, not even on the train coming back. Strictly speaking, of course, it was no longer any of her concern.

He'd nearly walked past the cross street when he recognized the Wilbraham out of the corner of his eye. It was a row of town houses knocked together. Reg collected his key and headed up the red-carpeted stairs. At the top of the house was their room, and Chris.

Chris had said he'd use the trip to do some

preliminary research in the British Museum reading room, where Marx himself had done his meaningful work. Reg was panting lightly after the second flight. At the top of the last one he had a little flash of déjà vu.

What did this place remind him of: the stair rods, the puckering cream paint on the walls, the floral prints, black framed? Then it came back to him. It felt like — it even smelled like — that country inn at Eureka Springs he and Margo used to go to at spring break, way back when they were still at the University of Missouri. They'd drive down there in that old Ford Fairlane on four bald tires. That far back.

Reg pulled in his paunch and slipped the key into the lock.

The house being quiet, Mrs. Smith-Porter decided on an early night. She took her time in the bathroom as Mrs. Steadman was out. She was on the stairs going down to the kitchen to make herself a milky drink when she heard a key in the front door. Against just such an eventuality, she still had her face on and hadn't bound up her hair. It was Mrs. Mayhew coming in, looking peaky. She seemed ready for her bed, but Mrs. Smith-Porter thought it was worth offering her refreshment. She'd pieced together bits of

Mrs. Mayhew's story and would be glad to hear of any recent developments if she cared to get them off her chest. People often did.

She directed her to a more comfortable chair than the one she was making for, and they talked quite half an hour. She was a beautifully spoken woman once you got past the accent, dwelling on the troubled daughter who had even before the parents' ill-timed divorce lacked self-confidence. Mrs. Smith-Porter had heard the term "self-confidence" often enough from various visitors to assume that the lack of it was a problem of epidemic proportions in the States. An interesting chat, but then Mrs. Mayhew began to droop in earnest. It wouldn't have been a kindness to keep her any longer.

Afterward, Mrs. Smith-Porter found herself bolt awake, the hot drink failing to do its work. She sat in a little slipper chair beside the bed in her box room, glancing through yesterday's papers, until she heard Mrs. Steadman mounting the last flight. Mrs. Smith-Porter allowed her a moment before slipping across the hall to give her door a light rap.

Julia jumped a foot, grabbing her heart with one hand and the priceless nightstand with the other. She cried out something, and the door began to open.

Mrs. Smith-Porter's head appeared around it, right at the top. "My dear, I hope I didn't startle you," she said, entering. The contrast between the fully made-up face and the ratty old chenille bathrobe made her something of an apparition. The bedroom shoes peering out from under her hem were corduroy and roomy. "I see your roses are holding their own."

Julia's heart began to settle down.

"I've just sent Mrs. Mayhew off to her bed."

"I wonder what kind of day she's had," Julia said.

"Not productive." One of Mrs. Smith-Porter's hands sketched something in the air. The other clutched the robe against her ropy neck. "I thought I'd just plant a seed in your mind, though you may well have worked it out on your own. I could be wrong, but I rather think I'm not."

Julia hung there, suspended.

"This complicated business of Mrs. Mayhew's daughter. It wasn't for me to raise a question, naturally. But they're taking the girl at her word, aren't they, and I wonder if it's wise of them because it all hinges on that, don't you see?"

Julia didn't.

"I shouldn't think the girl is pregnant at all."

On Tuesday Les meant to be downstairs first, to link up with Julia for the day and to be there when Margo came down. Thrown together in a rush, Les checked at the hall mirror to make sure she was all there.

She hadn't taken time for the tea in her room. Now as she began browsing the breakfast buffet for yogurt, Julia came up from behind and reached past her for the coffeepot.

"Good, Julia, you're up. Listen, when Margo comes down, she's going to try to put a brave face on, but we need to —"

Margo materialized in the doorway to the kitchen. Les spun around, and the cup danced a jig in Julia's saucer. Margo looked faintly entertained at the two of them caught red-handed. Brave face indeed, Julia thought. Margo was very well put together this morning, every hair in place. Practically rested. "Julia, you've had a call from Hugh."

Les spotted a cup on the table with dregs in it. Margo had been up for ages, wearing her dark pantsuit with the long tunic top. It was the best thing she had, not so matronly.

"I'm afraid it wasn't good news."

"Sir Ludovic is dead," Julia said.

"Hugh wanted you to know. Cremation and no fuss, he said, and he'll be getting in touch." Margo read from the note she'd

259

taken. "Friday, after Bermondsey."

Margo and Les exchanged a look. Les's theory was that Hugh and sly Julia had some long-standing friendship dating back to Julia's earlier London trips. Maybe more than a friendship.

"Was he someone important to Hugh?"

"He was his landlord, very elderly, and Hugh looked out for him."

The table was set for three, and when they took their places, Margo was more brave-faced than ever. If this is a cover-up, Les thought, she's overdoing it. "Margo, how are you? I mean really."

"Les, I'm all right." Ever the comforter, Margo reached out for Les's hand. Even in Julia's bleary view there was a change in Margo, something for the better. "I'm taking a day off from the summit conference."

"You're going to let Reg and Kimberly duke it out on their own," Julia said, beginning to emerge.

"And Kevin," Margo said. "It's dawning on me that I'm going to be able to live with whatever they decide."

"Listen, Margo, after what you've been through," Les said, "nobody's going to blame you for throwing in the sponge."

"She's not giving up," Julia said.

"No, I'm disengaging."

Les had been itching to reach across and butter Margo's croissant for her, but Margo pushed back from the table.

"Then you can spend the day with us," Les said. Her original plan had been for a matinee. "We'll get back on our itinerary. Julia has to drop by Colefax and Fowler to swatch some sources or whatever, but after that —"

"Les, I need a day on my own."

Les felt a sharp crack on her ankle from Julia's direction.

"I've got some new thoughts to think," Margo said, "all thanks to Chris Barnabas."

Les looked for direction to Julia, who was beginning to smile, so it seemed that these two were communicating on a level that left her out. "But, Margo, what do you have to thank him for?"

"An overwhelming sense of relief. All this time I'd thought he'd be a woman."

Julia sat back. "Of course."

Les's head was spinning. "Margo, wouldn't it have been more *understandable* if he *had* been a woman?"

"Les, I'd always thought that if any man ever loved me, it was going to have to be me, not my body."

"But you *are* a good-looking woman," Les said in anguish. "Isn't she, Julia?"

"We're all three reasonably good-looking women if you ask me," Julia said mildly, "but why don't you shut up and let her talk, Les?"

"I thought I was the plainest girl in the Cape, and then I thought I was the plainest woman in the United States. The plainest and the most awkward. When Reg wanted to marry me, I thought the heavens had opened."

"You were too grateful," Julia said.

"I was too goddamn grateful."

Les's eyes popped, and Julia thought Margo had never looked better than she did this minute.

"I know Reg is a bore, but that's all I thought I could get. I've never said that before. I've never even let myself think it, but it's the God's truth. Besides, I thought he was brilliant at first, academically. I fell hard for him during his lecture on Eugene V. Debs and the Pullman strike of 1894. I didn't know he'd cribbed every word of it. And even after I realized he was faking his career, I still didn't know he was faking his whole life."

"And yours," Julia said.

"And mine. But, you see, I didn't know I had any rights," Margo said. "Nobody ever read me my rights."

"And you never once questioned his sexuality," Julia said.

"Julia, why would I? If he wasn't interested, it had to be my fault. I spent years on end waiting for him to come home and tell me he'd developed a meaningful relationship with some size-two coed. He could have justified it to himself. He could have justified it to *me*.

"I built my life on my fears. I walked on eggs the whole time. Then one day — yesterday, as it happens — I heard about Chris. I was right about the age, but I got the sex wrong. So none of it had ever been about me. I could have been — anybody. For a minute I couldn't think. But then suddenly I just felt so . . . free."

They sat there in silence, nothing stirring. It was one of the best silences they'd ever had.

Then Les said, "I hate that. Margo, I hate it that you lived in fear all those years and had to walk on eggs. That shouldn't have happened to you. You —" Les struggled with herself and closed her eyes for a moment. "You're the least awkward person I ever knew."

Margo reached out for her again but looked aside. Rain was beginning to streak the windowpanes, blurring the garden. Julia

263

swallowed hard.

They heard a sound from the front of the house. Gemma stuck her head around the living-room door to see if it was time to clear away breakfast. She went on upstairs to do their beds.

In her aftermath, Les said, "Margo, Julia and I have met Chris Barnabas, and you want to know something? He's not that good-looking."

Les thought they were going to fall off their chairs. Margo had reason for hysteria, but Julia was just showing off. A thin white mustache of yogurt along Les's upper lip added to the effect, though of course she couldn't see that.

When they finally settled down, Julia said, "Margo, Reg will be back," and both of them looked at her. "He'll find out Chris isn't a permanent solution."

"There's the age difference," Les offered.

"And Reg is weak, isn't he?" Julia said.

"Yes."

"And you're not. He'll be back. Be ready for that. Be sure you're where you want to be that day."

"Reg back? As if I won't have my hands full with Kimberly."

"I thought you were disengaging."

"Julia, she's my daughter."

The three of them sat there, Les wondering where they went from here, but out of the blue Julia said, "Margo, has it crossed your mind that Kimberly isn't pregnant?"

Les caught her breath.

"Oh, Julia, I never thought for a moment she was. Poor kid, she wishes. I even tried to believe it. I didn't like being lied to, but I know her and how her mind works. No, I don't believe she's pregnant. If she'd had morning sickness, you could have heard her for a mile. She was always a difficult patient, even with a head cold."

Chapter 15

As Gemma had everything in hand and her visitors were gone their ways, Mrs. Smith-Porter launched herself forth for one of her excursions. There was a bring-and-buy at St. Savior's Church hall, and she wanted to be early in the queue. The weather was undecided, rain on the windowpane one moment, only dripping branches the next, so she was in her mac and her rainproof hat and pulling on her string gloves.

Of all the little markets and sales that cropped up in London, St. Savior's had a flavor all its own. It was in Knightsbridge only a stone's throw from the back doors of Harrod's. The last place you'd look for a jumble sale, but this one was decidedly up-market. Quite well-off-seeming women brought in castoffs from their last year's wardrobes and the backs of their cupboards and occasionally something really good in the way of small silver and tortoiseshell. They were the sort of women who would throw out the hardly worn and bottles of bath salts never opened and Irish linens still tied up in their original green ribbon. But they could drive a bargain and were every bit as hardhanded and hard-faced as Bermondsey and the Portobello Road, though their accents were a world apart.

All of Mrs. Smith-Porter's handbags had come from St. Savior's, suede-lined with good labels inside, and not a few of her underthings. If nothing struck her fancy, there was always the refreshment table. Danish pastries and fruit salads and you could sit and look on, everybody else being too toffee-nosed to speak.

Along by the Chelsea Potter, she consulted her watch. With better weather she was tempted to walk by way of the Walton Street shops and still be there before the opening hour, but she decided not to risk it.

The number 49 bus took its time coming, so she drew today's *Telegraph* out of her shopping bag and turned as usual to the obituaries. She did not quite make it to the notice of Sir Ludovic before the bus hove to at last. But as she was transferring at South Ken, the number 14, provokingly, was pulling away. Another wait then, unless she crossed the street and took the tube one stop. She decided on this as a spatter of rain gusted up, promising more. She was crossing over to the tube station, against the light but other people were doing it, when she looked suddenly to one side.

An enormous lorry filled her whole field of vision, a real juggernaut, great headlamps round in surprise at seeing her there in the crosswalk. She heard no scream of brakes and felt nothing. But suddenly she was someplace else.

Margo spent the morning going from one bookstore to another up Charing Cross Road, looking at children's books. Then for herself, an afternoon with the Turners at the Tate. When she got to the museum, she decided to splurge and lunch in the grand dining room with the murals. It was late afternoon by the time she got back to Radnor Walk, and the phone was ringing when she came in.

Moments later she was out of the house again, leaving a note behind in her Palmer Method where Les and Julia couldn't miss it:

> *Mrs. S-P "knocked down in road"*
> *and in hospital. No details.*
> *I've gone (4:35). Hold the fort.*
> *Margo*

Mrs. Smith-Porter lay in Sergeant Sandowski's arms, feeling weeds and bits of

268

mown grass on her legs and his hand up her skirt. The concert was over and the band had packed up and everyone else was drifting away, leaving them alone on this slope. A barrage balloon had broken loose, and its cables had wrapped themselves around a tree. People were looking at that, off in the distance through the hazy heat.

She lay enfolded by the sergeant, cozy as a cat with the sun baking through her utility frock. She was as tall as he was, but it didn't matter lying down. The Yanks treated you like a film star, like Greta Bloody Garbo: hold the door for you and your chair when they stood you a meal. They made Englishmen look sick. No wonder the Yanks so often fetched up in dark alleys, beaten to jellies. The sergeant had taken her to the Corner House at Marble Arch for her lunch, with egg mayonnaise, the first egg she'd seen since Easter, and he'd be wanting payment for that. He was wondering why she didn't wear the stockings he'd given her, as if she'd wear them in summer or chance laddering them on the stubble of Regent's Park.

He'd be wanting payment for the stockings too and the tablet of chocolate that tasted of before the war, but just at the moment she felt too lazy to bother. It was easier to look adoringly up at him whilst he told her all about Milwaukee. He was like a film star himself, with a chin smooth as a baby's behind. She lay there, ever so comfortable and dazzled by the sun. A speck got in her eye. She blinked it away, and Mrs. Mayhew was looking down at her.

She knew her at once but couldn't think from where. Trying to answer the question in Mrs. Mayhew's face, she started to speak but couldn't get the words out. That nonsense about Sergeant Sandowski was donkey's years ago, a dream from the old days. But where was she now?

A man in a white coat with a brown face was there on the other side of the bed. Yes, she was in bed, and by what right were these people crowding round? She would get up in a minute and put them all straight. And why, for that matter, was she wearing her rain-proof hat in bed? Though she couldn't reach up to be sure, she felt the hat tight across her forehead. It all wanted sorting, and she would see to it shortly, after she'd rested. She rather thought there'd be a firework display over the river tonight, and she had only to close her eyes to see it.

"We will keep waking her up," the little doctor told Margo outside the curtains, in the full flow of the casualty ward. "The head does not look disastrous to our eyes, but there is often no exterior evidence of subdural hematoma." He spoke with the lilt, Margo thought, of Bombay. "It is of course impossible now to judge her mentation. You are the daughter?"

"She's our landlady. I don't know —"

"We have nothing but her National Health Insurance number. She is not registered with a local GP in her catchment area." The doctor looked up severely from his clipboard. "Her ribs are fractured. You may depend upon that, but we will not bind them until we know where they have got to. But she is a lucky woman. These lorries!" Surprisingly, he flashed a sudden grin, gold-filled.

"How long will she —"

"Who can say?" The doctor shrugged elaborately. "The tests will be thorough, and she will be a sick girl! The pain, you see, in the ribs, and if we have to knock a hole in the skull."

Margo maintained her usual control. "Will you be the doctor who —"

"Oh no," he said, already starting away. "I shouldn't think you will set eyes on me again! Fractured clavicle?" He nodded to her sling. Then he was gone.

When she'd come to the hospital, Margo had thought the trip merited a cab. But as she left, she saw there was a bus stop just across the street. She took the first bus that came along, a number 14. Then when it turned the wrong way off Fulham Road, she got out and started walking. Coming past St. Luke's, she was drawn into the churchyard.

The long afternoon cast shadows across prim, mounded flower beds planted like a small-town park. Julia and Les would be waiting to hear, but she settled on a bench for a breather. The church rose honey colored and mock Gothic on one side, and the tombstones had all been moved back to form an almost solid wall of thin, lichened granite around the other sides. People leading subdued dogs strolled the gravel paths. Others lay on the grass, holding above their upturned faces books to catch the evening light.

Thinking she could give herself ten minutes, Margo slipped at once under the spell of this space. It was a little miracle of tranquillity within the endless city, a rare oasis appearing just when you needed it most. It seemed so modest that she hoped it didn't appear in any tourist guidebook. Then she had to know and reached in her purse for her Fodor's, to learn that the church was famous as the place where Dickens was married. And a none too successful marriage at that, she recalled.

She felt duty-bound to conjure up as many Dickens characters as she could without writing down a list: Scrooge, Mr. Macawber, Martin Chuzzlewit, Miss Havisham and Estella, Oliver. Once they'd marched past her mind, Tiny Tim in the rear, she found herself on some more profound level of calm. Working backward from Mrs. Smith-Porter lying in the casualty ward, she tried to trace in some kind of orderly sequence all the turns in her life that had led her to this unexpected spot. After all, she couldn't remember ever before sitting separate and anonymous on a park bench.

When she reached her mother, she thought this was really going back too far. But her mother appeared, and Margo let her.

It was a memory without words. Margo was still a child, at the sink with her eyes just at the bottom of the medicine-cabinet mirror, seeing themselves and the scene. She must have been brushing her teeth — possibly flossing, given the child she was. Behind and above, her mother stood leaning over her for a closer look in the mirror. In her mother's hand was the chrome contraption she used to curl her eyelashes. Surgical metal that near the eye had made Margo's stomach lurch. But there was something more that hadn't quite registered at the time: the carefully, coquettishly curled lashes in her mother's otherwise hard face. She'd never worn much makeup, saying men didn't really like it.

She was going out. Margo wondered if memory really did serve her and if her mother had actually gone out every night of her life. Margo rather thought she had. Surely a whole evening with her mother would have been long enough to remember.

So there was this memory: her mother thrust over her, leaning into the mirror. Margo could feel the pressure of her breasts clamped into the Maidenform bra, as near an embrace as this mother and this daughter ever came. A close call. And the tobacco smell in the flimsy dress and the liquor on her mother's breath. She always had a drink before she went out drinking.

Margo's mind moved on ahead, lightly chilled by the thought that nothing between a mother and a daughter is ever quite resolved. Even death and distance don't do it.

A tremor of panic brushed her, a sense of being set adrift in a world of connected people, but it passed. Then she was nagged — only nibbled, really — by old habit: that need to use every minute, to be at somebody's beck and call, to get her children's grades in on time, to justify her existence. But she sat through that too, and once it ebbed, she was visited by something harder to evaluate, something that started with fatigue and moved on to euphoria. She wondered if she was beginning to experience the onslaught of mood swings and all that implies. But she let whatever it was wash over her. By now it was time to be going.

She stood, then turned back, thinking she'd left something behind. But her purse was hanging from her good shoulder. She strolled on toward the Britten Street gate with the distinct impression that she'd at last left her earlier life behind, all her earlier lives, and that included her marriage, like a parcel abandoned under a park bench. It can't be that easy, she thought, but what a wonderful sensation. A flight of suddenly released birds singing and winging above her would have completed the mood and given a nice lyrical touch, but the square of sky above the churchyard was only an uninterrupted blue going purple at its eastern edge.

On the front step at Radnor Walk she encountered Les just going out. Les was making a run up to Marks & Spencers to bring things home to thaw for dinner. As they had the place to themselves, they might as well eat in. She'd discovered Mrs. Smith-Porter's second-best string bag wedged beside the below-the-counter refrigerator. All over London, Les saw people carrying the plastic shopping bags they give you at Marks and Spencers, but she liked the idea of her own personal string bag.

The sidewalk was in the midst of evening rush hour: thirty-something executives with loosened neckties bringing laptops home and stopping by the pubs for a quick one. Well-kept matrons who'd slipped out of superior residences to pick up something last-minute for dinner. Les felt herself weaving into this pattern, borne along and belonging, not like a tourist at all.

Turning as if from old habit into Marks & Spencers, she walked past the flower stall and along by men's socks and the fall fashions displayed on utilitarian racks, back to the groceries and wines. There she nearly ran riot, wanting everything she saw. She wouldn't mind cooking if she could get convenience stuff like that. And everything practically gift-wrapped, even new potatoes. She laid in some things for breakfast too because who knew?

When she got back to Radnor Walk, she found Julia lying on the kitchen floor with a flashlight and a wooden match, trying to light the oven.

In the dining room Margo went through the Welsh dresser, finding hunt-scene place mats you could sponge off because she hesitated using the linen. A muffled explosion in the kitchen meant Julia had lit the oven. A scent of lemon verbena wafted in from the garden, making the candle flames dance above a tabletop smooth as black ice.

They dined in the fading light and finished off with rhubarb crumble, Les and Julia with clear consciences because they'd had only salads for lunch, up on the fifth floor at Peter Jones. Candlelight brought the French window curtains alive: chrysanthemums and turquoise pagodas against sulfur yellow. "Who would have thought of adding tarnished silk fringe to chintz?" Les wondered.

"And don't think I'm not going to steal the idea," Julia said. Then, since Les didn't call the meeting to order, Julia did.

"We're missing a landlady, and we seem to be in charge, so we're going to have to decide some things. Margo, what did her prognosis look like to you?"

"Just what I told you. She was semi-conscious, if that. They hadn't done any tests. I don't know, and I have the feeling they keep you in a hospital longer here. Julia, she didn't look very good, the poor soul."

"And we're going home Sunday," Julia said. "What are our options? Hang on and hope she gets out of the hospital by the weekend?"

"I don't think she will," Margo said.

"Some people would move to a hotel tonight," Julia said. "Leave their keys behind and write back for a refund."

"Julia, I can't believe you said that." Les was scandalized. "We *couldn't*. For one thing, she's got a king's ransom of stuff in this house, and anybody could just barge in and clean her out." Les shuddered over her shoulder at the doors open to the garden. "It would be all right to look in her desk, wouldn't it? Up in Margo's room? Go through her papers and things to see what we could turn up. Who do you suppose her next of kin is?"

"Why do I have the feeling we are?" Julia said.

They spent a long night rifling the drawers of Mrs. Smith-Porter's writing table and a box of files they found beneath it, unearthing no one in her address book but Americans with indecipherable symbols by their names and all obviously her paying guests. No one local who looked like a friend, no Radnor Walk neighbor, and it was the same with her correspondence. They learned that the

NatWest bank addressed her as Mrs. Olivia Smith-Porter, and so did all the utilities and the Royal Borough of Kensington and Chelsea. Julia made a mental note to drop by the bank tomorrow.

"She runs a tight ship on very little paperwork," Julia said, easing back on Margo's sleigh bed. "It's as if she invented herself. I'm for searching her bedroom. Are we all up for that?" This felt like a more desperate act, and they traded glances all around.

"I'm not entirely comfortable with this," Margo said in a quiet voice. The door just opposite Julia's opened onto a small room with a slanting ceiling, and decor stopped at the threshold. Les felt around for a switch, and the light was a shaded bulb hanging from the ceiling. A small chair, an iron bed, and a chest of drawers painted a chipped white with a mirror above it, hung with hats. Les crossed over and closed the curtains. There was hardly room for three to maneuver. Margo and Julia started through the drawers, and Les took the closet. Under the shelf paper beneath a pile of purses she found a yellowed clipping, Mr. Smith-Porter's obituary out of the *Telegraph*. They sat on the bed to read it. "Look, widow in Barnes and four children, but they're all abroad." Julia and Margo were looking at each other past Les. "What?"

"I don't think our Mrs. Smith-Porter is the widow in Barnes," Julia said.

"You mean she's an earlier wife?"

"Or not a wife at all."

"This is too creepy," Les said.

They were up and coffeed next morning, waiting for Gemma, and Les was already wondering if Margo was going out to Richmond.

"No, I'm sticking by my guns. I'll go to the hospital and try to find out what I can. They won't let more than one of us in to see her. I'll take charge of things at that end."

From the dining room they heard the front door open and then smelled smoke. Into the living room shuffled a woman easily old enough to be Gemma's grandmother. She was the size of a gnome and about the same shape, aproned, with a hat down to her bifocals and a cigarette hanging from the corner of her mouth. And wearing, weirdly, wedgies.

Margo said, "If you're —"

"I work here. Mondays, Wednesdays, and Fridays, like clockwork. Mrs. Dowdel. Take no notice of me."

"I'm afraid Mrs. Smith-Porter has met with an accident."

"Never!" Mrs. Dowdel appeared to cross herself, but she was only adjusting a bra strap.

"She was hit by a truck, a lorry, and she's at the Chelsea and Westminster. Do you know if she has any family? Anybody at all?"

Mrs. Dowdel squinted through blue smoke. Ash rained down her apron.

"I keep myself to myself, and so does she." A look of sudden concern fell over Mrs. Dowdel's face. "But, 'ere, who's going to pay me?"

They got no more out of Gemma.

July

Chapter 16

Julia and Hugh lunched on Friday in the paved garden of the World's End pub down at the jog in the King's Road, under masses of red and blue flowers blazing in hanging baskets. Hugh had a pleasantly buttoned-down look even in an open collar, and Julia thought she'd never seen a man who looked better with his shirtsleeves rolled up. There was something almost irresistibly attractive about his forearms. Not a bad pair of wrists either. She couldn't take her mind off them. "What are you thinking?" he asked.

"I was thinking that World's End is a somewhat existential name for a London pub."

"Ah. You've hit on the only piece of tourist information I happen to know. It was a coaching inn to begin with. One of the King Charleses changed horses here or dismounted to stretch his legs or something, on his way to Hampton Court. This was right at the edge of town in his day, so the Londoners called it the world's end."

"How New York of them," Julia said.

Hugh had already described the restrained ripple that Sir Ludovic's death had created in his corner of Kent. "You didn't see the notice in the paper?" he asked. But Julia hadn't, and the conversation turned on Mrs. Smith-Porter's accident. Margo was back and forth between home and hospital. Julia had gone to the bank and to every other bureaucratic office she could think of, trying to find out if anybody knew more about Mrs. Smith-Porter than they did themselves. It had kicked a big hole in her business week. She'd missed the Wednesday market at Islington and a hotel show in the Bayswater Road, and at this point, neither she nor Margo was any the wiser. Les had taken over at Radnor Walk, to be there if anybody called up and to secure the house against break-ins. But she showed signs of turning into head housekeeper. Julia expected to find a large ring of keys depending from Les's waist any day now. "I'd like to kick that Mrs. Dowdel's butt," Les had said last night. "If she moved any slower, she'd be running in reverse, and she doesn't even move the furniture when she uses the vacuum."

"Hoovers," Julia had said.

"Why does everything here have to have a different name?"

"And we're going home Sunday," Julia said to Hugh, "after a trip that will go down in our annals as by far the most misfiring plan that Les ever cooked up."

"Don't," he said. "Don't go home. Stay. At least spend tomorrow at Ravenscote. It's up to me to sort through Ludo's things, and I don't know where to begin. You can't think how much there is. You didn't begin to see, and a lot of it is good and some of it rather better than that. There's going to have to be a sale once all the legalities are worked through, more likely several, all catalogued and publicized. Otherwise we'll have every dealer in the south of England baying at our gates at all hours and parking in the lawn. It's that or let the London auction houses in, and they'll sell short, take the profit, and run. Their noses are already to the wind. You could have a look now ahead of the hounds, earmark what you want, and we could set it aside."

Julia nearly rose to that but held back.

"Alternatively," he said, "we could spend the day arm in arm, roaming the countryside, kicking clods, and discussing the future."

"The future?" Julia said faintly.

"As you've seen for yourself, I don't run an awfully smooth operation. All very well for the way I've been going on, but now that I'm buried alive under everything in Ravenscote, I'm going to have to think bigger, to employ an American phrase. Surely this is the ideal time for us to . . . join forces?"

American efficiency and English charm, Julia thought but didn't say. "I don't see how —"

"No more do I at the moment. I'm only trying to devise some scheme to keep you on the hook. I can't speak plainer than that, can I?"

Julia supposed he couldn't, but said, "Not tomorrow. It's our last day."

"Then now," he said, standing up. "Let's go now. You haven't seen anything yet."

They'd moved Mrs. Smith-Porter to another ward, a long double line of beds filled with elderly women, their heads like rows of dandelions gone to seed. And with few visitors. Margo had been here yesterday when they took her for X rays. They'd set up an IV, ready for hydration because she was going to be sick at her stomach with pain when she cleared enough to feel it, according to a passing nurse.

Then on Friday Mrs. Smith-Porter's bed was empty, and Margo fought a momentary panic. She was turning to ask someone when a man in a white coat appeared. He was beside her before she knew. "I'm Dr. Jellicoe, the consultant on this ward. You're here for

288

Mrs. Smith-Porter?"

He was checking down a clipboard file, impatiently, Margo thought. "We've had to bind the ribs because the X rays indicated displacement. We don't like doing that because of the possibility of atelectasis — collapse of the lungs — but there you are."

"Where is she now?"

"MRI. You were here yesterday, I believe?"

"Yes," Margo said. They'd let her in only at intervals for a look. "She seemed to be asleep."

"She's proved to be sensitive to her pain medicine. We haven't found the proper dosage yet, but it's only a matter of adjustment. Would you like a coffee downstairs? I could use one."

In the lift he said, "Canadian?"

"American."

"I have a daughter who's gone as an au pair to some extraordinary people at Pacific Palisades. Anywhere near you?"

"No, Chicago. My friends and I are on vacation, at least it was a vacation, and we're staying at Mrs. Smith-Porter's house. We can't seem to find if she — has anybody."

"You'd be surprised how many we get like that."

"MRI?" Margo asked when they were at a table in the clattering hospital cafeteria.

"Magnetic resonance imaging. It's rather like a long doughnut the patient is sent through to see if there's a clot on the brain."

"And if there is?"

"The neurosurgeon will have to drill a burr hole and draw out the blood to ease the pressure."

"Serious?" Margo said.

"It can be, and she's not young. Good spirits?"

"Yes, I'd say so. I'd say she was a very proud and decided kind of woman. But in the bed she looked so" — Margo searched for the exact word — "diminished."

She hadn't needed this coffee. Now as the doctor was finishing his, she noticed he was an attractive man, a little frayed around the edges and careworn and — attractive, though she wasn't given to looking at men like —

"My name's Paul Jellicoe. I don't think I know yours."

"Margo Mayhew."

"Mrs.?" He couldn't see her left hand at the end of the sling below table level. It was a quick look, and he was wearing glasses halfway down his nose, but she saw, and it caught her off guard. Of course it was Mrs., but she wobbled while he looked on.

"I've just been through a divorce." She didn't mind saying it. She'd just never said it to a stranger.

"And you don't know where you are just at the moment."

That was close enough to the state she was in. Margo smiled. She often thought she ought to smile more.

"I know what it's like."

He might have said no more, but she gave him her most attentive look. "Not a divorce. My wife died, and I found myself very much at a . . . loose end," he said. "And you've had a nasty break."

Margo stared at him, but he was nodding at her sling. "Did you have a fall?"

"In fact, no," she said. "Gunshot."

"Ah yes." He nodded. "You said Chicago."

She was out of her depth, and when he asked how long she'd been in the sling, she had to close her eyes and compute. "Just about six weeks."

"Then you're due for an X ray yourself. Raise your elbow, slowly. Take your time."

She did, and when the elbow was nearly level with her shoulder, she felt a twinge.

"Yes, well, you'll need therapy, but first an

X ray to see where we are. You may not need to live in that sling any longer."

"I'll be home next week."

"No need to wait. You'll find we're quite equal to the job. Why stay as you are any longer than you need?"

When they'd drawn up in the forecourt, Ravenscote looked unchanged. The stickered blackberries hadn't yet woven the porch shut, and the miniature man who'd wanted Julia to be the Duchess of Windsor had faded fastidiously away. No wreath hung on the door.

But inside, Hugh threw open double doors at the foot of the principal staircase, and Julia gasped. "You haven't seen the rooms this side of the house," he said. "I don't suppose Ludo himself had been in here since Jubilee Year."

The first room, what she could see of it, was doubtless a perfectly proportioned cube. Sections of an elaborate cornice were missing, along with most of the ceiling, but more than that she couldn't tell. The room was more crammed than Hugh's barn. "He bought next to nothing, though he let nothing at all go." But this much accumulation was beyond explanation. He led her along a narrow passage past a japanned commode that stopped her cold. Everything was piled on top of everything else, and legs thrust out at them: cabriole and reeded and pad-footed. It all smelled of the ages, of sour cider, and Julia was half drunk when they came to the stone fireplace on the far wall.

Another room lay beyond, though you had to go through the back of a bookcase. This one was marginally more intimate, with the remains of landscape wallpaper, and here were rugs stacked and rolled, supine and leaning against walls. Julia's toe unfurled one, and it was a Savonnerie in a pattern of ribbons crisscrossing to make squares, and within each square a gathering of roses. There were Bessarabians and what looked to her like very early Wiltons and Persians enough to pave a major mosque.

"These rooms were done up and the conservatory added for the prince's visit, though there's no record of him stopping the night. But —"

He opened a door to another magnificent cube, less cluttered than the others, but done and overdone for a prince's repose. Deep damask chairs and a gout stool drew up to another priceless fireplace. Below a pocked mirror a wide-winged gilded eagle supported a red marble top. "Can that be —"

"Yes, William Kent. Latish, and one of a

pair. I've seen the other one about the house, though I couldn't say where."

Then the bed, grander by far than Sir Ludo's upstairs, with yellow moiré hangings that swagged down from a gold crown at the ceiling. Bed steps led up to it, and Hugh lifted the hinged top of the second one to reveal the chamber pot underneath. Julia was examining the needlework treads, and then somehow she was in his arms again, remarkably near the towering bed.

Catching her unawares, Hugh swept her up and was ascending the steps. So this was clearly one of those Regency romances, available at any Barnes & Noble. The bed alone gave it away, and being carried wasn't even necessary. They could both simply have scampered up the mounding mattress and kept going till they reached the dip in the center. God knows, she was willing. But they'd reached the dip anyway, and rough hands nestled her gently into this valley miles from escape. Her last coherent thought was that in this vast museum of antiquities she herself ought to appear reasonably young. But now Hugh had slipped free of his shirt and was at work on the buckle of his belt, and Julia's mind went obligingly out of focus.

Some sea change seemed to roll in a gentle

tide over Les. She had the house to herself —
Julia out to lunch with Hugh and not back,
Margo at the hospital. Les wondered idly
why she wasn't feeling either bored or caged,
even nerve-racked. A day this long and un-
structured at home in St. Louis, even without her mother, and she'd be climbing the
curtains. All of London lay just outside the
door, and they hadn't scratched the surface,
but she was perfectly content to putter
around like she owned the place.

Out of her travel money she'd paid Mrs.
Dowdel, who wanted her wage at the end of
each morning's work, and Gemma's weekly
salary. Tying on one of Mrs. Smith-Porter's
aprons, she'd gone over the house with a
dust rag where they'd missed, though you
wouldn't catch her doing her own dusting at
home. She'd made a sort of inventory of the
kitchen cabinets. Then everything on the
Welsh dresser and behind the doors beneath.
She'd found a perfect Spode cup and saucer,
apparently a spare, and made herself a cup of
mint tea in the middle of the afternoon, carrying it out into the garden. Distantly, she
thought of all the places she'd planned for
teatime this week. The Dorchester. Brown's.
The Park Lane. The Waldorf . . .

But the garden cleared her mind completely. She couldn't see as far as tomorrow,

which ought to be driving her to distraction. She didn't even know if she ought to start packing for home, but instead of fidgeting, she found herself unwinding, almost unraveling.

She supposed she must be falling under the spell of this house. It struck her as exactly the right size. When she thought of going home to Portland Place, she couldn't picture it, like one of those dreams when you walk through room after echoing room, and it's all so familiar, but you don't recognize it. She couldn't quite remember Portland Place even when she tried to concentrate on the two bedrooms she meant to do over. Do over for what?

She let her mind drift beyond inventories and lists out into unknown territory. Little Harry crossed her mind. She'd made a note to pick out a necktie for him at Turnbull & Asser, but he probably wouldn't wear it anyway. And Harry . . .

She ought to pull herself together, but shadows in leaf patterns played around her feet, and the sundial gave no particular time. She couldn't believe how quiet this secret place was. Blissful and perfect as if she'd been heading here all her life. She barely had time to set the cup and saucer aside before she drifted into some dreamless state.

★ ★ ★

Margo had been in the ward when they'd brought Mrs. Smith-Porter back from radiology, either deeply asleep or unconscious. But Margo didn't like to leave her, and nobody had come along to shoo her out.

She sat at the bedside unconsciously cradling her own arm, but she was out of the sling, thanks to Paul, who'd expedited the X rays, read them himself, and freed her of the thing. He'd ceremoniously wadded it up and dumped it in the waste can. Though that arm was still useless and cramped, she felt like the last day of school. She felt, in fact, weightless, a distinctly unfamiliar sensation.

Paul had come back later to find her in the ward, saying that they'd need to operate on Mrs. Smith-Porter.

"Soon," he'd said. "The sooner the better, though neurosurgeons schedule as little as possible for a Saturday."

"Then will she —"

"It's one fence to clear. We take them as they come."

Then he'd run a professional hand lightly over Margo's shoulder and gone away again, looking more careworn this late in the day. She'd listened to his footfalls receding over the crackling linoleum.

Now they were beginning to bring the dinner trays, and she thought there wasn't any point in staying longer, but Mrs. Smith-Porter stirred. She'd been motionless, like a graven image in a turban, Egyptian in profile, and deeply sunk in the pillow. But she moved now as if she was naturally easing herself out of sleep. One foot jerked under the sheet.

She opened her eyes, squinted against the light, and searched the ceiling, suspiciously, Margo thought. She took a shallow breath, and when her head began to turn, she winced. Her pink-rimmed eyes found Margo, who leaned forward.

There was immediate recognition, or maybe only surprise. Mrs. Smith-Porter's mouth opened. Her lips were a shade grayer than her face. She looked away from Margo while wheels turned almost visibly in her mind. Then her eyes shifted back, and she reached out, the thinnest arm imaginable, lost in the sleeve of the hospital gown. She hadn't spoken in days, but she was trying to now. She must need water, though Margo didn't know if she should hold up the container with the straw. Mrs. Smith-Porter was motioning her closer. Then in a hoarse whisper she said, "Mrs. Baldridge."

"No, I'm —"

"Not you." Mrs. Smith-Porter's fragile hand waved Margo away. *"Listen.* Mrs. Baldridge. Best front. Mrs. Farwell. At the back. Miss Lindquist. At the top."

Margo hung on every word, her lips moving automatically.

Mrs. Smith-Porter swallowed, and her eyes commanded Margo to understand.

"Lubbock Garden Club."

At least that's what it sounded like. Then in voice enough to carry: "Sunday!"

Mrs. Smith-Porter's eyes closed after immense effort. She snored suddenly, and Margo sat back, stunned by new awareness.

Chapter 17

When she finally rolled in, after ten, Julia found Les giving Margo a manicure in the living room. They were both in their robes, and the scene was a cross between a sleep-over and two moms waiting up. Julia entered, trying to look as little seduced as possible. It took her a moment to grasp the significance of the manicure.

"Margo, you're out of your sling."

Margo put out both arms in a gesture of small triumph.

"Julia, do you take lunches this long in New York?" Les said. "Listen, you'll never guess. We hadn't even thought about it, but —"

"Could I sit down first. I've had a big day." Julia settled on the banquette. "I keep having these big days."

"Margo, tell her."

"Mrs. Smith-Porter is having an operation in the morning. There's a clot. She was able to speak a few words this afternoon. Names, actually."

"What names?"

"She has a house full of new guests coming

in on Sunday. Apparently from the Lubbock Garden Club."

"Hell," Julia said softly. "Why didn't we realize —"

"That's what I said. Julia, what are we going to do?"

"Margo, how long do you think Mrs. Smith-Porter's recovery will take?"

"I don't know, but they're drilling a hole in her head tomorrow morning."

"We can't just leave the keys and go," Les said. "It'll be Sunday. Gemma won't even be here, and I don't see her putting herself out, and that Dowdel woman's as useless as —"

"We ought to be able to find the guests' addresses upstairs in the desk," Julia said. "Surely we could get through to one of them in Lubbock or wherever and head them off."

"That's what Margo said but, Julia, that's terrible. They'll be all packed, and they've put down their deposits and everything. They've probably already left. They've probably gone to New York first like I wanted to do. And they're from Lubbock."

"Les, what does that have to do with anything?"

"Well, they're Texans. They like to have a good time."

"Being Texans," Julia said, "they could probably have a good time at Claridge's."

"Julia, that wouldn't be nearly as nice as here. That's a hotel. What are they going to think? We know this place, but they don't. We can't just hand this house over to complete strangers. And what about Mrs. Smith-Porter? This is her livelihood." Having finished Margo's manicure, Les was sawing away on her own nails. "As far as we know, this is all she has. I'll bet it is."

"Les, how did you get us in a fix like this? It almost amounts to genius."

"That's not fair, and we ought to be thinking about Mrs. Smith-Porter. Julia, sometimes you can be a little bit hard."

Margo snorted slightly.

"All right, Les. What do you suggest?"

The doorbell rang then, and they all jumped and looked at their watches. It rang again, shrill and insistent. Margo was half out of her chair, but Les said, "You go, Julia. You're dressed, but be careful." Nothing much would have surprised Julia, not even the whole membership of the Lubbock Garden Club out there in the dark.

But before she could get the door all the way open, a voice said, "Where the hell's my mother?"

Kimberly stood out there, her hair in a halo against a streetlight, her luggage in a

302

heap. She picked up a suitcase and stalked in past Julia, who marveled at how quickly a teenager can reduce you to a servant.

Margo was standing, putting out her hands, but Kimberly stopped in the living-room door. Working out of her backpack, she said, "I'm not talking about anything tonight. Forget that. I'm going up to my room."

She turned to the darkened hall, but Julia was there, not an inch away. Kimberly thought about pushing past her, but hesitated. "Your mother's out of her sling. You might notice that," Julia said in an undertone.

"Who do you think you —"

"Get in there and talk to your mother, or I'll kick your fat ass out in the street. Don't tempt me." Julia's lips seemed scarcely to move. Kimberly spun around.

All too aware of Julia still behind her in the door, she eased down on the edge of the midget's throne, which Julia thought put her at a slight disadvantage.

Margo sat back in her chair, though she'd rather have gone over to take her child in her arms. Whatever else she was feeling, relief seemed to be foremost. "Honey, what's happened?"

"Why weren't you there? Then you'd

know. You . . . abdicated authority."

"That sounds like your dad speaking."

"I hate every one of them. My goddamn dad and his fruit friend. And —" Her voice broke, and her face dissolved. Julia imagined it melting down the gaping neck of her sweatshirt. Her eyes overflowed, and she was fighting a sob straight out of childhood.

"And Kevin?" Margo said gently.

She was racked with sobs now, so Margo could go over and put her arms around her.

If she'd only reach back to her mother, Julia thought, but Kimberly pushed her away. She made angry swipes at her eyes with her sweatshirt sleeve. Then after a deep, shuddering breath: "Kevin's betrayed me too." She stared hard at the floor. "Like the rest of you." Something hopeless surfaced in the sullenness of her voice.

"Margo, do you want Les and me to leave you?" Julia said, but Margo shook her head.

"How did Kevin betray you, Kimberly?"

"He called his parents."

"Didn't you think that sooner or later he'd have to?"

"He called his parents, and they told him I'd have to have proof I was pregnant. Like from a doctor. He'd have to see it. They'd have to see it. Can you believe that shit?"

"Do you have proof from a doctor?"

Margo said, calmer, quieter than before.

"Not here. Why would I have it *here?* It was like he was accusing me. Like he wouldn't take me at my word. Like there wasn't any trust. I just started screaming at him, you know? I couldn't help it. He's just like Dad. You think they're there, but they aren't."

"What about your dad?"

"He doesn't care. What does he care? He acts like he does. He gets that real serious look on his face, but it's a big show. All he wants to do is get back to his boyfriend and —"

"Don't, Kimberly."

A silence lingered that recalled to Julia long-ago visits of her own to the guidance counselor's office.

"Are you pregnant?"

Every kind of denial crossed Kimberly's face. She gave Margo a well-practiced unseeing stare. But then as if from some separate compartment of her brain she said, "No."

She shrugged, and Julia tried to interpret that. Could she merely be shrugging off her lie, ready to walk away from it? She heaved herself out of the chair and looked almost at Julia, wondering if she could get past her now.

"Why did you say you were pregnant?" Margo asked.

"So he'd marry me. Now."

"Someday you'll —"

"No. Now."

"So what shall we do, Kimberly?"

She stood there, looking past all of them. "We forget about it. That'll be the best thing for me. We just forget the whole f—"

"We can't do that."

"I suppose you want me to go to college."

"No, you're not ready for college," Margo said. "You wouldn't know why you were there. I see that now."

"Then what am I supposed to do?"

"You'll have to get a job."

Kimberly's glance just grazed the top of Margo's head. "Why?" she said. "You have one."

Julia came down early, past Les's closed bedroom door, and Kimberly's. Against all odds, Julia had slept like a log, and dreamed intently of bulldogs.

She found Margo in the garden, fully dressed, sitting in a lacy iron chair with a pen in her hand. There was coffee, but Julia was already bolt awake. A pad of ruled paper lay on Margo's lap.

"Don't tell me you're recording this trip for posterity."

"Actually, I was drafting a letter I may or

may not send. I wanted to see what it looked like written out." She reached down to prop the pad against a chair leg, and this seemed to change the subject. "It's almost like an autumn morning, isn't it?"

Julia breathed in the cool morning damp. "Yes, I was just thinking that."

She drew up another chair. "I'd already forgotten your sling."

"Yet that's why we're here, isn't it?"

"That was the reason given. You'll go to the hospital?"

"Later," Margo said. "She'll be in the operating room this morning. I need to be here when Reg comes for Kimberly."

Julia's eyes widened.

"I've talked to him. They're taking an afternoon flight. She'll be ready to go back when she thinks about it. She has no reason to stay another day here."

"You meant it about disengaging."

"I do now. Kimberly expects us to go back to the way we've been, and that wouldn't be good for either of us. She and Reg will have to work something out."

They sat there among the morning scents. London didn't seem to get up any earlier on a Saturday morning than New York did.

"I just realized," Julia said. "Do you know what day this is?"

"The Fourth of July," Margo said. "Independence Day."

And still they sat. This was one of those calms too good to last, and Julia let herself bask in Margo's presence, wondering only vaguely why Les wasn't down.

"She's probably overslept," Margo said. "She was up half the night."

"Packing?"

"I doubt it. I think she was just overstimulated. You heard her last night. She's gotten very proprietary about this house. But it's more than that. She doesn't want to go home."

"This house is about to fill up with other people."

"There's Mrs. Smith-Porter's own room," Margo said in a musing voice, "and the little one I'm sleeping in. I think it's three women for the three other rooms."

Julia checked over her shoulder to make sure Les wasn't making an approach. "I can't believe I'm hearing this. What's Les going to do, bring them cups of tea every morning in Mrs. Smith-Porter's apron?"

But Margo's face wore a sphinxlike expression that Julia couldn't begin to read. "There's another question," Margo said, "and we haven't asked it. Why didn't we gang up on her last night? Why didn't you and I just overrule her and charge upstairs to find the addresses of those women and call them? Or get through to directory assistance in Lubbock and track them down? We could have, Julia. Why didn't we?"

The question hung in the air against a frieze of gently stirring wisteria. "Les doesn't want to go home. She really doesn't. What does she have to go home to?"

But Julia held out instinctively. "A house the size of San Simeon and a hyperactive social calendar and a line of credit that would choke a —"

"And her mother," Margo said. "And Harry."

This struck a somber note, and Julia cast another look at the door.

"Let's back her up, Julia. She'd do anything for us. You know that. She wants some more time here. Why shouldn't she have it? Let's give her the permission."

"How?"

Margo was quiet for a moment. "You do it your way, and I'll do it in mine."

"All right," Julia said, "but let's give her a little hell first."

"Give who hell?" Les appeared in the French doors, having approached by stealth.

"We were just having a little chat," Julia said, which was hell enough for Les, who'd been left out. "Actually, we were thinking that we can't just walk away from this place tomorrow."

"But Julia, that's what I said." Les teetered on the doorsill.

"Did you? Did she, Margo?"

"Get on with it, Julia," Margo said.

"And going back tomorrow is out of the question for me," Julia said. "I'm helping Hugh inventory Sir Ludovic's estate, and I'm setting aside as much of it as I can afford, and I don't know how many containers I'll need for shipping. Hugh's thinking of having a sale, and we'll need to catalogue everything for —"

"Julia, you mean you'll stay on here till —"

"There's no room for me *here*. I'll need to be in the country. I'll have to stay down there with — near Hugh."

"Julia, what are we talking about here, days, weeks?"

"I have no idea. I'm going to have to contact Mrs. Lederer to see if she can handle things from her end."

Les stood there, looking like Christmas morning, Julia thought.

"Is anybody interested in my plans?" Margo remarked.

"Margo." Les froze. "What?"

"I couldn't possibly go tomorrow either.

This shoulder needs therapy, and I've arranged to have it at the Chelsea and Westminster. I have a doctor here, you know."

Les gaped. "Margo, you didn't say. Is it Mrs. Smith-Porter's?"

"No. Thank heaven I didn't need a neurosurgeon." Margo turned over a hand, her left one. "I have my own doctor."

Now who's giving the hell? Julia thought.

"Margo, that's wonderful. That's perfect. You can stay in the room you're already in." Les looked around for something to make a list on, then whirled back. "What about Kimberly?"

"She's going home today with Reg."

Les longed to make eye contact with Julia. "Margo, how do you feel about that?"

"It's my idea. I think I've done all I can do for her. Julia thinks I've done too much, and I expect you think the same, Les."

"Margo, I never —"

"I'm always going to be there for my daughter, and right now I think this is about the right distance."

Les's eyes were still sloping to find Julia's. Margo was so in control, sitting there with the garden arranged behind her. She was just the way Les wanted her to be.

Then she pulled herself together. "Well, that's settled then. You both better call the airline and put your reservations on hold."

"I already have," Julia said.

"Les is right," Margo said. "You are sly, Julia."

Les wanted to hug herself. She wanted to hug *them,* but it felt like pushing her luck. "I'll call Harry. It'll be fine. Harry won't care."

She was ready to bolt for the phone, and Julia calculated that she was about to jolt Harry out of a deep sleep at two-thirty in the morning, if he was at home at all. But Les turned back. "And don't forget, you two. Tea this afternoon. Reservations at the Ritz. First seating."

Julia and Margo stared. "Les —"

"You know that was part of the original plan, and there's no reason not to. Never mind about hats, Margo. We won't wear any. Julia, you can call Hugh and tell him to join us. I'll ring the Ritz and tell them to pull up another chair."

"Les, what makes you think Hugh is going to want to lose half a day's work and drive all the way up here in traffic on a hot Saturday afternoon to have tea in a room full of tourists?"

"Because you'll be there, Julia. That's why. I just wish you'd drop this pose about you and Hugh being all business. He's nuts about you."

"How could you possibly think you know —"

"For heaven's sake, Julia. You're absolutely gorgeous. And a little bit mean. Men like that."

Margo suppressed some sound.

"And you've fallen for him, and you've fallen hard. Any fool can see that." Les turned on her heel. "And listen, now that we're all staying, we're going to have to find a good hairdresser. Think roots, Julia." Then Les made one of her best exits.

After a measured pause, Margo said, "Remember that the next time you feel like giving her any hell."

Then after another interval: "Julia, how long have you known Hugh?"

"Let's see." Julia thought. "What day is this?"

"All right," Margo said. "Don't tell if you don't want to."

Chapter 18

When the all clear went, Mrs. Smith-Porter sat up suddenly. The damp of the stone floor had worked right through her combinations to her bones.

She was dizzy when she stood, and it was too dark to know which way was up. She'd spent the night slumped against a packing crate, surrounded by the shapes of strangers. It wasn't even a proper shelter, only the basement of a block of flats backing up to Chelsea Manor Street, but they charge you three halfpence for a ticket to doss down in the tube.

She hadn't slept a wink for fear she'd wake up dead, and how could she? They came over in waves all night, droning, and you could hear the *crump* of the bombs falling, far off, then nearer. But the sound of the antiaircraft guns was worse. It tore through your head, and shrapnel rained on roofs and clanged in the street. People said the antiaircraft fire did more damage than the Germans.

People talked through the night whenever the noise let up, voices in the dark droning like the planes. Nobody she knew. They said if the swimming baths next door took a direct hit, this basement would flood, and we'd all be for it.

She'd come in hungry, and she was hungry still. Fear of being blown to bits, buried alive, and drowned didn't take the edge off her appetite, and she'd kept her shoes on. They were her only pair, and she couldn't have them nicked in the dark.

She had to find her way out now, along with the others, hoicking herself over all sorts of rubbish she couldn't see. Once they knew they could leave, they were all mad keen to go, wondering what they'd find up above. No queues in the shelter, and she fought her way along with the rest. A big hand with fingers like bangers closed over her breast, but she turned and brought her knee up in a sharp jab where it might be most instructive. Then they all walked over each other up steps past dustbins into a courtyard littered with twists of metal.

It was gray morning, just, and when she turned up the street, the pavement was like a shingle beach, thick with crumbled glass, wicked shards sticking up. She watched her every step and didn't take any notice of where she was till the King's Road.

And then she wouldn't have known it. The

air was hot as noon — summer noon, not September — and the stench of gas and cordite and everything that burns caught in her throat. The street was only rough mounds of rubble, and already the AFS was out, dragging hoses. Opposite, the windows of the big grocer's framed fire. She couldn't think, and people were everywhere about her. People in their nightclothes, barefoot on this glass. A woman stood stock-still in the middle of the road with an electric iron in her hand, the flex hanging down.

She ran where she could, past the town hall signboard that read TITTLE-TATTLE LOST THE BATTLE. At Oakley Street a bus lay on its side, and people were running with a ladder. She came upon a pair of curtains, lovely lined silk with bobbles, still clinging by their rings to a rod. Now the air was full of leaves skating on the wind, except they were bits of patterned wallpaper.

Her feet found the way, and when she got to the corner shop, it was alight, the panes of the upper windows still exploding out, one at a time. When she turned into the narrow side street, it was nothing she'd known. The fire brigade had found their way in at the far end, and people milled about, draped in blankets, counting their children. The roofline and the chimney pots that had once made such a monotonous line against the sky were as broken as distant hills.

She hadn't come home for a year, hadn't bothered, and now she couldn't find the house. Along this stretch of street the house-fronts had thrown themselves out onto the pavement, and you could see whatever was left inside, grayed with plaster dust, but she couldn't find her mother's house. She hadn't set eyes on her since the early days of the war, but now she had to know, and when she finally found the house, it wasn't there.

The fire brigade swarmed over a hill of rubble held high by the houses either side. But she turned away because perhaps her mother had gone to a shelter, perhaps she'd moved house. She'd find another place to look for her, but now they had their steam drills out, hammering the rubble, looking for life. How could they hear if her mother cried out from under that mountain of broken brick? The sound of the drills would drive her mad if she stopped here another minute. They seemed to be drilling her head.

She turned to run. The surface of the street was oddly clear now, and she could sprint headlong away. She seemed to run for years until she couldn't draw another breath. When she looked up at last, they were standing there beside her bed.

The doctor in the white coat, whom she seemed almost to recognize, and with him three women. Though they weren't as distinct as where she'd been, she could almost call them by their names. They were her three visitors, all looking round the doctor at her with gratifying concern. And how smartly they were turned out, dressed in their best for this visit to her bedside. Very kind of them indeed, and she must gather herself, rise to the occasion and remember why she was here.

It came to her in a blinding flash. In running like a panicked child away from the ruin of her mother's house, she hadn't watched where she went. She'd run into the King's Road and looked up just too late to see the lorry there, bearing down on her, though it must have been an ambulance because the bell still rang in her head.

She couldn't find her voice so she reached out to them, but she'd been doped, given something to make her sleep, and so she did.

The first seating for tea at the Ritz was overbooked, chiefly with Italians as far as Julia could tell: Armani on all sexes from wall to wall. Julia had gone all out herself in one of Susan Lazar's citrus sheaths and propped in her hair sunglasses with rims that matched the dress. Fifteen years too young for her, but she was in go-for-it mode. Les was in a shantung two-piece from Neiman's last year, but as she said, nobody would have seen it here. Margo wore the dress she'd worn the day they buried Dorothy, and it looked pleasantly loose on her.

When Margo had issued an airy invitation to Paul Jellicoe to join them and he'd accepted, Les's jaw had hit the hospital floor. There was something so un-Margo-ish about the way she'd conjured him up. Call *me* sly, Julia had thought.

They were still waiting for Hugh, fending off the waiter, who wasn't going to put up with much more delay at a first seating.

"After the recovery room," Paul was saying, "she'll be in neurological intensive care, a couple of days I should think, until she's back on the ward, that is if all her neurological signs are stable. Then if the ribs look like mending . . ."

He isn't a bad-looking man, Julia thought, a little jowly, but better out of the white coat. His suit was crumpled, but a good cut. Or was this a thought she was picking up from Les, who was at her most alert? Julia reflected on how companionably Margo and Paul sat there together. She was beginning to explore the ironies of the situation when the waiter made another threatening pass. Then a hand fell on Julia's shoulder.

She looked up to find Hugh over her, golden in the room. He bent and brushed her cheek with his lips. "How un-English," she murmured. Then in full voice: "I believe you know these ladies, and this is Dr. Jellicoe."

The two men shook hands across the low table, and Julia thought how audaciously handsome Hugh looked. Midnight blue blazer, clubby tie, slightly threadbare Jermyn Street shirt. And that carelessly cropped blond hair going not a bit thin even around back. So she was besotted. Sue her.

"Kent?" Paul Jellicoe said to him, frowning in thought. "My people were from there."

Margo looked on with lightly invested interest. Les was sopping it all up. Julia —

"Was Ludovic —"

"Yes, actually," Hugh said.

"What a pleasure to meet you, Sir Hugh."

Julia blanked, and the waiter obtruded with the bread-and-butter, cucumber-and-cress course.

Les looked lost, Margo suddenly thoughtful. A chair slid in under Hugh, and he was reaching for Julia's hand.

"Sir Hugh?" Her head turned slowly his way.

"Darling, I didn't quite find the moment to tell you." He spoke low, but Les and Margo leaned nearer. Dr. Jellicoe had the look of a man who's just put his foot in it and can't fathom how. "I'd hoped you'd see it in the paper, Ludo's death notice. I'm his nephew."

The room revolved. Julia noticed marble columns marching past her. "And his heir."

"And his heir," Hugh said. "House, holdings —"

"Title," Julia said.

"Not an old title," Hugh said. "Nothing very —"

"And why did I never ask you who his heir was?" Julia fingered her chin. "How smoothly we skated past that."

"One doesn't just — and as you're an American —"

"Careful."

"And I had the impression you'd had — revolutionary leanings in your youth, your earlier youth."

"She did. She'd come home from college in combat boots," Les said, only trying to help.

"Les, you pour," Margo said.

321

"I'm over that now, Hugh." Julia spoke in the level voice of a woman from whom information has been withheld.

"I only thought that . . . in the fullness of time —"

"Hugh, 'the fullness of time' is a hopelessly pompous phrase."

"Not here, surely," he said, looking around the room. "I only thought that if things — progressed as I hoped they would, you might fight shy of the idea."

"What idea?"

"Your being Lady Dalrymple."

Les banged the teapot down and shrieked, bringing two waiters on the run, though at a stately pace.

Les stood at the front window of Mrs. Smith-Porter's best bedroom, looking down. The street was Sunday-silent, misted with light rain. The potpourri had been stirred, and garden flowers for nosegays were in the rooms, and she and Margo had made up the beds. But now Margo had gone off to breakfast at the hospital with Paul before he had to make rounds. Les had the house to herself in this interlude, and it was like standing in the wings before the curtain went up. She felt a buzz behind her breastbone.

Brakes shrieked through her thoughts, and

she looked down to see the cab at the door. She counted three women as they got out and put their heads together about the fare and the tip. She could see at a glance they'd overpacked. Now they were trying to decide if it was worth putting up their umbrellas. Les started down through the house.

She opened to the second ring, and a big, smiley-faced woman wearing Lalaounis gold earrings and a Burberry filled the door. "Mrs. Smith-Porter? I'm Mrs. T. J. Baldridge. From Lubbock?"

Les blinked and took a longer look. "You are not," she said. "You're Cissy Metcalfe from the UT chapter. Onetime national chaplain."

"Oh my God." Cissy Metcalfe Baldridge faltered backward. "Who were you?"

"Les Vogel, University of Missouri, regional alumnae corresponding secretary five years running."

"I want you to *hush*." Cissy lunged for Les and seized her in a hug like a hammerlock. Then over her shoulder, "Girls — Jo-Nell, Mary Kate, you're not going to *believe* this," and Radnor Walk was rent with their cries, Pi Phis all.

Chapter 19

The days opened and closed like a fan in Mrs. Smith-Porter's mind. She knew moments of stark clarity, often at night when she found herself surrounded by quite old women. And she called herself to attention for the neurologist's daily visit. He tickled the bottoms of her feet and watched her toes with interest. He shone lights in her eyes.

Early on, she'd blotted her copybook with him. When he'd asked her who she was, she'd answered absently with her earlier name, which made her sound gaga. Now she was emphatic when he asked, answering Olivia Smith-Porter in as much voice as she could muster. This, of course, gave the impression that she was progressing, though merely speaking her own name left her breathless. On the whole she preferred the other doctor, the one who sparked Mrs. Mayhew's interest. Good of her to call so often. Mrs. Smith-Porter would have thought it time Mrs. Mayhew and her friends were going home, along with the daughter, but apparently not, and that was comforting too. The days moved at such a strange pace here.

She slept endlessly, and that naturally threw her thoughts right off. But now at least she wasn't back in the war every time she closed her eyes. She dreamed of the sea instead, though the beach was made of broken glass. The meaning of this dream escaped her. She cared nothing for the sea and hadn't been near it except for that time when she'd gone away to Dawlish to leave her old life behind and school herself for the new.

But here she stood with the tide coming in and the seabirds wheeling. Quite near the sea she was, with the nasty wet weed tangling her feet and the waves rolling in until she could hardly see sky. She couldn't think how often she dreamed of the sea, ebbing and flowing, and now she was walking right out into the foaming water, mad as a March hare, but the sea drew her. She felt it rising around her, making her hospital gown cling. It rose until she had to hold her chin high.

Then she knew it wasn't the sea at all. She was in the shelter, and the swimming baths next door had taken a direct hit. The water burst through the bulging bricks, invisible in the darkness but pounding in her head. She was awash, swept off her feet, breathing the black water. And of course there was no way out.

★ ★ ★

"You didn't learn that in England." Julia lay tangled with Hugh in the early morning, upstairs in the enchanted cottage. Morning light entered through the screen of ivy at the window. The ceiling was nearly low enough to touch, and she had only moments ago nearly gone through it.

Hugh said it had been his mother's room. Her dressing table stood at the foot of the bed with rings on the surfaces where her scent bottles had been.

"It wouldn't be the same if we were an old titled couple."

"No." He ran a callused hand over her. "You'd be wearing a flannel nightdress you refused to take off. And complicated knickers."

"And a mobcap bearing the Dalrymple crest."

"Tucked up with hot-water bottles and a mustard plaster on your chest."

"Three pugs snoring on the foot of the bed, and the chamber pot within easy reach."

"And I'd have to apply for my connubial rights through the offices of an upper servant."

"Chain of command," Julia murmured, "and naturally never in the morning."

Unaccountably, this dismal prophecy inspired them both to another round of what seemed to Julia adolescent behavior. They might as well have been in the backseat of a Chevrolet. Then Hugh was saying, "I hope I've made it perfectly clear."

His face was so near that Julia could see nothing else. "What, exactly?"

"That I can't imagine life without you. In fact I don't remember life before you."

"You remember nothing of before we met?"

"Not much. The odd impression. Very sketchy."

"Ah," said Julia, remembering very little herself.

"You see," Hugh said, "I love you. I'd pursue you to the ends of the earth. So please don't go."

"Go?" Julia said. "Where?"

Later, she thought she should get serious about the day. She'd spent all week poking through the prince's rooms while Hugh listened to an ominous agenda of probate and death duties in legal offices. The seed of an idea was beginning to thrive in her mind: a line of furniture, minor pieces at first, out of top-quality seasoned wood and employing local craftsmen if possible. Reproductions of some of the furniture in the house. Rescaled, of course. "The Ravenscote Collection," possibly. She envisioned a brochure of austere line drawings against a summery water-color of the house and made a mental note to put a call through to Jim Lumsden in Los Angeles to find out how he'd promoted his Las Palmas line.

It was something to get onto even while the estate was tied up, that and some preliminary thinking about turning the ballroom into permanent showroom space. Other stately homes had made the transition to commercial enterprises. Julia's thoughts opened to a vista of every dealer on Lexington Avenue being brought up the lane in a fleet of minibuses that met the train.

"What would you think of copying some of the more likely pieces?" Hugh said as innocently as if he couldn't read minds. "Go down well in the States? Your Mrs. Lederer could run the New York office, and we could set up showrooms in the house, if we can manage to hang on to it. And marketed — how? As 'the Lady Dalrymple Range'? Something on that order?"

The phone rang, and it was Margo, calling from the hospital. "Julia, can you come up to London today? I think you'd better. It's urgent."

Cissy Metcalfe had made a pledge before God and T.J. to see every show in London she and the girls could cram into two weeks, and once they recovered from the shock of finding Les Vogel as their landlady, they made a place for her in their plans. Cissy meant business: *Miss Saigon* and everything in the West End, along with all the fringe theater they could find, including one memorable performance upstairs at the Man in the Moon pub, performed entirely in the nude. "You say nude," Jo-Nell said. "I say mother-naked, and how are we going to tell it in Lubbock?"

They couldn't believe how much Les knew about London — like the palm of her hand. It was the same as having their own personal tour guide. She could point you in the right direction every time and knew the cutest places for tea. Right from the get-go they all said this was the best trip yet, and they went someplace every year. "Catch me in Cozumel again," Mary Kate said.

And this precious house. They could hardly get themselves going in the morning. They'd gladly just sit in that garden all day, drinking it in, except for the sale at Harrod's. Then they couldn't believe Les, who only wanted to buy tea towels and glass cloths for the kitchen at Radnor Walk.

On Thursday, Les left them after a matinee and came home because she had a hundred things to do. She'd aimed them at Fortnum's for an early supper in the cafe before an evening performance at the Criterion, which they could walk to from there. Then she'd volunteered to bring home their shopping for them so they didn't have to lug it around any longer. With all this to carry, she'd splurged on a cab. Now, before she could dig for her key, she had to line up the shopping bags on the doorstep. Aquascutum, Liberty, Dickens Jones, Liberty again because they'd done Regent Street this morning. She meant to stack the bags inside and sprint up to Waitrose for groceries.

But inside, she glanced into the living room. Margo was home. And Julia was there too. They sat on either side of the fireplace, almost posed, waiting for her. Les just noticed that Margo was white as a sheet. "What is it? What's happened?"

"Come in and sit down," Julia said.

"Oh no, what is it?" Les didn't want to sit down.

"It's Mrs. Smith-Porter," Margo said, her voice tinny, not like her. "Les, she just slipped away."

Away?

"Paul said that the combination of the strapped ribs and the general anesthesia during the operation tipped her into pneumonia."

Pneumonia. Les looked through to the doors open on the garden. It was flooded with warm, late-day light.

"They'd had her on oral antibiotics. Then antibiotics by IV, and today . . . the neurosurgeon saw her this morning, but later on they couldn't wake her. She was gone." A sob tugged at Margo's voice. Her head dipped, and she ran a hand over her eyes.

"Margo, were you there?"

She shook her head. "I didn't go till nearly noon, and when I got there, Paul . . ."

Les was beside her, crouched on the floor so their heads were close. "Margo, you were there all these past days. You were right there for her."

Les had an arm around Margo, and Julia could just reach out to touch Les's shoulder, so they were all connected. The sense of loss that overcame her, overcame all of them, bewildered Julia. They'd hardly known —

Les stood, straightening her skirt. She did something definite with her hands and said, "We've already tried our best to find out if she has any relatives or anybody, so we've done all we can do there. Somebody at her bank can help with arrangements. Julia, you know the bank people." Les was beginning to organize, and delegate, but then she pressed a fist against her lips and stood motionless a moment. "Wasn't she a fine lady?" she said at last, something shrill and spiraling in her voice. "And brave too. Gutsy. Didn't she build herself a good life?"

Julia's eyes filled suddenly. She had the distinct impression that Mrs. Smith-Porter was standing outside on the stairs, listening. Every detail of the room spoke her name.

"What will happen to this house?" Julia said.

And out of nowhere Les said, "I want this house."

Julia and Margo exchanged looks.

"I mean it," Les said. "Don't look at each other. I'm serious. I want to live in these rooms. On nice mornings I want to have breakfast in that garden.

"I don't know how you buy houses here from people's estates, but there must be a way, and I suppose it'll take forever, but what's time for anyway? I guess you have to get lawyers onto it, but Hugh would know one, wouldn't he?"

She spoke in a rush, and Julia tried to gauge the degree of hysteria in her voice. "Les, wait a minute. What would you do? Do you mean you'd live in London —"

"Julia, Cissy Metcalfe knows fifty people

she'll be sending. And they'll know fifty people. I've got a few contacts of my own. I could run this place till the next ice age on Pi Phis alone, not to mention Mrs. Smith-Porter's repeaters. I can show them around the town, the shopping and all that. I know what they like. Julia, I'd be good at it. I *am* good at it."

When Julia shot another glance at Margo, there was a look of immense wonder on her face. "Les, this is pretty spur-of-the-moment," Julia said, "and it might not be the moment to be thinking about —"

"Oh yes, Julia," Les said. "This is exactly the moment. I never even knew this moment could happen. I'm not going to walk away from it. I'm not going to sit this one out, Julia, and neither should you."

"Where do I come into this?"

"Because we're all three in the same boat when you think about it. What in the hell do any of us have to lose except a load of tired old habits? We all three ought to take flying lessons. Julia, you always think you have to hole up by yourself to be safe. You always did think commitment was a cage."

"Wasn't it for you?"

"For me it was. Yes. You and I were always opposites. Now I want out." Then rounding on Margo, Les said, "And you're always there for everybody else and never there for yourself. We've all been hiding from who we are, and that's you too, Margo."

In the quiet she'd created, Les could hear her own breathing. "But I was the worst. I was just playing out my hand. But now I want to deal myself a new hand. I want a whole new ball game."

Julia was lost among Les's mixed metaphors, but the speech had reached her on a deeper level. Then Margo said very calmly, "Les, you have more sense than Julia and me put together."

"You'll stay then, Margo? At least till the end of the summer. For one thing, I want to fire that Mrs. Dowdel."

"Les, you want me to do floors?"

"No, I don't want you to do floors, Margo. Stop being a martyr. We'll get somebody. But there's plenty to do, and we'll do it together."

"All right," Margo said, to Julia's astonishment.

"Les, what about your mother?" she said.

"Harry can find her a place in a retirement community. A unit in one of those places with a clubhouse and . . . crafts. She can pay for it herself when the house at the Cape sells. She wouldn't want to go back to the Cape. She'll want to be in St. Louis because she knows a lot of people there. She'll like it."

"And if she doesn't?"

"I won't be there to hear it."

That alone deserved a moment of silence, but Julia said, "What about Harry? Will he buy this house for you?"

"Yes."

"You here. Harry there."

"Yes."

"Les, I think you and Harry both ought to know that there's a single piece of furniture upstairs worth two hundred thousand pounds all by itself."

"Julia, some of the more valuable pieces may have to be sold. I'll count on you to make the arrangements and find tasteful replacements. If this place can be paid off by the sale of some of its contents, so much the better. Then nobody's beholden to anybody."

This financial wizardry crossed with a divorce settlement stunned Julia finally into silence. It was Margo who said, "Les, Harry —"

"Harry won't care. Harry has somebody else."

Margo dodged Julia's quick look. "Les, are you leaving Harry?"

"I'm already gone."

August

Chapter 20

The day they were to move back home broke the heat record for Chicago. To keep the price down to a half-day job for the movers, a firm called Two Deadheads with a Truck, Reg had tried to get everything into an orderly pile in the living room of the apartment. He'd boxed his books and the PC and everything from the kitchenette, and he was overwhelmed by how much there was. The window unit was going full blast, but Reg was still sweating like a — not a Turk, but a lot.

Since Chris had left, he'd been sleeping in the living room. Chris had been offered an academic appointment in the California system he thought was too good to pass up. Reg had wanted to talk it over, weigh the pros and cons from the perspective of his own longer and hard-won experience, but Chris was too focused, and in fact left the apartment a couple of weeks before he actually had to make the move.

Kimberly had their room, and Reg would be in there now, knocking down the bed, if she wasn't still presumably in it. He checked his watch and saw he'd sweated through the band.

He'd enrolled Kimberly at Oakton. When Margo, in one final power play, told her she wasn't college material, Kimberly was motivated to give it a try. She hadn't developed the self-image to apply for a job in what remained of the summer. She'd hardly left her room since they came back from England, but this was the inevitable result of Margo's final rejection in that grandstanding refusal to return. But Reg was confident that with some modest success in an unpressured academic setting, Kimberly would overcome the worst of her formative influences.

In another week they'd both be in school, so Reg's countdown was to get settled back in the house, reorganize his old work space, and get his files in order and his books on the shelves. At this point, he'd have expected to be confronting Margo with the necessity of her moving out of it, selling the property and contents, and dividing the proceeds. He'd taken counsel and had reason to believe he was on fairly sound legal grounds.

Then Margo dropped her bombshell, calling up to say she was staying in England, apparently on a permanent basis, whatever that meant. She'd called two days after Chris left, and Reg was still considering the juxtaposition of the two events. Could she have known?

She'd sent in her letter to Crestwood, announcing her retirement. She had her twenty years in, but how she thought she was going to live on that minimal pension in London he didn't know, and clearly her own thinking was anything but logical. His early impression was that she was merely menopausal. In these past weeks, however, he'd come to the conclusion that Margo had suffered an emotional breakdown over the divorce, a separation anxiety to which she was making one of her inappropriate responses. She would see this differently later, but she'd said that the house was his as long as he was making a home for Kimberly, and he would hold her to that. Moreover, when Margo returned, inevitably chastened, Reg was open to the option of their living together again. Not a reconciliation per se, but a new arrangement with clearly defined parameters. In fact since Chris had left, the idea had crossed Reg's mind more than once.

A pounding on the door brought him around, and he went to let in the movers. Both Deadheads were dripping wet already, and looked none too encouraged at the amount to be moved. They were both white boys with dreadlocks, and the one built like an Adonis skinned off his shirt.

The bedroom door opened, and from the corner of his eye Reg seemed to see Margo standing there. But it was Kimberly of course, dressed, surprisingly, and pushing up her sweatshirt sleeves in a somehow businesslike way. She'd seen him watching the shirtless boy and said, "Oh for Christ's sake, Dad. Grow up."

Both Deadheads looked around at this, but seemed to have grasped nothing but the sofa, which they were now banging repeatedly against the front doorframe. Finally they were through it, and Kimberly was giving Reg the first direct look he could remember having from her. "Look," she said, "we're going to need to have some rules, right? No more Chrises in the house. Don't date or whatever. Don't do anything weird. Just be, like, a dad."

Reg was struck by the ghost of Margo's intonation in Kimberly's voice, though of course not the phrasing. "Kimberly —"

"Because it's just you and me now. Mother's not coming back."

"So she says now," Reg said reasonably, "but once she's had some time to —"

"Dad, she's got somebody else. We've talked on the phone, you know. You'll get the bill."

"And she told you she had someone else." Reg drew in his cheeks, an expression of amused and detached skepticism he often used in class.

"I could put it together," Kimberly said with all the certainty of seventeen.

And Reg let it go at that. The idea that Margo was seeing another man was well beyond the bounds of probability. But there was something touching in Kimberly's trying to plant a sad little seed of jealousy in Reg's mind. A perfectly natural ploy for a child of divorce in attempting to reunite the parents, though more typical of a younger adolescent, Reg would have thought.

That night Harry Hockaday flew to London, a trip fraught with evil omens right from the start. They'd sat on the runway an hour. Business class was jammed enough to feel like economy. The movie starred Bruce Willis, and both dinner and breakfast congealed into a cannonball in Harry's stomach. Sleepless all night, he dozed on his feet in the immigration line and again waiting for the luggage. Though he'd thought it was a regular weekday, here it was something called August Bank Holiday Monday, and they had to wait an hour for a cab.

Miraculously, their room at the Westbury

was ready. Helene fell across the bed, and Harry took a disposable razor into the shower to give himself a shave. Then he stood watching the foam and water run down the curve of his belly while he waited for revival. The phone calls from Les over this last month jangled in his mind. She always caught him at the office, calls anybody could monitor, but Les said this was business, and they ought to do it in business hours.

A retirement community for her mother he could go along with, gladly. He'd already taken some exploratory steps, but everything else had him completely baffled. He was still blocked by the basic idea of Les going off to London for a ten-day trip and just not coming back. All right, a lot of women went away for the summer. But if she wasn't back by Labor Day, they were looking at a whole new ball game. Not that he cared what other people thought. To hell with other people. He stepped out of the shower and toweled off.

Helene lay across the bed with her shoes on, dead to the world. She said she'd come over to shop, but nothing was open today. If he had any sense, he'd take a couple Nytols, crap out on the other bed, sleep till whenever, and then get up and decide. But no, he was rummaging through his suitcase, looking for a reasonably unwrinkled pair of pants, his linen jacket, a shirt and tie. He could do with a shine.

Down in the lobby he rang Les and then changed some more money without taking any particular notice of the exchange rate. Out in Bond Street it was warmer than he thought England ever got. Harry slipped out of his jacket to keep from sweating through it. The Burlington Arcade was shut, but he threaded through to Piccadilly Street, coming out within sight of the Ritz. He crossed over for a cab going in the right direction. A little more walking wouldn't do him any harm, so he strolled on past the pictures up for sale on the Green Park fence. He'd grab a cab before he got up to that big round intersection ahead, whatever it was called.

Harry found himself walking from one woman to another, and right at this moment he couldn't quite get a handle on that. Helene had wanted to come, and she didn't make a lot of demands. But why had he gone along with it? He'd been a little steamed by Les's calls, and it had something to do with evening up the sides, or a fallback position. He couldn't exactly spell it out. And since this walk wasn't clearing his head, he stepped off the curb to flag a cab.

He rang twice before Les opened the front door.

"Hi, babe," he said.

"Harry, for heaven's sake," she said. "You look like the country club at the Cape."

She was wearing something a little foreign-looking, a sleeveless top and a skirt with pale stripes, or maybe he just hadn't seen it before. She looked good. When she waved him inside, he felt cramped by the size of the room, hunched over, but he ought to work on his posture anyway.

"The garden's warm. Let's sit here." He caught her in profile, and she looked like maybe twenty years old, like way back. It was as if he hadn't seen her in years. "Do you want a drink?"

"I better not. I feel like I've been kicked in the head." He meant jet lag, but wondered if she thought he meant something else. "Your mother's fine."

"Fine?"

"As good as she gets. She's expecting you back."

"Is she."

"I got Mae Rafferty to stay with her while I'm away. Little Harry —"

"When you get home, you get in touch with Little Harry and tell him to call his mother."

"Oh well, you know how he is."

"Yes, I know. He's a chip off the old block."

"Is he? I can't see it," Harry said. "I couldn't have just gone off to Boston at his age and — done my thing."

"No, you couldn't. I wouldn't have let you. We cramped each other's style. But you'll get him back."

They sat there, somehow more companionable than they could remember being.

"Honey," he said, "what do you want?"

"You know what I want, Harry. I want you to buy me this house. I'll pay you back."

"Why? I can't understand why."

"Because I want to have people here. I want to entertain them, and I want them to have a good time. I want to see them coming and going and to hear their stories." She made a gesture, and he watched her hand against the light from the garden. "I want to make all the arrangements."

"Babe, you can do that at home. You do."

"Harry, I want them to pay. I want to be in business. I think I always did. Listen, with all the effort I put into Junior League alone, I could have run General Motors."

"You want — like a bed-and-breakfast?"

"Yes. The best one in town."

"You can do that in St. Louis. Not in

347

Portland Place. They wouldn't approve that, but we'll find you somewhere. Maybe St. Charles. Big old redbrick house, and you can fix it up. You're the best at that. And get somebody in to —"

"Harry, I'm not coming back."

"Oh babe," he said, watching the floor begin to slide out from under him. "Remember —"

"Let's not do that," she said, standing. "Let me show you the house."

She walked him through it and out to the little space she called a garden, and the out-of-date kitchen. He tried to see it as she saw it, but his mind was in retreat. As she led the way upstairs, he watched her bare legs below the switching skirt and wondered what she'd be like in bed, which is what jet lag can do to you.

At the top she said, "I'm full up right now, but you can take a peek at the rooms." They made the rounds, and she walked into one of them, the smallest, not much bigger than a closet. "Look at that writing table," she said. "Isn't it exquisite? This is Margo's room."

Margo Skinner? "Margo's here?"

"Yes, she stayed. We all did. Julia too. We're beginning to go our own ways again, like before, but we stayed. Margo's out today. She's seeing somebody, though she calls it therapy. Actually, I suppose it is."

"She's seeing some — Englishman?" Harry said, just for something to say.

"Yes. She's dating. She never got to date, you know. I don't know about marriage. I don't know if they're thinking about that, but I doubt if it would interest her. She's done that."

And Harry wondered if they were still talking about Margo. He and Les stood in the upstairs hall, close, but he knew he couldn't touch her.

"I could just say no," he said. "I could just say I wouldn't buy you this house."

"You could, Harry, and it would serve me right. I trapped you. It's ancient history now, but my mother and I trapped you into marrying me. I wasn't the bride, Harry. I was the bait. We never gave you a chance. You have every right not to give me mine."

"Honey, I never saw it like that. Did I ever make you feel —"

"No, Harry, you never did."

She led him back downstairs, and now an element of formality crept in between them. He wouldn't sit down again unless she did.

"Portland Place is too big for us now. It doesn't make a lot of sense now," he said, though he knew it sounded like grasping at straws. "How about we get a new house, maybe out in —"

"Harry, I want this one." They stood there together, and she was out of reach.

"So we just go our separate ways?"

"Harry, we've been going our separate ways for years."

"I was going my separate way, but I always came home."

"And that's how I feel now," Les said. "I feel like I've come home."

Her face was in shadow. He put out his hand, and she took it. They stood there, hands clasped, and all he wanted was to turn back the clock. And then the doorbell rang.

Les drew away, toward the front hall. It must be a visitor who'd forgotten a key. Cissy Metcalfe was forever forgetting hers when she and Jo-Nell and Mary Kate were here. People did. From the living room Harry heard her open the door, and the silence that followed. Then Les said, "Well for Pete's sake, Helene Rafferty. What on earth are you doing here?" Helene Rafferty, daughter of Mae, treasurer of the Herb Society, and general hanger-on. Divorced. Twice.

"I'm full up, but come in." Les led her into the living room, but Helene stopped in the doorway. Almost as tall as Les, but dark, wider in the hips. Les turned back and saw Helene's face. The look on it meant to be firm, but was merely fixed, a touch of fear in her eyes. Les couldn't imagine what was the matter with her, and then she looked at Harry.

The three of them stood there. Then new knowledge broke over Les's head and flowed through her like a river. All this time she'd thought it would be somebody younger, maybe a lot younger and bigger in the bust and nobody she could name.

Les was nearly panting with surprise, only that at first, as if they weren't Harry and Les and Helene Rafferty but strangers she'd just heard some gossip about. But then the wonderful, elegant simplicity of the situation hit her head-on. Helene Rafferty wanted Harry, and she didn't.

"Les, I'm sorry. But I wanted to come," Helene said, finding her voice. "I sort of forced the issue."

"Oh, Helene, honestly," Les said, "with Harry you have to."

As it was Bank Holiday Monday, Julia and Hugh decided they'd earned a day off. They rode in the Mini over the patchwork hills on country lanes past oasthouses under fleecy clouds and fetched up at Rye in time for lunch.

It was traditional and indigestible, roast beef and potatoes, hard-hearted sprouts and great elephant ears of Yorkshire pudding, the plate swilling in brown gravy. They ate it in the most authentic pub on the most picturesque cobbled street in Rye. Over the bloodred summer pudding, Hugh said, "It could be quite simple."

"Nothing ever is," Julia said. "What?"

Uncharacteristically, he was turning the signet ring on his hand. "We might just run up to town some morning — when we can find a moment — and stop by Chelsea Town Hall."

"Ah. Why?"

"The Registry Office. To be married."

Julia found herself lightly hallucinating, as on that first morning they'd met. She had a quick flash of Les and Margo in bottle green and claret like the last time, sweeping down some governmental hall behind her, their arms full of her veil.

"I suppose we might," she said, fighting an idiotic shyness.

They took a turn through the town, bypassing the antique shops, and ended with a stroll around the garden of Henry James's house, hand in hand. Driving back through the evening, Julia decided she was adjusting to the near-death element in the British way of driving.

That night when she was undressing in their room, she chased a comb down the back of the dressing table, her hand meeting some object wedged there, down low, balanced on the skirting board. She pulled it out — a framed picture. When she wiped the dust off the glass, she uncovered a photograph of Sylvia. Black and white, but she was wearing the same dress she'd had on that Sunday when Julia had met her upstairs at Ravenscote. She recognized the pattern. Sylvia posed against a stile, somewhere on the grounds probably, but in that same languorous way she'd stood against the fireplace when they'd met.

"Hugh." He was coming back from what passed as the bathroom, wrapped in a towel. "Look at this picture of Sylvia."

"Yes," he said, coming up behind her. "Had I mentioned her name?"

"No, you hadn't. I've been wondering who she is."

"Darling, have you? She was my mother. That picture was made before I was born. The 1940s, from the look of it, wouldn't you have thought?"

"No, Hugh, I wouldn't. I met Sylvia. It

was on the Sunday you came down to be with Sir Ludo. I was looking for a bathroom, and she was in that upstairs room with the Chinese screens."

"Ah," Hugh said.

"And she certainly wasn't your mother. I'm old enough to be hers."

"It would be very like my mother to come back at the age most flattering to herself."

"Don't, Hugh. Anything gothic makes my flesh creep. Besides, we talked. She and I had a chat."

"Did you? What about?"

Julia made herself remember. "I don't know. We exchanged names. She was very English and superior. She said, 'I couldn't think who you'd be,' something like that. She talked about the house, how she preferred something smaller."

"Yes, she loved this cottage."

"And she asked me if I was awfully in love with you."

"Then there you are," Hugh said.

"And she mentioned something about my having waited long enough, which I thought was rude."

"Nobody would have called her diplomatic. But of course she wanted to meet you and see you for herself. I am, after all, her only son."

"Hugh, you could talk me into practically anything, but people don't come back. That's just folklore and a — plot device in *Hamlet*. Besides, she was smoking."

"Yes," Hugh said, "all her life, like a chimney. Everybody did then."

"Ghosts don't smoke."

"I thought you didn't believe in them."

Julia's head throbbed. "Hugh, just for the sake of argument let's say it was your mother, back from the grave and complete with handbag and Dunhill lighter. And she's come back for a look at somebody you want to . . . well, me. You were married before, Hugh. Did she come back to give your first wife the once-over?"

"I don't know. My first wife, as you rather prematurely call her, never said. But then she was English and quite used to these old houses where —"

"Hugh, let's not pursue this conversation. Let's just drop it now and laugh about it later."

"Darling, I didn't bring it up. My idea of enjoying the evening was making love to you."

"Yes," Julia said, putting down the framed picture on the dresser, "let's do that."

"I really think we ought," Hugh said, turning the picture to the wall.

October Epilogue

They were married on a gusty autumn morning, and Julia carried a nosegay of blue gentians from the garden at Ravenscote. The *Telegraph* sent a photographer for a picture of the new American Lady Dalrymple, to run in the Saturday edition.

Les took charge of the arrangements. Having made a close study of Chelsea Town Hall weddings around the corner from Radnor Walk, she'd said, "Hats, Julia, and this time I mean it. Big, swoopy English hats we'll never wear again."

Of the three of them, Margo looked the most like a baronet's wife in hers, one that had hung on Mrs. Smith-Porter's mirror, retrimmed for the occasion. Les brought Baggies full of confetti, and the people queuing for the bus across the King's Road looked on when they came out under a watery October sun. "The first one of you two who addresses me as 'Lady' gets a fat lip," Julia had said. But Les would have dropped her a curtsy on the town hall steps if Margo hadn't gotten a grip on her.

The wedding lunch was at Radnor Walk,

Les presiding over a collation drawn largely from Marks & Spencers, with cheeses from Harrod's Food Hall. Paul Jellicoe brought the champagne as his wedding present, his and Margo's. Just the five of them, as all Les's visitors were out for the day, doing London.

They toasted Julia and Hugh, and Les, feeling pleasantly bee-stung by the champagne, proposed another toast to the three of them. Then when they peered out from under the brims of their hats, they were Julia Englehardt and Les Vogel and Margo Skinner, just the three of them against the world, dodging around under the snowball bushes beside the Vogels' porch, or up in Les's room with the after-school sunlight pouring in across the candlewick bedspread. "No," Les said. "Not to old times. To the future and wherever it takes us next."

There hadn't been a real engagement, but Hugh seized the moment to give Julia a ring to wear with her new wedding band, fumbling it out of a hidden pocket of his waistcoat. It was a magnificent aquamarine surrounded in diamonds that had belonged to his mother.